A Treasury of Old-Fashioned Christmas Stories

A Treasury of Old-Fashioned Christmas Stories

Presented by

Michele Slung

CARROLL & GRAF PUBLISHERS
NEW YORK

A Treasury of Old-Fashioned Christmas Stories

Carroll & Graf Publishers
An Imprint of Avalon Publishing Group, Inc.
245 West 17th Street, 11th Floor
New York, NY 10011

First Carroll & Graf edition 2006

Library of Congress Cataloging-in-Publication Data is available.

ISBN-10: 0-7867-1803-X
ISBN-13: 978-0-78671-803-0

9 8 7 6 5 4 3 2 1

Book design by Maria Fernandez

Printed in the United States of America
Distributed by Publishers Group West

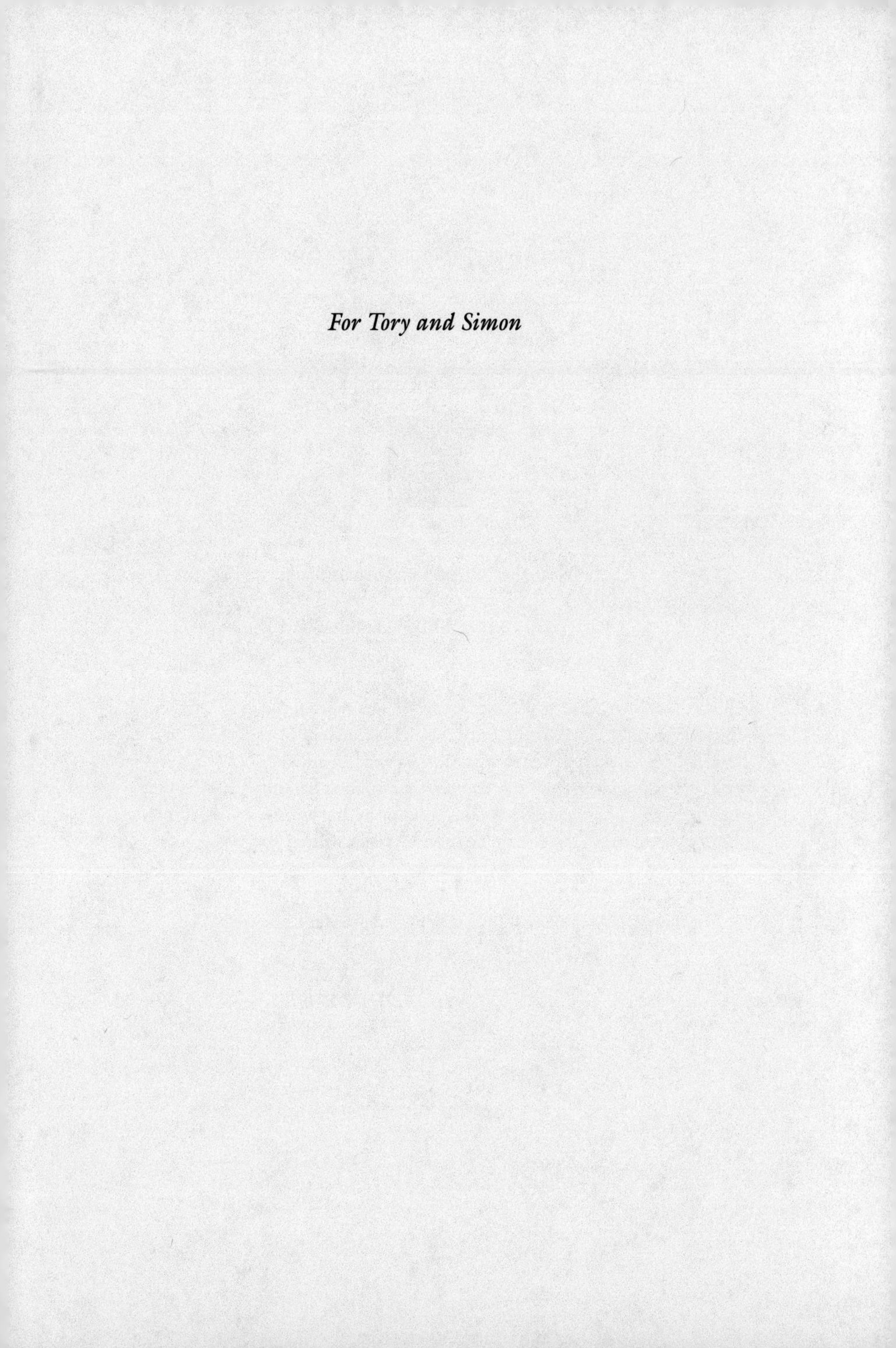

For Tory and Simon

Contents

Acknowledgments

For his always invaluable help, patience, and good humor, I must first thank the Library of Congress's Tom Mann. For their always loving friendship, Karen De Witt and Kathy Matthews have my equally loving gratitude. I also want to thank Claiborne Hancock for his early enthusiasm and support, and Will Balliett for his, as well. (There are many reasons to appreciate Will, and I've had occasion to know quite a few. He is a publisher for all seasons and not just for Christmas.)

Greetings to the Reader

"WHAT IS IT THAT'S WRONG with Christmas?" is a question posed in Stephen Leacock's charming fable "Merry Christmas." Replies the narrator swiftly: "Why . . . all the romance, the joy, the beauty of it has gone, crushed and killed by the greed of commerce and the horrors of war. . . ."

Continuing, he drifts into reverie: "I can conjure up, as anybody can, a picture of Christmas in the good old days of a hundred years ago—the quaint old-fashioned houses, standing deep among the evergreens, with the light twinkling from the windows on the snow—the warmth and comfort within—the great fire roaring on the hearth—the merry guests grouped about its blaze and the little children with their eyes dancing in the Christmas firelight, waiting for Father Christmas in his fine mummery of red and white and cotton wool to hand the presents from the Yuletide tree. I can see it . . . as if it were yesterday."

However, since the book containing this nostalgic glance backward was first published in 1918, what you've just read is a lament not for vanished Christmases of merely a hundred years ago but—since many decades more have gone by—for ones celebrated now almost 200 years in the past.

Still, how familiar it all sounds! Isn't what's being expressed the same sense of loss one has heard mourned each and every December over the course of our own lives? And isn't it true that complaining how "Christmas isn't what it used to be" long ago turned into a seasonal tradition all its own?

While *A Treasury of Old-Fashioned Christmas Stories* may not be the solution to the problem, it does offer a temporary antidote in the form of twenty-one richly memorable tales meant to transport readers straight into the heart of that twirling snow globe where lost Christmases are to be found. Mainly little known stories, or else wholly forgotten ones, they are by writers of acknowledged distinction (Louisa May Alcott, Anthony Trollope, Mary E. Wilkins Freeman, Max Beerbohm) or less current repute (Mary Elizabeth Braddon, Jacob A. Riis, Mark Lemon, Stephen Leacock) and even by some whose work has not, to my knowledge, been noticed at all for many decades (Willis Boyd Allen, Armando Palacio Valdés, Ida M. Starr, Myra Kelly).

The joy of finding and sharing such stories, taking them down from literature's attic, is a special pleasure of mine. I have an addiction, really, to popular fiction from bygone eras—it has to smell and look and feel a certain way—and it traces back a half-century ago to a childhood spent practically committing to memory the fiction shelves of my nearest local library. New titles rarely hold my attention. Since a book (or a story) is both a journey and a destination, I prefer one that, in all its particulars, shows its age; only then is it the silently humming time machine that enables me to escape with the most perfect satisfaction.

For example, coming across story of a 1920s Christmas by F. M. Mayor, author of the acclaimed minor classic *The Rector's Daughter*, was completely transporting. From the first sentence of "Innocents' Day," I was suddenly in a genteel ladies' London that no longer exists, a place where when one's circumstances were reduced, even one's least expectations had to be, as well. "She felt a tear roll down her cheek. Was she really so foolish as to cry because she was missing the Christmas tree?"

Or take the gloriously stocked late-nineteenth-century toy store described in Willis Boyd Allen's "Mrs. Brownlow's Christmas Party," with its enormous fleets of Noah's arks, regiments of tin soldiers, its vast population of "winking, crying, walking and talking dolls" and cacaphony of trumpets, drums and music boxes. Reading it, one inhales Cottlow & Co.'s "delicious smell of sawdust and paint and wax" along with the excited but cautiously browsing Brownlows.

And though almost everyone knows O. Henry's famous tale of Christmas sacrifice, "The Gift of the Magi," few will be acquainted with his boisterous "Christmas by Injunction," in which a wild west mining town is forced to import children to guarantee a would-be amateur Santa recipients for his largesse. "When the kids are rounded up," the volunteer hospitality committee is instructed, "light up the candles on the tree and set 'em to playing 'Pussy Wants a Corner' and 'King William.' When they get good and at it, why—old Santa'll slide in the door. I reckon there'll be plenty of gifts to go 'round." Meanwhile, humming along with those cheerful tunes, we wait happily to see what will happens next. (With O. Henry, remember, there's always a twist.)

The word "anthology" itself means "garland," an appropriately Christmassy term. But I chose to call this collection a treasury because of the reading magic, the possibility for surprise and strangeness, the romance, sentiment and drama, and even the inevitable eccentricity it embodies. Treasuries are large of spirit, in other words. Old-fashioned, that's what they are. The idea of a treasury seems to go with those Christmases that live in our imaginations, that exist where we no longer are—and maybe never have been—but wish we were.

Wrote John Edgar Park (whose "The Christmas Heretic" offers many surprises), "There are three strands in the Christmas tradition. There is the gold thread of religion. There is the silver thread of benevolence. And then there is a gaily colored thread of homespun yarn, that's laughter."

You'll find each here, festively twined together in a garland of reading for your pleasure. I wish you joy in it, one and all.

Mrs. Brownlow's Christmas Party

by WILLIS BOYD ALLEN

IT WAS FINE CHRISTMAS WEATHER. Several light snow-storms in the early part of December had left the earth fair and white, and the sparkling, cold days that followed were enough to make the most crabbed and morose of mankind cheerful, as with a foretaste of the joyous season at hand. Down town the sidewalks were crowded with mothers and sisters, buying gifts for their sons, brothers, and husbands, who found it impossible to get anywhere by taking the ordinary course of foot-travel, and were obliged to stalk along the snowy streets beside the curbstone, in a sober but not ill-humored row.

Among those who were looking forward to the holidays with keen anticipations of pleasure, were Mr. and Mrs. Brownlow, of Elm Street, Boston. They had quietly talked the matter over together, and decided that, as there were three children in the family (not counting themselves, as they might well have done), it would be a delightful and not too expensive luxury to give a little Christmas party.

"You see, John," said Mrs. Brownlow, "We've been asked, ourselves, to half a dozen candy-pulls and parties since we've lived here, and it seems nothin' but fair that we should do it once ourselves."

"That's so, Clarissy," replied her husband slowly; "but then—there's so many of us, and my salary's—well, it would cost considerable, little woman, wouldn't it?"

"I'll tell you what!" she exclaimed. "We needn't have a regular grown-up party, but just one for children. We can get a small tree, and a bit of a present for each of the boys and girls, with ice-cream and cake, and let it go at that. The whole thing sha'n't cost ten dollars."

"Good!" said Mr. Brownlow heartily. "I knew you'd get some way out of it. Let's tell Bob and Sue and Polly, so they can have the fun of looking forward to it."

So it was settled and all hands entered into the plan with such a degree of earnestness that one would have thought these people were going to have some grand gift themselves, instead of giving to others, and pinching for a month afterwards, in their own comforts, as they knew they would have to do.

The first real difficulty they met was in deciding whom to invite. John was for asking only the children of their immediate neighbors: but Mrs. Brownlow said it would be a kindness, as well as polite, to include those who were better off than themselves.

"I allus think, John," she explained, laying her hand on his shoulder, "that it's just's much despisin' to look down on your rich neighbors—as if all they'd got was money—as on your poor ones. Let's ask 'em all: Deacon Holsum's, the Brights, and the Nortons." The Brights were Mr. Brownlow's employers.

"Anybody else?" queried her husband, with his funny twinkle. "P'raps you'd like to have me ask the governor's family, or Jordan & Marsh!"

"Now, John, don't you be saucy," she laughed, relieved at having carried her point. "Let's put our heads together, and see who to set down. Susie will write the notes in her nice hand, and Bob can deliver them, to save postage."

"Well, you've said three," counted Mr. Brownlow on his fingers. "Then there's Mrs. Sampson's little girl, and the four Williamses, and"—he enumerated one family after another, till nearly thirty names were on the list.

Once Susie broke in, "O Pa, *don't* invite that Mary Spenfield; she's awfully stuck-up and cross!"

"Good!" said her father again. "This will be just the thing for her. Let her be coffee and you be sugar, and see how much you can sweeten her that evening."

In the few days that intervened before the twenty-fifth, the whole family were busy enough, Mrs. Brownlow shopping, Susie writing the notes, and the others helping wherever they got a chance. Every evening they spread out upon the sitting-room floor such presents as had been bought during the day. These were not costly, but they were chosen lovingly, and seemed very nice indeed to Mr. Brownlow and the children, who united in praising the discriminating taste of Mrs. B., as with justifiable pride she sat in the center of the room, bringing forth her purchases from the depths of a capacious carpetbag.

The grand final expenditure was left until the day before Christmas. Mr. Brownlow got off from his work early, with his month's salary in his pocket, and a few kind words from his employers tucked away even more securely in his warm heart. He had taken special pains to include their children for his party, and he was quietly enjoying the thought of making them happy on the morrow.

By a preconcerted plan he met Mrs. Brownlow under the great golden eagle at the corner of Summer and Washington streets; and, having thus joined forces, the two proceeded in company toward a certain wholesale toy-shop where Mr. Brownlow was acquainted, and where they expected to secure such small articles as they desired, at dozen rates.

And now Mr. Brownlow realized what must have been his wife's exertions during the last fortnight. For having gallantly relieved her of her carpetbag, and offered his unoccupied arm for her support, he was constantly engaged in a struggle to maintain his hold upon either one or the other of his charges, and rescuing them with extreme difficulty from the crowd. At one time he was simultaneously attacked at both vulnerable points, a very stout woman persisting in thrusting herself between him and his already bulging carpetbag, on the one hand, and an equally persistent old gentleman engaged in separating Mrs. Brownlow from him, on the other. With flushed but determined face he held on to both with all his might, when a sudden stampede, to avoid a passing team, brought such a violent pressure upon him that he found both Clarissa and bag dragged from him, while he himself was borne at least a rod away before he could stem the tide. Fortunately, the stout woman immediately fell over the bag, and Mr. Brownlow, having by this means identified the spot where it lay, hewed his way, figuratively speaking, to his wife and bore her off triumphantly. At last, to the relief of both, they reached the entrance of the toy-dealer's huge store. Mr. Brownlow at once hunted up his friend, and all three set about a tour of the premises.

It was beyond doubt a wonderful place. A little retail shop, in the Christmas holidays, is of itself a marvel; but this immense establishment, at the back doors of which stood wagons constantly receiving cases on cases of goods directed to all parts of the country, was quite another thing. Such long passageways there were, walled in from floor to ceiling with boxes of picture-blocks, labeled in German; such mysterious, gloomy alcoves, by the sides of which lurked innumerable wild animals with glaring eyes and rigid tails; such fleets of Noah's arks, wherein were bestowed the patriarch's whole family (in tight-fitting garments of yellow and red) and specimens of all creation, so promiscuously packed together that it must have been extremely depressing to all concerned; such a delicious smell of sawdust and paint and wax; in short such presentation of Toy in the abstract, and Toy in particular, and Toy overhead, and underfoot, and in the very air,—could never have existed outside of Cottlow & Co.'s, Manufacturers, Dealers, and Importers of Toys.

Mrs. Brownlow was fairly at her wits' end to choose. When she meekly inquired for tin soldiers, solid regiments of them sprang up, like Jason's armed men, at her bidding. At the suggestion of a doll, the world seemed suddenly and solely peopled with these little creatures, and winking, crying, walking and talking dolls crowded about the bewildered customers,—dolls with flaxen hair, and dolls with no hair at all; dolls of imposing proportions when viewed in front, but of no thickness to speak of, when held sideways; dolls as rigid as mummies, and dolls who exhibited an alarming tendency to double their arms and legs up backward. To add to the confusion, the air was filled with the noise of trumpets, drums, musical boxes and other instruments, which were being tested in various parts of the building, until poor Mrs. Brownlow declared she should go distracted. At length, however, she and her husband, with the assistance of their polite friend, succeeded in selecting two or three dozen small gifts, and, when the last purchase was concluded, started for home.

After a walk of ten minutes, they reached Boylston Market, where they were at once beset by venders of evergreen and holly wreaths, crosses and stars of every description. Mr. Brownlow bought half a dozen of the cheaper sort of wreaths, which the owner kindly threaded upon his arm, as if they were a sort of huge, fragrant beads. Then he selected a tree, and, after a short consultation with Mrs. Brownlow, decided to carry it home himself, to save a quarter. A horse-car opportunely passing, they boarded it, Mrs. Brownlow and her bag being with some difficulty squeezed in through the rear door, and Mr. Brownlow taking his stand upon the front platform, from which the tree, which had been tightly tied up, projected like a bowsprit, until they reached home.

Great was the bustle at 17 Elm Street that night. Parcels were unwrapped; the whole house was pleasantly redolent of boiling molasses; and from the kitchen there came at the same time a scratchy and poppy sound, denoting the preparation of mounds of feathery corn. Bob and his father took upon themselves the uprearing of the tree. On being carried to the parlor it was found to be at least three feet too long, and Mr. Brownlow, in his shirt-sleeves, accomplished wonders with a saw, smearing himself in the process with pitch, from head to foot.

The tree seemed at first inclined to be sulky, perhaps at having been decapitated and curtailed; for it obstinately leaned backward, kicked over the soapbox in which it was set, bumped against Mr. Brownlow, tumbled forward, and in short, behaved itself like a tree which was determined to lie on its precious back all the next day, or perish in the attempt. At length, just as they were beginning to despair of ever getting it firm and straight, it gave a little quiver of its limbs, yielded gracefully to a final push by Bob, and stood upright, as fair and comely a Christmas tree as one would wish to see. Mr. Brownlow crept out backward from under the lower branches, (thereby throwing his hair into the wildest confusion and adding more pitch to himself), and regarded it with a sigh of content. Such presents as were to be disposed of in this way were now hung upon the branches; then strings of pop-corn, bits of wool, and glistening paper, a few red apples, and lastly the candles. When all was finished, which was not before midnight, the family withdrew to their beds, with weary limbs and brains, but with light-hearted anticipation of to-morrow.

"Do you s'pose Mrs. Bright will come with her children, John?" asked Mrs. Brownlow, as she turned out the gas.

"Shouldn't—wonder"—sleepily from the four-poster.

"Did Mr. Bright say anything about the invitation we sent, when he paid you off?"

Silence. More silence. Good Mr. Brownlow was asleep, and Clarissa soon followed him.

Meanwhile the snow, which had been falling fast during the early part of the evening, had ceased, leaving the earth as fair to look upon as the fleece-drifted sky above it. Slowly the heavy banks of cloud rolled away, disclosing star after star, until the moon itself looked down, and sent a soft "Merry Christmas" to mankind. At last came the dawn, with a glorious burst of sunlight and church-bells and glad voices, ushering in the gladdest and dearest day of all the year.

The Brownlows were early astir, full of the joyous spirit of the day. There was a clamor of Christmas greetings, and a delighted medley of shouts from the children over the few simple gifts that had been secretly laid aside for them. But the ruling thought in every heart was the party. It was to come off at five o'clock in the afternoon, when it would be just dark enough to light the candles on the tree.

In spite of all the hard work of the preceding days, there was not a moment to spare that forenoon. The house, as the head of the family facetiously remarked, was a perfect hive of B's.

As the appointed hour drew near, their nervousness increased. The children had been scrubbed from top to toe, and dressed in their very best clothes; Mrs. Brownlow wore a cap with lavender ribbons, which she had a misgiving were too gaudy for a person of her sedate years. Nor was the excitement confined to the interior of the house. The tree was placed in the front parlor, close to the window, and by half-past four a dozen ragged children were gathered about the iron fence of the little front yard, gazing open-mouthed and open-eyed at the spectacular wonders within. At a quarter before five Mrs. Brownlow's heart beat hard every time she heard a strange footstep in their quiet street. It was a little odd that none of the guests had arrived; but then, it was fashionable to be late!

Ten minutes more passed. Still no arrivals. It was evident that each was planning not to be the first to get there, and that they would all descend on the house and assault the door-bell at once. Mrs. Brownlow repeatedly smoothed the wrinkles out of her tidy apron, and Mr. Brownlow began to perspire with responsibility.

Meanwhile the crowd outside, recognizing no rigid bonds of etiquette, rapidly increased in numbers. Mr. Brownlow, to pass the time and please the poor little homeless creatures, lighted two of the candles.

The response from the front-yard fence was immediate. A low murmur of delight ran along the line, and several dull-eyed babies were hoisted, in the arms of babies scarcely older than themselves, to behold the rare vision of candles in a tree, just illumining the further splendors glistening here and there among the branches.

The kind man's heart warmed towards them, and he lighted two more candles. The delight of the audience could now hardly be restrained, and the babies, having been temporarily lowered by the aching little arms of their respective nurses, were shot up once more to view the redoubled grandeur.

The whole family had become so much interested in these small outcasts that they had not noticed the flight of time. Now some one glanced suddenly at the clock, and exclaimed, "It's nearly half-past five!"

The Brownlows looked at one another blankly. Poor Mrs. Brownlow's smart ribbons drooped in conscious abasement, while mortification and pride struggled in their wearer's kindly face, over which, after a moment's silence, one large tear slowly rolled, and dropped off.

Mr. Brownlow gave himself a little shake and sat down, as was his wont upon critical occasions. As his absent gaze wandered about the room, so prettily decked for the guests who didn't come, it fell upon a little worn, gilt-edged volume on the table. At that sight, a new thought occurred to him. "Clarissy," he said softly, going over to his wife and putting his arm around her, "Clarissy, seein's the well-off folks haven't accepted, don't you think we'd better invite some of the others in?" And he pointed significantly toward the window.

Mrs. Brownlow, despatching another tear after the first, nodded. She was not quite equal to words yet. Being a woman, the neglect of her little party cut her even more deeply than it did her husband.

Mr. Brownlow stepped to the front door. Nay more, he walked down the short flight of steps, took one little girl by the hand, and said in his pleasant, fatherly way,

"Wouldn't you like to go in and look at the tree? Come, Puss" (to the waif at his side), "we'll start first."

With these words he led the way back through the open door, and into the warm, lighted room. The children hung back a little, but seeing that no harm came to the first guest, soon flocked in, each trying to keep behind all the rest, but at the same time shouldering the babies up into view as before.

In the delightful confusion that followed, the good hosts forgot all about the miscarriage of their plans. They completely outdid themselves, in efforts to please their hastily acquired company. Bob spoke a piece, the girls sang duets. Mrs. Brownlow had held every individual baby in her motherly arms before half an hour was over. And as for Mr. Brownlow, it was simply marvelous to see him go among those children, giving them the presents, and initiating their owners into the mysterious impelling forces of monkeys with yellow legs and gymnastic tendencies; filling the boys' pockets with popcorn, blowing horns and tin whistles; now assaulting the tree (it had been lighted throughout, and—bless it—how firm it stood now!) for fresh novelties, now diving into the kitchen and returning in an unspeakably cohesive state of breathlessness and molasses candy,—all the while laughing, talking, patting heads, joking, until the kindly Spirit of Christmas Present would have wept and smiled at once, for the pleasure of the sight.

"And now, my young friends," said Mr. Brownlow, raising his voice, "we'll have a little ice-cream in the back room. Ladies first, gentlemen afterward!" So saying, he gallantly stood on one side, with a sweep of his hand, to allow Mrs. Brownlow to precede him. But just as the words left his mouth there came a sharp ring at the door-bell.

"It's a carriage!" gasped Mrs. Brownlow, flying to the front window, and backing precipitately. "Susie, go to that door an' see who 't is. Land sakes, *what* a mess this parlor's in!" And she gazed with a true housekeeper's dismay at the littered carpet and dripping candles.

"Deacon Holsum and Mrs. Hartwell, Pa!" announced Susie, throwing open the parlor door.

The lady thus mentioned came forward with outstretched hand. Catching a glimpse of Mrs. Brownlow's embarrassed face she exclaimed quickly—

"Isn't this splendid! Father and I were just driving past, and we saw your tree through the window, and couldn't resist dropping in upon you. You won't mind us, will you?"

"Mind—you!" repeated Mrs. Brownlow, in astonishment. "Why of course not—only you are so late—we didn't expect"—

Mrs. Hartwell looked puzzled.

"Pardon me,—I don't think I quite understand"—

"The invitation was for five, you know, ma'am."

"But we received no invitation!"

Mr. Brownlow, who had greeted the deacon heartily and then listened with amazement to this conversation, now turned upon Bob, with a signally futile attempt at a withering glance.

Bob looked as puzzled as the rest, for a moment. Then his face fell, and he flushed to the roots of his hair.

"I—I—must have—forgot"—he stammered.

"Forgotten what?"

"The invitations—they're in my desk now!"

Thus Bob, with utterly despairing tone and self-abasement.

Mrs. Hartwell's silvery little laugh rang out—it was as near moonlight playing on the upper keys of an organ as anything you can imagine—and grasped Mrs. Brownlow's hand.

"You poor dear!" she cried, kissing her hostess, who stood speechless, not knowing whether to laugh or cry, "so that's why nobody came! But who has cluttered—who has been having such a good time here, then?"

Mr. Brownlow silently led the last two arrivals to the door of the next room, and pointed in. It was now the kind deacon's turn to be touched.

" 'Into the highways'!" he murmured, as he looked upon the unwashed, hungry little circle about the table.

"I s'pose," said Mr. Brownlow doubtfully, "they'd like to have you sit down with 'em, just's if they were folks—if you didn't mind?"

Mind! I wish you could have seen the rich furs and overcoat come off and go down on the floor in a heap, before Polly could catch them!

When they were all seated, Mr. Brownlow looked over to the deacon, and he asked a blessing on the little ones gathered there. "Thy servants, the masters of this house, have suffered them to come unto thee," he said in his prayer. "Wilt thou take them into thine arms, O Father of lights, and bless them!"

A momentary hush followed, and then the fun began again. Sweetly and swiftly kind words flew back and forth across the table, each one carrying its own golden thread and weaving the hearts of poor and rich into the one fine fabric of brotherhood and humanity they were meant to form.

Outside, the snow began to fall once more, each crystaled flake whispering softly as it touched the earth that Christmas night, *"Peace—peace!"*

Rosa's Tale

BY LOUISA MAY ALCOTT

"Now, I believe everyone has had a Christmas present and a good time. Nobody has been forgotten, not even the cat," said Mrs. Ward to her daughter, as she looked at Pobbylinda, purring on the rug, with a new ribbon round her neck and the remains of a chicken bone between her paws.

It was very late, for the Christmas tree was decorated, the little folks in bed, the baskets and bundles left at poor neighbors' doors, and everything ready for the happy day which would begin as the clock struck twelve. They were resting after their mother's words reminded Belinda of one good friend who had received no gift that night.

"We've forgotten Rosa! Her mistress is away, but she shall have a present nevertheless. As late as it is, I know she would like some apples and cake and a Merry Christmas from the family."

Belinda jumped up as she spoke, and having collected such remnants of the feast as a horse would relish, she put on her hood, lighted a lantern, and trotted off to the barn to deliver her Christmas cheer.

As she opened the door of the loose box in which Rosa was kept, Belinda saw Rosa's eyes shining in the dark as she lifted her head with a startled air. Then, recognizing a friend, the horse rose and came rustling through the straw to greet her late visitor. She was evidently much pleased with the attention and gratefully rubbed her nose against Miss Belinda. At the same time, she poked her nose suspiciously into the contents of the basket.

Miss Belinda well knew that Rosa was an unusually social beast and would enjoy the little feast more if she had company, so she hung up the lantern, and sitting down on an inverted bucket, watched her as she munched contentedly.

"Now really," said Miss Belinda, when telling her story afterwards, "I am not sure whether I took a nap and dreamed what follows, or whether it actually happened, for strange things do occur at Christmastime, as everyone knows.

"As I sat there, the town clock struck twelve, and the sound reminded me of the legend, which affirms that all dumb animals are endowed with speech for one hour after midnight on Christmas Eve, in memory of the animals who lingered near the manger when the blessed Christ Child was born.

"I wish this pretty legend were true and our Rosa could speak, if only for an hour. I'm sure she has an interesting history, and I long to know all about it.

"I said this aloud, and to my utter amazement the bay mare

stopped eating, fixed her intelligent eyes upon my face, and answered in a language I understood perfectly well—'You shall indeed know my history, for whether the legend you mention is true or not, I do feel that I can confide in you and tell you all that I feel,' sweet Rosa told me.

" 'I was lying awake listening to the fun in the house, thinking of my dear mistress so far away across the ocean and feeling very sad, for I heard you say that I was to be sold. That nearly broke my heart, for no one has ever been so kind to me as Miss Merry, and nowhere shall I be taken care of, nursed, and loved as I have been since she bought me. I know I'm getting old and stiff in the knees. My forefoot is lame, and sometimes I'm cross when my shoulder aches, but I do try to be a patient, grateful beast. I've gotten fat with good living, my work is not hard, and I dearly love to carry those who have done so much for me. I'll carry them about until I die in the harness if they will only keep me.'

"I was so astonished by Rosa's speech that I tumbled off the pail on which I was sitting and landed in the straw staring up at Rosa, as dumb as if I had lost the power she had gained. She seemed to enjoy my surprise, and added to it by letting me hear a genuine horse laugh—hearty, shrill, and clear—as she shook her pretty head and went on talking rapidly in the language which I now perceived to be a mixture of English and the peculiar dialect of the horse country.

" 'Thank you for remembering me tonight, and in return for the goodies you bring I'll tell my story as quickly as I can, for I have often longed to recount the trials and triumphs of my life. Miss Merry came last Christmas Eve to bring me sugar, and I wanted to speak, but it was too early and I could not say a word, though my heart was full.'

"Rosa paused an instant, and her fine eyes dimmed as if with tender tears at the recollection of the happy year, which followed the day she was bought from the drudgery of a livery stable to be a lady's special pet. I stroked her neck as she stooped to sniff affectionately at my hood, and eagerly said—

" 'Tell away, dear. I'm full of interest, and understand every word you say.'

"Thus encouraged, Rosa threw up her head, and began once again to speak with an air of pride, which plainly proved what we had always suspected, that she belonged to a good family.

" 'My father was a famous racer, and I am very like him, the same color, spirit, and grace, and but for the cruelty of man, I might have been as renowned as he. I was a happy colt, petted by my master, tamed by love, and never struck a blow while he lived. I won one race for him, and my future seemed so promising that when he died, I brought a great price.

" 'I mourned the death of my master, but I was glad to be sent to my new owner's racing stable, where I was made over by everyone. I heard many predictions that I would be another Goldsmith Maid or Flora Temple. Ah, how ambitious and proud I was in those days! I was truly vain in regard to my good blood, my speed, and my beauty, for indeed, I was handsome then, though you may find it difficult to believe now.' Rosa sighed regretfully as she stole a look at me, and turned her head in a way that accentuated the fine lines about her head and neck.

" 'I do not find it hard to believe at all,' I answered. 'Miss Merry saw them, though you seemed to be nothing more than a skeleton when she bought you. The Cornish blacksmith who shod you noted the same. It is easy to see that you belong to a good family by the way you hold your head without a check-rein and carry your tail like a plume,' I said, with a look of admiration.

" 'I must hurry over this part of my story because, though brilliant, it was very brief, and ended in a way that made it the bitterest portion of my life,' continued Rosa. 'I won several races, and everyone predicted that I would earn great fame. You may guess how high my reputation was when I tell you that before my last, fatal trial, thousands were bet on me, and my rival trembled at the thought of racing against me.

" 'I was full of spirit, eager to show my speed, and sure of success. Alas, how little I knew of the wickedness of human nature then, how dearly I bought the knowledge, and how completely it has changed my whole life! You do not know much about such matters, of course, and I won't digress to tell you all the tricks of the trade, only beware of jockeys and never bet.

" 'I was kept carefully out of everyone's way for weeks and only taken out for exercise by my trainer. Poor Bill! I was fond of him, and he was so good to me that I never have forgotten him, though he broke his neck years ago. A few nights before the great race, as I was enjoying a good sleep carefully tucked away in my stall, someone stole in and gave me a dish of warm mash. It was dark, and I was but half awake. I ate it like a fool, even though I knew by instinct that it was not Bill who left it for me.

" 'I was a trusting creature then, and used to all sorts of strange things being done to prepare me to race. For that reason, I never suspected that something could be wrong. Something was very wrong, however, and the deceit of it has caused me to be suspicious of any food ever since. You see, the mash was dosed in some way, it made me very ill and nearly allowed my enemies to triumph. What a shameful, cowardly trick.

" 'Bill worked with me day and night, trying desperately to prepare me to run. I did my best to seem well, but there was not time for me to regain my lost strength and spirit. My pride was the only thing that kept me going. "I'll win for my master, even if I die in doing it," I said to myself. When the hour came, I pranced to my place trying to look as well as ever, though my heart was heavy and I trembled with excitement. "Courage, my lass, and we'll beat them in spite of their dark tricks," Bill whispered, as he sprang into place.

" 'I lost the first heat but won the second, and the sound of the cheering gave me strength to walk away without staggering, though my legs shook under me. What a splendid minute that was when, encouraged and refreshed by my faithful Bill, I came on the track again! I knew my enemies began to fear. I carried myself so bravely that they fancied I was quite well, and now, excited by that first success, I was mad with impatience to be off and cover myself with glory.

" 'Rosa looked as if her 'splendid moment' had come again, for she arched her neck, opened wide her red nostrils, and pawed the straw with one little foot. At the same time, her eyes shone with sudden fire, and her ears were pricked up as if to catch again the shouts of the spectators on that long ago day.

" 'I wish I had been there to see you!' I exclaimed, quite carried away by her ardor.

" 'I wish you had indeed,' she answered, 'for I won. I won! The big, black horse did his best, but I had vowed to win or die, and I kept my word. For I beat him by a head, and as quickly as I had done so, I fell to the ground as if dead. I might as well have died then and there. I heard those around me whispering that the poison, the exercise, and the fall had ruined me as a racer.

" 'My master no longer cared for me and would have had me shot if kind Bill had not saved my life. I was pronounced good for nothing, and Bill was able to buy me cheaply. For quite a long time, I was lame and useless, but his patient care did wonders. And just as I was able to be of use to him, he was killed.

" 'A gentleman in search of a saddle horse purchased me because my easy gait and quiet temper suited him, for I was meek enough now, and my size allowed me to carry his delicate daughter.

" 'For more than a year, I served little Miss Alice, rejoicing to see how rosy her pale cheeks became, how upright her feeble figure grew, thanks to the hours she spent with me. My canter rocked her as gently as if she were in a cradle, and fresh air was the medicine she needed. She often said she owed her life to me, and I liked to think so, for she made my life a very easy one.

" 'But somehow my good times never lasted long, and when Miss Alice went west, I was sold. I had been so well treated that I looked as handsome and happy as ever. To be honest though, my shoulder never was strong again, and I often had despondent moods, longing for the excitement of the race track with the instinct of my kind, so I was glad when, attracted by my spirit and beauty, a young army officer bought me, and I went to the war.

" 'Ah! You never guessed that, did you? Yes, I did my part gallantly and saved my master's life more than once. You have observed how martial music delights me, but you don't know that it is because it reminds me of the proudest hour of my life.

I've told you about the saddest—now listen as I tell you about the bravest and give me a pat for the courageous act that won my master his promotion though I got no praise for my part of the achievement.

" 'In one of the hottest battles, my captain was ordered to lead his men on a most perilous mission. They hesitated; so did he, for it was certain to cost many lives, and, brave as they were they paused an instant. But, I settled the point. Wild with the sound of drums, the smell of powder, and the excitement of the hour, I rebelled. Though I was sharply reined in, I took the bit between my teeth and dashed straight ahead into the midst of the fight. Though he tried, my rider could do nothing to stop me. The men, thinking their captain was leading them on, followed cheering loudly and carrying all that was before them.

" 'What happened just after that I never could remember, except that I got a wound here in my neck and a cut on my flank. The scar is there still, and I'm proud of it, though buyers always consider it a blemish. When the battle was won, my master was promoted on the field, and I carried him up to the general as he sat among his officers under the torn flags.

" 'Both of us were weary and wounded. Both of us were full of pride at what we had done, but he received all the praise and honor. I received only a careless word and a better supper than usual.

" 'It seemed so wrong that no one knew or appreciated my courageous action. Not a one seemed to care that it was the horse, not the man, who led that fearless charge. I did think I deserved at least a rosette—others received much more for far less dangerous deeds. My master alone knew the truth of the matter. He thanked me for my help by keeping me always with him until the sad day when he was killed in a skirmish and lay for hours with no one to watch and mourn over him but his faithful horse.

"Then I knew how much he loved and thanked me. His hand stroked me while it had the strength, his eye turned to me until it grew too dim to see, and when help came at last, I heard him whisper to a comrade, "Be kind to Rosa and send her safely home. She has earned her rest."

" 'I had earned it, but I did not get it. When I arrived home, I was received by a mother whose heart was broken by the loss of her son. She did not live long to cherish me. The worst of my bad times were only beginning.

" 'My next owner was a fast young man who treated me badly in many ways. At last the spirit of my father rose within me, and I ran away with my master and caused him to take a brutal fall.

"To tame me down, I was sold as a carriage horse. That almost killed me, for it was dreadful drudgery. Day after day, I pulled heavy loads behind me over the hard pavement. The horses that pulled alongside me were far from friendly, and there was no affection to cheer my life.

" 'I have often longed to ask why Mr. Bergh does not try to prevent such crowds from piling into those carriages. Now I beg you to do what you can to stop such an unmerciful abuse.

" 'In snowstorms it was awful, and more than one of my mates dropped dead with overwork and discouragement. I used to wish I could do the same, for my poor feet, badly shod, became so lame I could hardly walk at times, and the constant strain on the upgrades brought back the old trouble in my shoulder worse than ever.

" 'Why they did not kill me, I don't know. I was a miserable creature then, but there must be something attractive that lingers about me, for people always seem to think I am worth saving. Whatever can it be, ma'am?'

" 'Now, Rosa, don't talk so. You know you are an engaging, little animal, and if you live to be forty, I'm sure you will still have certain pretty ways about you—ways that win the hearts of women, if not of men. Women sympathize with your afflictions, find themselves amused with your coquettish airs, and like your affectionate nature. Men, unfortunately, see your weak points and take a money view of the case. Now hurry up and finish. It's getting a bit cold out here.'

"I laughed as I spoke, and Rosa eyed me with a sidelong glance and gently waved her docked tail, which was her delight. The sly thing liked to be flattered and was as fond of compliments as a girl.

" 'Many thanks. I will come now to the most interesting portion of my narrative. As I was saying, instead of being knocked on the head, I was packed off to New Hampshire and had a fine rest among the green hills, with a dozen or so weary friends. It was during this holiday that I acquired the love of nature Miss Merry detected and liked in me when she found me ready to study sunsets with her, to admire new landscapes, and enjoy bright, summer weather.

" 'In the autumn, a livery stable keeper bought me, and through the winter, he fed me well. By spring, I was quite presentable. It was a small town, but a popular place to visit in the summertime. I was kept on the trot while the season lasted, mostly because ladies found me easy to drive. You, Miss Belinda, were one of the ladies, and I never shall forget, though I have long ago forgiven it, how you laughed at my odd gait the day you hired me.

" 'My tender feet and stiff knees made me tread very gingerly and amble along with short, mincing steps, which contrasted rather strangely with my proudly waving tail and high carried head. You liked me nevertheless because I didn't rattle you senseless as we traveled down the steep hills. You also seemed pleased that I didn't startle at the sight of locomotives and stood patiently while you gathered flowers and enjoyed the sights and sounds.

" 'I have always felt a regard for you because you did not whip me and admired my eyes, which, I may say without vanity, have always been considered unusually fine. But no one ever won my whole heart like Miss Merry, and I never shall forget the happy day when she came to the stable to order a saddle horse. Her cheery voice caught my attention, and when she said after looking at several showy beasts, "No, they don't suit me. This little one here has the right air," my heart danced within me and I looked 'round with a whinny of delight. "Can I ride her?" she asked, understanding my welcome. She came right up to me, patted me, peered into my face, rubbed my nose, and looked at my feet with an air of interest and sympathy that made me feel as if I'd like to carry her clear around the world.

" 'Ah, what rides we had after that! What happy hours trotting merrily through the green woods, galloping over the breezy hills, and pacing slowly along quiet lanes, where I often lunched luxuriously on clover tops while Miss Merry took a sketch of some picturesque scene with me in the foreground.

" 'I liked that very much. We had long chats at such times, and I was convinced that she understood me perfectly. She was never frightened when I danced for pleasure on the soft turf. She never chided me when I snatched a bite from the young trees as we passed through sylvan ways, never thought it any trouble to let me wet my tired feet in babbling brooks, and always kindly dismounted long enough to remove the stones that plagued me.

" 'Then how well she rode! So firm yet light in the seat, so steady a hand on the reins, so agile a foot to spring on and off, and such infectious spirits. No matter how despondent or cross I might be, I felt happy and young again whenever dear Miss Merry was on my back.'

"Here Rosa gave a frisk that sent the straw flying and made me shrink into a corner. She pranced about the box, neighing so loudly that she woke the big, brown colt in the next stall and set poor Buttercup to lowing for her lost calf, which she had managed to forget about for a few moments in sleep.

" 'Ah, Miss Merry never ran away from me! She knew my heels were to be trusted, and she let me play as I would, glad to see me lively. Never mind, Miss Belinda, come out and I'll behave as befits my years,' laughed Rosa, composing herself, and adding in a way so like a woman that I could not help smiling in the dark—

" 'When I say "years," I beg you to understand that I am not as old as that base man declared, but just in the prime of life for a horse. Hard usage has made me seem old before my time, but I am good for years of service yet.'

" 'Few people have been through as much as you have, Rosa, and you certainly have earned the right to rest.' I said consolingly, for her little whims and vanities amused me.

" 'You know what happened next,' she continued, 'but I must seize this opportunity to express my thanks for all the kindness I've received since Miss Merry bought me, in spite of the ridicule and dissuasion of all her friends.

" 'I know I didn't look a good bargain. I was very thin and lame and shabby, but she saw and loved the willing spirit in me. She pitied my hard lot and felt that it would be a good deed to buy me even if she never got much work out of me.

" 'I shall always remember that, and whatever happens to me hereafter, I never shall be as proud again as I was the day she put my new saddle and bridle on me. I was led out, sleek, plump, and handsome with blue rosettes at my ears, my tail cut in the English style, and on my back, Miss Merry sat in her London hat and habit, all ready to head a cavalcade of eighteen horsemen and horsewomen.

" 'We were the most perfect pair of all, and when the troop pranced down the street six abreast, my head was the highest, my rider the straightest, and our two hearts the friendliest in all the goodly company.

" 'Nor is it pride and love alone that bind me to her. It is gratitude as well. She often bathed my feet herself, rubbed me down, watered me, blanketed me, and came daily to see me when I was here alone for weeks in the winter. Didn't she write to the famous friend of my race for advice, and drive me seven miles to get a good smith to shoe me well? Didn't she give me weeks of rest without shoes in order to save my poor, contracted feet? And am I not now fat and handsome, and barring the stiff knees, a very presentable horse? If I am, it is all owing to Miss Merry, and for that reason, I want to live and die in her service.

" 'She doesn't want to sell me and only told you to do so because you didn't want to care for me while she is gone. Dear Miss Belinda, please keep me! I'll eat as little as I can. I won't ask for a new blanket, though this old army one is thin and shabby. I'll trot for you all winter and try not to show it if I am lame. I'll do anything a horse can, no matter how humble, in order to earn my living. Don't, I beg you, send me away among strangers who have neither interest nor pity for me!'

"Rosa had spoken rapidly, feeling that her plea must be made now or never. Before another Christmas, she might be far away and speech of no use to win her wish. I was greatly touched, even though she was only a horse. She was looking earnestly at me as she spoke and made the last words very eloquent by preparing to bend her stiff knees and lie down at my feet. I stopped her and answered with an arm about her neck and her soft nose in my hand—

" 'You shall not be sold, Rosa! You shall go and board at Mr. Town's great stable, where you will have pleasant society among the eighty horses who usually pass the winter there. Your shoes shall be taken off so that you might rest until March at least. Your care will be only the best, my dear, and I will come and see you. In the spring, you shall return to us, even if Miss Merry is not here to welcome you.'

"Thanks, many, many thanks! But I wish I could do something to earn my board. I hate to be idle, though rest is delicious. Is there nothing I can do to repay you, Miss Belinda? Please answer quickly. I know the hour is almost over,' cried Rosa, stamping with anxiety. Like all horses, she wanted the last word.

" 'Yes, you can,' I cried, as a sudden idea popped into my head. "I'll write down what you have told me and send the little story to a certain paper I know of. The money I get for it will pay your board. So rest in peace, my dear. You will have earned your living after all, and you may rest knowing that your debt is paid.'

"Before she could reply, the clock struck one. A long sigh of satisfaction was all the response in her power. But, we understood each other now, and cutting a lock from her hair for Miss Merry, I gave Rosa a farewell caress and went on my way. I couldn't help wondering if I had made it all up or the charming beast had really broken a year's silence and freed her mind.

"However that may be, here is the tale. The sequel to it is that the bay mare has really gone to board at a first-class stable," concluded Miss Belinda. "I call occasionally and leave my card in the shape of an apple, finding Madam Rosa living like an independent lady, her large box and private yard on the sunny side of the barn, a kind ostler to wait upon her, and much genteel society from the city when she is inclined for company.

"What more could any reasonable horse desire?"

The Christmas Masquerade

by MARY E. WILKINS FREEMAN

ON CHRISTMAS EVE THE MAYOR'S stately mansion presented a beautiful appearance. There were rows of different-colored wax candles burning in every window, and beyond them one could see the chandeliers of gold and crystal blazing with light. The fiddles were squeaking merrily, and lovely little forms flew past the windows in time to the music.

There were gorgeous carpets laid from the door to the street, and carriages were constantly arriving, and fresh guests tripping over them. They were all children. The Mayor was giving a Christmas Masquerade to-night, to all the children in the city, the poor as well as the rich. The preparation for this ball had been making an immense sensation for the last three months. Placards had been up in the most conspicuous points in the city, and all the daily newspapers had at least a column devoted to it, headed with THE MAYOR'S CHRISTMAS MASQUERADE in very large letters.

The Mayor had promised to defray the expenses of all the poor children whose parents were unable to do so, and the bills for their costumes were directed to be sent in to him.

Of course there was a great deal of excitement among the regular costumers of the city, and they all resolved to vie with one another in being the most popular, and the best patronized on this gala occasion. But the placards and the notices had not been out a week before a new Costumer appeared, who cast all the others into the shade directly. He set up his shop on the corner of one of the principal streets, and hung up his beautiful costumes in the windows. He was a little fellow, not much larger than a boy of ten. His cheeks were as red as roses, and he had on a long curling wig as white as snow. He wore a suit of crimson velvet knee-breeches, and a little swallow-tailed coat with beautiful golden buttons. Deep lace ruffles fell over his slender white hands, and he wore elegant knee-buckles of glittering stones. He sat on a high stool behind his counter and served his customers himself; he kept no clerk.

It did not take the children long to discover what beautiful things he had, and how superior he was to the other costumers, and they begun to flock to his shop immediately, from the Mayor's daughter to the poor rag-picker's. The children were to select their own costumes; the Mayor had stipulated that. It was to be a children's ball in every sense of the word.

So they decided to be fairies, and shepherdesses, and princesses, according to their own fancies; and this new costumer had charming costumes to suit them.

It was noticeable, that, for the most part, the children of the rich, who had always had everything they desired, would choose the parts of goose-girls and peasants and such like; and the poor children jumped eagerly at the chance of being princesses or fairies for a few hours in their miserable lives.

When Christmas Eve came, and the children flocked into the Mayor's mansion, whether it was owing to the Costumer's art, or their own adaptation to the characters they had chosen, it was wonderful how lifelike their representations were. Those little fairies in their short skirts of silken gauze, in which golden sparkles appeared as they moved, with their little funny gossamer wings, like butterflies, looked like real fairies. It did not seem possible, when they floated around to the music, half supported on the tips of their dainty toes, half by their filmy, purple wings, their delicate bodies swaying in time, that they could be anything but fairies. It seemed absurd to imagine that they were Johnny Mullens, the washwoman's son, and Polly Flinders, the charwoman's little girl, and so on.

The Mayor's daughter, who had chosen the character of a goose-girl, looked so like a true one that one could hardly dream she ever was anything else. She was, ordinarily, a slender, dainty little lady, rather tall for her age. She now looked very short and stubbed and brown, just as if she had been accustomed to tend geese in all sorts of weather. It was so with all the others—the Red Riding-hoods, the princesses, the Bo Peeps, and with every one of the characters who came to the Mayor's ball; Red Riding-hood looked round, with big, frightened eyes, all ready to spy the wolf, and carried her little pat of butter and pot of honey gingerly in her basket; Bo Peep's eyes looked red with weeping for the loss of her sheep; and the princesses swept about so grandly in their splendid brocaded trains, and held their crowned heads so high that people half believed them to be true princesses.

But there never was anything like the fun at the Mayor's Christmas ball. The fiddlers fiddled and fiddled, and the children danced and danced on the beautiful waxed floors. The Mayor, with his family and a few grand guests, sat on a dais covered with blue velvet at one end of the dancing hall, and watched the sport. They were all delighted. The Mayor's eldest daughter sat in front and clapped her little soft white hands. She was a tall, beautiful young maiden, and wore a white dress, and a little cap woven of blue violets on her yellow hair. Her name was Violetta.

The supper was served at midnight—and such a supper! The mountains of pink and white ices, and the cakes with sugar castles and flower-gardens on the tops of them, and the charming shapes of gold and ruby-colored jellies! There were wonderful bonbons which even the Mayor's daughter did not have every day; and all sorts of fruits, fresh and candied. They had cowslip wine in green glasses, and elderberry wine in red, and they drank each other's health. The glasses held a thimbleful each; the Mayor's wife thought that was all the wine they ought to have. Under each child's plate there was a pretty present; and every one had a basket of bonbons and cake to carry home.

At four o'clock the fiddlers put up their fiddles and the children went home; fairies and shepherdesses and pages and princesses all jabbering gleefully about the splendid time they had had.

But in a short time what consternation there was throughout the city! When the proud and fond parents attempted to unbutton their children's dresses, in order to prepare them for bed, not a single costume would come off. The buttons buttoned again as fast as they were unbuttoned; even if they pulled out a pin, in it would slip again in a twinkling; and when a string was untied it tied itself up again into a bow-knot. The parents were dreadfully frightened. But the children were so tired out they finally let them go to bed in their fancy costumes, and thought perhaps they would come off better in the morning. So Red Riding-hood went to bed in her little red cloak, holding fast to her basket full of dainties for her grandmother, and Bo Peep slept with her crook in her hand.

The children all went to bed readily enough, they were so very tired, even though they had to go in this strange array. All but the fairies—they danced and pirouetted and would not be still.

"We want to swing on the blades of grass," they kept saying, "and play hide-and-seek in the lily-cups, and take a nap between the leaves of the roses."

The poor charwomen and coal-heavers, whose children the fairies were for the most part, stared at them in great distress. They did not know what to do with these radiant, frisky little creatures into which their Johnnys and their Pollys and Betseys were so suddenly transformed. But the fairies went to bed quietly enough when daylight came, and were soon fast asleep.

There was no further trouble till twelve o'clock, when all the children woke up. Then a great wave of alarm spread over the city. Not one of the costumes would come off then. The buttons buttoned as fast as they were unbuttoned; the pins quilted themselves in as fast as they were pulled out; and the strings flew round like lightning and twisted themselves into bow-knots as fast as they were untied.

And that was not the worst of it; every one of the children seemed to have become, in reality, the character which he or she had assumed.

The Mayor's daughter declared she was going to tend her geese out in the pasture, and the shepherdesses sprang out of their little beds of down, throwing aside their silken quilts, and cried that they must go out and watch their sheep. The princesses jumped up from their straw pallets, and wanted to go to court; and all the rest of them likewise. Poor little Red Riding-hood sobbed and sobbed because she couldn't go and carry her basket to her grandmother, and as she didn't have any grandmother she couldn't go, of course, and her parents were very much troubled. It was all so mysterious and dreadful. The news spread very rapidly over the city, and soon a great crowd gathered around the new Costumer's shop, for every one thought he must be responsible for all this mischief.

The shop door was locked; but they soon battered it down with stones. When they rushed in the Costumer was not there; he had disappeared with all his wares. Then they did not know what to do. But it was evident that they must do something before long, for the state of affairs was growing worse and worse.

The Mayor's little daughter braced her back up against the tapestried wall and planted her two feet in their thick shoes firmly. "I will go and tend my geese!" she kept crying. "I won't eat my breakfast! I won't go out in the park! I won't go to school. I'm going to tend my geese—I will, I will, I will!"

And the princesses trailed their rich trains over the rough, unpainted floors in their parents' poor little huts, and held their crowned heads very high and demanded to be taken to court. The princesses were, mostly, geese-girls when they were their proper selves, and their geese were suffering, and their poor parents did not know what they were going to do, and they wrung their hands and wept as they gazed on their gorgeously-appareled children.

Finally, the Mayor called a meeting of the Aldermen, and they all assembled in the City Hall. Nearly every one of them had a son or a daughter who was a chimney-sweep, or a little watch-girl, or a shepherdess. They appointed a chairman and they took a great many votes, and contrary votes; but they did not agree on anything, until some one proposed that they consult the Wise Woman. Then they all held up their hands, and voted to, unanimously.

So the whole board of Aldermen set out, walking by twos, with the Mayor at their head, to consult the Wise Woman. The Aldermen were all very fleshy, and carried gold-headed canes which they swung very high at every step. They held their heads well back, and their chins stiff, and whenever they met common people they sniffed gently. They were very imposing.

The Wise Woman lived in a little hut on the outskirts of the city. She kept a Black Cat; except for her, she was all alone. She was very old, and had brought up a great many children, and she was considered remarkably wise.

But when the Aldermen reached her hut and found her seated by the fire, holding her Black Cat, a new difficulty presented itself. She had always been quite deaf, and people had been obliged to scream as loud as they could in order to make her hear; but, lately, she had grown much deafer, and when the Aldermen attempted to lay the case before her she could not hear a word. In fact, she was so very deaf that she could not distinguish a tone below G-sharp. The Aldermen screamed till they were quite red in their faces, but all to no purpose; none of them could get up to G-sharp, of course.

So the Aldermen all went back, swinging their gold-headed canes, and they had another meeting in the City Hall. Then they decided to send the highest Soprano Singer in the church choir to the Wise Woman; she could sing up to G-sharp just as easy as not. So the high-Soprano Singer set out for the Wise Woman's in the Mayor's coach, and the Aldermen marched behind, swinging their gold-headed canes.

The high-Soprano Singer put her head down close to the Wise Woman's ear, and sang all about the Christmas Masquerade, and the dreadful dilemma everybody was in, in G-sharp—she even went higher, sometimes—and the Wise Woman heard every word. She nodded three times, and every time she nodded she looked wiser.

"Go home, and give 'em a spoonful of castor-oil, all 'round," she piped up; then she took a pinch of snuff, and wouldn't say any more.

So the Aldermen went home, and each one took a district and marched through it, with a servant carrying an immense bowl and spoon, and every child had to take a dose of castor-oil.

But it didn't do a bit of good. The children cried and struggled when they were forced to take the castor-oil; but, two minutes afterward, the chimney-sweeps were crying for their brooms, and the princesses screaming because they couldn't go to court, and the Mayor's daughter, who had been given a double dose, cried louder and more sturdily: "I want to go and tend my geese! I will go and tend my geese!"

So the Aldermen took the high-Soprano Singer, and they consulted the Wise Woman again. She was taking a nap this time, and the Singer had to sing up to B-flat before she could wake her. Then she was very cross, and the Black Cat put up his back and spit at the Aldermen.

"Give 'em a spanking all 'round," she snapped out, "and if that don't work put 'em to bed without their supper!"

Then the Aldermen marched back to try that; and all the children in the city were spanked, and when that didn't do any good they were put to bed without any supper. But the next morning when they woke up they were worse than ever.

The Mayor and the Aldermen were very indignant, and considered that they had been imposed upon and insulted. So they set out for the Wise Woman's again, with the high-Soprano Singer.

She sang in G-sharp how the Aldermen and the Mayor considered her an imposter, and did not think she was wise at all, and they wished her to take her Black Cat and move beyond the limits of the city. She sang it beautifully; it sounded like the very finest Italian opera-music.

"Deary me," piped the Wise Woman, when she had finished, "how very grand these gentlemen are." Her Black Cat put up his back and spit.

"Five times one Black Cat are five Black Cats," said the Wise Woman. And, directly, there were five Black Cats, spitting and miauling.

"Five times five Black Cats are twenty-five Black Cats." And then there were twenty-five of the angry little beasts.

"Five times twenty-five Black Cats are one hundred and twenty-five Black Cats," added the Wise Woman, with a chuckle.

Then the Mayor and the Aldermen and the high-Soprano Singer fled precipitately out the door and back to the city. One hundred and twenty-five Black Cats had seemed to fill the Wise Woman's hut full, and when they all spit and miauled together it was dreadful. The visitors could not wait for her to multiply Black Cats any longer.

As winter wore on, and spring came, the condition of things grew more intolerable. Physicians had been consulted, who advised that the children should be allowed to follow their own bents, for fear of injury to their constitutions. So the rich Aldermen's daughters were actually out in the fields herding sheep, and their sons sweeping chimneys or carrying newspapers; while the poor charwomen's and coal-heavers' children spent their time like princesses and fairies. Such a topsy-turvy state of society was shocking. Why, the Mayor's little daughter was tending geese out in the meadow like any common goose-girl! Her pretty elder sister, Violetta, felt very sad about it, and used often to cast about in her mind for some way of relief.

When cherries were ripe in spring, Violetta thought she would ask the Cherry-man about it. She thought the Cherry-man quite wise. He was a very pretty young fellow, and he brought cherries to sell in graceful little straw baskets lined with moss. So she stood in the kitchen-door, one morning, and told him all about the great trouble that had come upon the city. He listened in great astonishment; he had never heard of it before. He lived several miles out in the country.

"How did the Costumer look?" he asked respectfully; he thought Violetta the most beautiful lady on earth.

Then Violetta described the Costumer, and told him of the unavailing attempts that had been made to find him. There were a great many detectives out, constantly at work.

"I know where he is!" said the Cherry-man. "He's up in one of my cherry-trees. He's been living there ever since cherries were ripe, and he won't come down."

Then Violetta ran and told her father in great excitement, and he at once called a meeting of the Aldermen, and in a few hours half the city was on the road to the Cherry-man's.

He had a beautiful orchard of cherry-trees, all laden with fruit. And, sure enough, in one of the largest, way up amongst the topmost branches, sat the Costumer in his red velvet short-clothes and his diamond knee-buckles. He looked down between the green boughs. "Good-morning, friends," he shouted.

The Aldermen shook their gold-headed canes at him, and the people danced round the tree in a rage. Then they began to climb. But they soon found that to be impossible. As fast as they touched a hand or foot to the tree, back it flew with a jerk exactly as if the tree pushed it. They tried a ladder, but the ladder fell back the moment it touched the tree, and lay sprawling upon the ground. Finally, they brought axes and thought they could chop the tree down, Costumer and all; but the wood resisted the axes as if it were iron, and only dented them, receiving no impression itself.

Meanwhile, the Costumer sat up in the tree, eating cherries, and throwing the stones down. Finally, he stood up on a stout branch and, looking down, addressed the people.

"It's of no use, your trying to accomplish anything in this way," said he; "you'd better parley. I'm willing to come to terms with you, and make everything right, on two conditions."

The people grew quiet then, and the Mayor stepped forward as spokesman. "Name your two conditions," said he, rather testily. "You own, tacitly, that you are the cause of all this trouble."

"Well," said the Costumer, reaching out for a handful of cherries, "this Christmas Masquerade of yours was a beautiful idea; but you wouldn't do it every year, and your successors might not do it at all. I want those poor children to have a Christmas every year. My first condition is, that every poor child in the city hangs its stocking for gifts in the City Hall on every Christmas Eve, and gets it filled, too. I want the resolution filed and put away in the city archives."

"We agree to the first condition!" cried the people with one voice, without waiting for the Mayor and Aldermen.

"The second condition," said the Costumer, "is that this good young Cherry-man here, has the Mayor's daughter, Violetta, for his wife. He has been kind to me, letting me live in his cherry-tree, and eat his cherries, and I want to reward him."

"We consent!" cried all the people; but the Mayor, though he was so generous, was a proud man. "I will not consent to the second condition," he cried angrily.

"Very well," replied the Costumer, picking some more cherries, "then your youngest daughter tends geese the rest of her life, that's all!"

The Mayor was in great distress; but the thought of his youngest daughter being a goose-girl all her life was too much for him. He gave in at last.

"Now go home, and take the costumes off your children," said the Costumer, "and leave me in peace to eat cherries!"

Then the people hastened back to the city and found, to their great delight, that the costumes would come off. The pins staid out, the buttons staid unbuttoned, and the strings staid untied. The children were dressed in their own proper clothes and were their own proper selves once more. The shepherdesses and the chimney-sweeps came home, and were washed and dressed in silks and velvets, and went to embroidering and playing lawn-tennis. And the princesses and the fairies put on their own suitable dresses, and went about their useful employments. There was great rejoicing in every home. Violetta thought she had never been so happy, now that her dear little sister was no longer a goose-girl, but her own dainty little lady-self.

The resolution to provide every poor child in the city with a stocking full of gifts on Christmas was solemnly filed, and deposited in the city archives, and was never broken.

Violetta was married to the Cherry-man, and all the children came to the wedding, and strewed flowers in her path till her feet were quite hidden in them. The Costumer had mysteriously disappeared from the cherry-tree the night before, but he left, at the foot, some beautiful wedding presents for the bride—a silver service with a pattern of cherries engraved on it, and a set of china with cherries on it, in hand-painting, and a white satin robe, embroidered with cherries down the front.

Christmas in Possession

by M. E. Braddon

"But oh, Gus!" said a faltering voice as two little white hands clung about the captain's stalwart arm, "suppose that dreadful man should do what he threatened, and there should be an execution!" And Captain Hawthornden's pretty, pale-faced wife shuddered, as if she had been talking of one of those sanguinary performances which, in the good old times of English history, were wont to attract crowds to Tower Hill.

"Nonsense, my love! there's not the remotest chance of such a thing," cried the captain sturdily. "Do you suppose if there were I'd go away and leave my precious petsy-wetsy in danger of falling into the hands of the Philistines?"

"And Toodleums!" exclaimed Mrs. Hawthornden piteously. Toodleums was a pet name for that domestic miracle of beauty and genius, the first baby. "Imagine dreadful men taking away Toodleum's coral, that my own darling mother sent him!"

"I should like to see the bailiff that would put a finger on that coral!" cried the warrior fiercely. "But now let's talk dispassionately, my darling, for time's nearly up. It's half-past eleven. The express leaves King's Cross at 12:40, so my precious Clara must dry her pretty eyes and listen to her devoted Augustus."

The devoted Augustus looked very handsome and bright and cheerful as he bent over his tearful young wife, while two brisk little serving-maids scudded up and down stairs in quest of innumerable canes, overcoats, and courier bags, and a noble russia leather despatch-box, and skirmished with the cabman, who was groaning under the captain's portmanteau and gun-case in the hall.

"You see, my darling, all we have to do is to look things in the face. Absalom holds a bill of mine which he refuses to renew—having, in point of fact, renewed it two or three times already—which cursed bond falls due on the twenty-fourth, Christmas Eve; the idea of any bloodsucking-fellow having the heart to refuse to renew a bill falling due on Christmas Eve! and the black-hearted scoundrel swears if it isn't paid he'll put in an execution upon these goods before the day is out. Was there ever such a dastard?"

"But you do owe him the money, don't you, Gus darling?"

"Well, yes, I owe him *some* of it, of course; but you can't call compound interest at forty per cent, a just debt."

"But you knew what the interest was to be when you borrowed the money, didn't you, Gus darling?"

"Of course, the iniquitous rascal traded on my desperation. Women don't understand these things, you see, my love. However, scoundrel as I believe Absalom to be, I don't suppose him capable of putting in an execution on Christmas Eve, especially after the diplomatic letter I wrote him this morning. But I'll tell you what, Clara; be sure to let no stranger into the house on any pretence whatever. Sport the oak, my love, and tell your servants not to let a living creature cross the threshold."

"Yes, dear, I'll tell them. And there's the butcher, and the grocer, and the baker, and even the milkman, Augustus dear. You don't know how insolent their young men have been lately; and, you see, you won't answer their letters, and that makes them angry."

"Selfish bloodhounds!" cried the captain; "what the deuce do they want? Do they expect me to coin money? And upon my word, Clara, I don't think it's very generous on your part to torture me in this way, just as I'm off to spend Christmas with my uncle, Sir John Strathnairn—whose only son Douglas, a precious muff, by the way, stands between me and one of the oldest baronetcies and finest estates in North Britain—and am going to bore myself to death deer-stalking, and that kind of thing, entirely on your account; since this is about my only chance of squaring the old miser, and reconciling him to the idea of my imprudent marriage. It's positively selfish of you, Clara; and I hate selfishness."

At this the young wife's tears flowed afresh. She was very young, very inexperienced, the fifth daughter of a small gentleman farmer in Somersetshire, with no better fortune than her pretty face and bright winning manner. Augustus Hawthornden, late captain of hussars, had put the finishing stroke to a career of imprudence by falling in love with this bright hazel-eyed damsel, and marrying her off-hand, in his own impetuous way. This event had happened about eighteen months ago, immediately after the sale of the captain's commission, the price of which he had anticipated to the last penny by means of his friends the money-lenders. Since this time the captain and his wife had lived as mysteriously as the young ravens. They were now the inhabitants of a charming little villa at Kensington, prettily furnished by a crack West End upholsterer, and the proud and happy parents of an infant prodigy, whose laundress's account alone was no trifle, and whose baby-existence required to be sustained by the produce of one especial cow, charged extra in the dairyman's bill.

This was the aspect of affairs on the 21st of December, when Captain Hawthornden prepared to leave his Penates, on a journey to the extreme north of Scotland, where he was to spend some weeks at the grim feudal castle of a fabulously rich uncle, Sir John Kilmarnock Strathnairn, from whom he hoped to obtain a new start in life.

"That's what I want, Clara," he told his confiding little partner. "The army was a mistake for a man with nothing but a beggarly younger son's portion of three hundred a year. As if any fellow in the Eleventh could live on his pay and a paltry three hundred a year! So, of course, I got my poor little estate mortgaged up to the eyes; and there's nothing left but the reversion to Toodleums, which no doubt he'll dispose of to the Jews before he gets it."

Mrs. Hawthornden shook her head at this.

"Oh, yes, he will, or he's not the Toodleums I take him for," said the captain resolutely.

So it was that Augustus Lovat Hawthornden, scion of two good old Scottish houses, departed on his northern journey, with a view to softening the heart of his wealthy maternal uncle, and with a vague idea that Sir John Strathnairn would be induced to give him a start in some new profession—say the Church or the Bar. He knew some fellows who were doing wonders at the Bar, and he had heard of snug sinecures in the Church.

"Egad! if the worst comes to the worst, I suppose I must go in for a Government employment, and devote my mind to the investigation of the cattle plague, or the control of sewers, or some such low drudgery," said the captain.

So he caught his little wife in his arms, gave her a hearty kiss, and hurried off to the loaded cab that was to convey him on the first stage of his journey.

The tender young wife could not be satisfied with so brief a parting. She ran out to the cab, and there was a passionate clasping of hands, and murmured blessings made inaudible by the sobs. And at the last——"

"O Gus!" she cried, "*can* you go without kissing Toodleums?" And she beckoned to the little nurse who was holding the baby up to his parents' view at a first-floor window.

"Oh, d——!" exclaimed the captain, "I can't lose the train for this kind of tomfoolery. King's Cross, cabby, as hard as you can pelt!"

The cruel cab horse went tearing off, and Mrs. Hawthornden returned to the house with her pretty pale hair dishevelled by the bitter winter wind, and her face wet with more bitter tears. In the hall she met the cook, a fiery-faced young person, whom the inexperienced little wife always encountered with fear and trembling.

"Oh, if you please, ma'am," said this domestic, in a breathless, gasping voice that was very alarming, "did master leave the money for my wages—two quarters one month and three weeks azact—as you *said* you'd arst him?"

"No, Sarah," faltered Mrs. Hawthornden; "I'm sorry to say he could not settle *everything* this time; but directly he comes back from Scotland, he—I—I am sure all will be made right."

"Settle everythink, indeed!" cried the cook contemptuously. "I should like to see anythink as *he* has settled. Settling ain't much in his way. Here I have been slaving myself to death in his service—and to wait on a gentleman that wants devilled kidneys and briled bones promiscous, for hisself and his friends, up to twelve o'clock at night and later, is not what I've been used to—going on three-quarters of a year and never seen the colour of his money. And I can't stand it no longer. So, if you please, ma'am, I shall leave this afternoon; and if I can't get my doo by fair means, I must get it by foul; which summonsing at the County Court by his cook won't bring much credit on Captain Orthongding, I should think."

"Oh, and if you please, mum, I should wish to leave at the same time as cook," said the brisk young housemaid; "not that I've got anythink to say agen you, ma'am, which you have always been a kind missus; but flesh and blood can't bear to be put off, and to be sworn at into the bargain without no more consideration than if we was Injy slaves."

"Oh, very well, Sarah and Jane," replied Mrs. Hawthornden hopelessly, "you must do as you please, and go away when you please. I am sure my husband will pay to the last farthing if you can only wait patiently till his affairs are arranged; but if you can't—"

"No, mum, we can't," answered the cook resolutely. "We're tired of waiting. The line must be drawed somewheres; and when the tradespeople declines to call for orders the time has come to draw it."

Mrs. Hawthornden left the deserters and went upstairs.

"It was unkind of them to leave it till Gus was gone," she thought; and then, with a thrill of horror, she considered what would happen if the nurse should also revolt. "I can live without dinner, and I can do the housemaid's work myself," she thought; "but baby is used to Hannah, and if she went away——"

The picture was too awful for contemplation. The poor little woman ran straight to the nursery—the pretty chamber which had been so daintily furnished in the days when, rich in the sense of an open account at the upholsterers, the captain had given his orders with a noble recklessness.

Here she found the nursemaid, a good-tempered-looking girl of eighteen, bending over the pink-curtained bassinet.

"He's a little fretful with his teeth to-day, mum," she said.

"Oh, Hannah," cried Clara Hawthornden, casting herself on her knees before this homely young person, "you won't leave me, will you—you won't de-de-desert the baby?"

"Leave Toodleums, ma'am? Bless his dear little heart! I'd as soon cut my head off as leave him. Why, Mrs. Hawthornden, if you haven't been crying! Oh, do, please, mum, get up! What could have put such a notion into your pretty head? Oh, please, mum, don't take on so!"

"I can't help it, Hannah. The others are going, and I thought you would go too; and my darling would cry for you. Oh, Hannah, we shall be all alone in the house; and the tradespeople won't call anymore till Captain Hawthornden's affairs are arranged—and we shall have n-n-nothing to eat!"

"Oh, yes, we will, mum," replied the dauntless Hannah. "Don't you be downhearted, mum; we'll manage somehow, depend upon it."

"I don't know, Hannah. In the hurry of his going away I forgot to ask my husband for a little ready money; and I haven't so much as a shilling to buy baby's biscuits."

The girl looked aghast at this.

"Oh, how I wish mamma would send me a hamper this

Christmas!" said Mrs. Hawthornden piteously. "She sends one to my married sister, Mrs. Tozer, every year; but papa was so angry when I married Captain Hawthornden—it was a runaway match, you know, Hannah—that he won't let my name be mentioned at home; and I haven't a friend in the world except mamma, who daren't be kind to me for fear of papa."

"Never you mind, mum," replied Hannah cheerfully; "we'll get biscuits for baby, somehow, or my name's not Hannah Giles. Isn't there anything in the house I could take to——"

Here this excellent girl made a discreet and significant pause.

"Yes, Hannah, you good and faithful creature, I know what you mean. My jewellery has gone ever so long ago; all but this poor little wedding ring, and I could scarcely part with that—unless Toodleums were starving. But there's my cashmere shawl, and the silver-grey moiré that I wear at dinner parties; and if you really wouldn't mind——"

"Lor' bless you, mum, not a bit! Wait till after tea to-night. I know where to take them."

"Bless you!" cried the disconsolate young wife; "you're a true friend, Hannah."

At this juncture mistress and maid were interrupted by the sudden awakening of Master Toodleums; and after this diversion they went downstairs to reconnoitre the enemy's country, Toodleums crowing and dribbling on his nurse's shoulder. Below all was desolation. Curiously they explored the snug little kitchen and offices, into which the timid young housekeeper had rarely ventured to intrude during the cook's stern dominion. Awful was the havoc revealed by the present investigation: broken crockery, bottomless saucepans, knife-blades without handles, forks without prongs, grease, rags, waste, ruin, were visible in every corner. The larder was bare of everything except the heel of a stale loaf and a box of sardines, the latter being a species of *hors d'oeuvres* which the lower powers had not affected.

"Oh, Hannah, what can have become of the sirloin of beef we had for the late dinner yesterday? Such a monstrous joint, too, as the cook ordered, though I told her a little piece of roast beef. Why, you and I could have lived upon it for a week!"

"And the cook has taken it off in her box, I dare say," cried Hannah. "Oh, the barefaced hussy!"

There was evidently nothing edible in the house except the sardines, so mistress and maid were fain to wait until the shades of evening should permit the faithful Hannah to execute the somewhat delicate transaction in relation to the silver-grey moiré and the cashmere shawl.

"If you don't mind taking care of the baby for an hour, mum, I'll tidy up the kitchen a bit and get the tea things ready; and then, while the kettle's boiling, I can run around to where I spoke of; and get some tea and sugar, and a rasher or so of bacon, and the baby's biscuits, and a fancy loaf as I come back. I don't suppose you'll care much about dinner to-day, mum."

"Dinner!" cried Mrs. Hawthornden; "I feel as if I should never be able to eat anything more as long as I live. Oh, Gus, if you only knew what we have to go through! Oh, my precious popsy, when you grow up and marry, you must never leave your poor little wife alone at Christmas-time, with all the debts unpaid, and everybody angry."

This apostrophe was addressed to the six-months-old infant, who looked supremely indifferent to the fond appeal. Mrs. Hawthornden took the child in her arms and went to the drawing-room, where she sat in a low chair by the dull fire, and indulged in that dismal refreshment which women call "a good cry."

She was very desolate, very miserable. The short winter day was already darkening, the prospect without looked bleak; but in the windows of other villas the firelight shone cheerily and the lonely young wife thought sadly of happy families assembled in those rooms; families across whose hearth the dread spectre Insolvency had never cast his gloomy shadow. And then she thought of her own distant home. The good old-fashioned rooms, always made especially gay and pleasant at this season. The chintz room and the blue room, the oak room and the cedar parlour; the bright winter flowers, and ever-blossoming chintz curtains; the fires glowing red on every hearth; the noble Worcester punch-bowl brought from its retirement; the chopping and mincing, and cake- and pastry-making, and bustle and preparation in the housekeeper's room; the gardener coming into the kitchen with his pile of holly and mistletoe, laurel, and bay; the odour of Christmas that pervaded the house; and the dear friends with whom she might never spend that holy festival again.

"Oh, if papa could see me now, I don't think he could be angry with me anymore," she said to herself despairingly.

For nearly two hours she sat alone, singing softly to her baby, and crying more or less all the time. And then Hannah came in with the tea-tray, and lighted candles, and the daintiest little dish of fried bacon, and baby's biscuits, and a jug of milk for that young gentleman's consumption.

"It's all right, mum, one pound fifteen-fifteen on the shawl, and a pound on the moiré; but you'd never believe the trouble I had to screw him up to it. And he made me have a ticket for each. That's their artful way. I've heard father say they make mints of money out of the tickets alone. And now do cheer up, and take your tea, that's a dear lady."

The brisk little maiden stirred the fire, drew the curtains, arranged the table, and made all things as cheerful and pleasant as circumstances would permit. Her mistress insisted that she should share the meal; and the two took their tea together—the girl almost overcome by so great an honour, the young wife's thoughts speeding northward with the gallant captain, who sat in the *coupé* of an express train, smoking Henry Clays, at eighteenpence apiece.

"Now don't you be downhearted, mum," said the faithful handmaid, as she bade her mistress good-night. "I only spent three shillings this evening; one pound twelve will carry us on till master comes home."

This was comfort; but poor Clara had not forgotten the threatened horror of the twenty-fourth, Christmas Eve, that day to which she used to look forward at the dear old home, an old-fashioned festival enough, with its simple dissipations in the way of acted charades, snapdragon, and egg-flip.

"Oh, what a child I was!" she exclaimed; and she had been indeed a joyous and innocent creature in those days. If she had been a calculating person, given to weigh advantages, and not the most unselfish and devoted of wives, she might have asked herself whether the proprietorship of a dashing *cidevant* cavalry officer and his superb moustache was a privilege absolutely worth all it had cost her.

The dreaded twenty-fourth arrived, and the weary hours crept by with leaden feet. Every sound of a step in the street set Clara's heart beating. No ominous single knocks came to the door, except the faint appeal of a shivering dealer in boot-laces; for the angry tradespeople knew the captain was away, and did not care to torment his helpless young wife uselessly, any more than they cared to supply her with goods without hope of payment. Even that long day wore itself out at last; and the mistress and the maid took their tea and rasher again together before a cheerful fire, and discussed the probability that Mr. Absalom's stony heart had been melted by the softening influences of the season, and that there would be no execution.

"The very word is so dreadful," said Mrs. Hawthornden; "and yet that's better than calling a cruel thing that makes a man prisoner an 'attachment.' I remember Augustus telling me he had an 'attachment' out against him; and it didn't sound dreadful at all; but the very next week he was taken to Whitecross Street. I wonder what they are doing at home now?—at tea, I dare say. When I shut my eyes I can see them all sitting round the great fireplace. I wonder whether any one thinks of me? I do wish mamma had contrived to send me a hamper, with a home-made pound-cake, and some mince pies and one of our famous geese; not on my own account, but on yours, Hannah, for you've been so good to me; and I should like you to have a nice Christmas dinner, and something to take home to your poor mother to-morrow evening. But I'm a famous goose to think of such a thing; for mamma couldn't send me a hamper without papa's knowledge, and he is so *dreadfully* angry with me."

A sharp rat-tat, something between a single knock and a postman's sounded on the door at this moment, and gave maid and mistress a kind of galvanic shock.

"Don't let anyone in, Hannah," cried Mrs. Hawthornden. "My husband said we were not to admit a creature."

Hannah had skipped to the window-curtains, and was peering out at the doorstep. She jumped back into the room as if she had been shot.

"Oh, be joyful, mum!" she cried. "You've got your wish. It's a 'AMPER!"

"No!"

"Yes, mum; and *such* a big one! Ain't it lovely! And mince pies, and pound-cake, and gooses too, I'll wager. And baby shall suck a bit of roast goose to-morrow, bless him! My brother Joe's baby ain't five months old yet, and will suck the gravy out of anything as well as if he was a grown man. Oh, won't we have a merry Christmas, mum—you, and me, and baby? And ain't I glad that cross old cook's gone!"

"It's like magic!" exclaimed Mrs. Hawthornden, as the imitation postman's knock was repeated impatiently. "Run to the door, Hannah. You're sure it *is* a hamper?"

"Lor' bless your heart, mum, as if I didn't know a Christmas 'amper when I see one!" and the girl flew into the little hall.

It was a foolish thing to be moved, perhaps, by such a vulgar trifle as a Christmas hamper; but Clara Hawthornden wept tears of pleasure as she waited for the welcome basket. It was not of the famous home-reared goose or home-made mince pies she thought; but of the love that had contrived the gift, the tender motherly strategems and plottings and contrivings that must have been gone through in order to compass the seasonable surprise.

"God bless the dear mother!" she murmured as she went out into the hall, where the queer-looking little old man was just depositing a noble hamper, the very straw oozing from the interstices of which looked quite appetising. Mrs. Hawthornden was too much moved to remember that the little old man standing in the hall was there in direct disobedience of the captain's solemn mandate that no stranger should be admitted within that door.

"Here is sixpence for yourself, my good man," said Clara politely. "Good evening." She looked towards the open door, gently indicating that the little old man could depart; but the old man, instead of so doing, gave a little whistle, and beckoned to some one without.

In the next moment a portly stranger stood on the threshold, gaily attired in a drab overcoat and olive-green trousers, and with gold chains and lockets twinkling on his expensive waistcoat.

"Sorry to have recourse to stratagem, miss," said this gentleman, removing the newest of white hats from the blackest and curliest of *chevelures,* "but really, you see, the captain's one of those people with whom one must be deeper than Garrick. Here is my warrant, miss, all correct and regular, as you may perceive. Suit of Shadrach Absalom. This old gent and I will take an inventory, miss; and he can remain on the premises afterwards."

"What!" cried Clara, growing very white; "do you mean to say that hamper is not from my mother at Somerton Manor?"

"That hamper, my dear young lady, is like the wooden horse that went into Troy. Don't trouble yourself to open it, my good girl; there's nothing but straw inside, and a brickbat or two just to give it solidity. All stratagems are fair in love and war, and the recovery of a just debt, especially when a bill has been renewed three times, as this one has. Shadrach Absalom is my first cousin, miss, and as good a fellow as ever lived; but the captain has really been too bad."

"I'm sure my husband means to pay everything when he comes from Scotland, where he has gone to visit his uncle, Sir John Strathnairn," faltered the horror-stricken Clara.

"What, do you mean to say that Captain Hawthornden has got such a pretty young creature as you for his wife, and that he can have the heart to go away and leave you to bear the brunt of his difficulties?" cried Laurence Absalom, the sheriff's officer, with honest indignation.

"I beg, sir, that you will not remark upon my husband's conduct. He always acts for the best. Oh, Hannah, what are we to do?"

"I know what I should like to do," answered the handmaiden spitefully, "and that is to scratch that nasty, deceiving old man's face."

"If you could scratch some of the dirt off it you'd be doing him a service, my dear," said Mr. Laurence Absalom, with easy good nature, while the old man sat quietly on the delusive hamper, the picture of grimy meekness.

Mr. Absalom called for a candle, and proceeded to explore the house, attended by the meek old man, who wiped his dirty face upon the dingiest of blue cotton handkerchiefs, and breathed very hard as he followed his commanding officer. Together the two men ransacked drawers and wardrobes, peered into chiffoniers, and violated the sanctity of writing desks, and carefully catalogued furniture and bedding, books and electro-plate, china and glass, table linen and pictures. All Clara's pretty dresses, her dainty ribbons and laces, her coquettish little bonnets and innocent girlish jackets, were set down on a sheet of greasy foolscap, while the two women looked on, one of them utterly helpless and miserable, wondering what would come next.

At last the inventory was complete, and Mr. Absalom prepared to take his departure.

"Of course, you'll be writing to the captain, ma'am," he said; "and you'll please tell him that unless this business is squared in five days' time his property will go to the hammer. I'm sure I'm very sorry on your account; but, you see, the captain knew what he had to expect, and he really ought to have provided against it. Good evening, Mrs. Hawthornden. The old gent will stay till the sale. You'll find him very quiet."

"What!" cried Clara aghast, "is that dreadful old man to stop in the house?"

The dreadful old man gave a grunt of assent.

"Upon my word, ma'am, I wish I was the party," said Mr. Absalom gallantly; "I should consider it quite a privilege; but old Jiffins does that part of the work, and you'll find him as harmless as an old spaniel, if you don't mind his appetite; that is rather alarming, I admit. Good night."

And with an easy nod Mr. Laurence Absalom departed, leaving the mistress and maid staring in consternation at the man in possession, who was refreshing himself with a pinch of snuff out of a screw of paper. He certainly was by no means a prepossessing individual; indeed, it is impossible to imagine grubbiness more dingy than the grubbiness of this old man's aspect. He wore a long great coat, and of shirt or shirt collar there were no traces visible; but in lieu of these conventionalities he displayed a dirty wisp of neckerchief that had once been white, but which was now a sickly yellow. His boots seemed to have been the dress boots of a giant, and were wrinkled like the skins of French plums. On one hand he wore a roomy black glove, also of the texture of French plums. His grey hair straggled over the greasy velvet collar of his coat, in an eminently patriarchal fashion, and his bottle nose—nay, indeed, his complexion generally—was of that rubicund hue produced by copious consumption of malt and spirituous liquors, in conjunction with exposure to all kinds of weather. Such as he was, he seemed to Mrs. Hawthornden the living embodiment of a nightmare. She stood rooted to the ground, staring at him hopelessly and helplessly, and it was only the brisk Hannah who aroused her from the waking trance.

"Hadn't the old gentleman better step into the master's study?" suggested the girl. "He'll want to sit somewhere, you see, ma'am."

"To sit? Yes, and he is going to live here. Oh, Hannah, *what* shall we do?"

"Don't you be frightened, mum," whispered the girl; "I've lived where there's been a man in possession, and it's nothing when you're used to it. Step this way, if you please, sir," she added briskly, and she pointed to a little box of a room opposite the drawing-room.

The old man walked to the door of this apartment, then suddenly turned back and approached Mrs. Hawthornden, who quailed before him. To her horror he lifted his dirty hand and laid it—oh, so gently!—on her soft hair, patting her head as if she had been a child.

"Don't you be frightened, my pretty!" he said; "I've seen a deal of trouble in my time, and I can feel for them as have their homes broke up, though it is my business to break 'em. It's the business that's hardhearted, my pretty, not me. You bear that in mind, and don't worry yourself about old Jiffins no more than if he was an old tomcat. He'll keep his place, depend upon it, and won't give no trouble to no one."

"I'm sure you're very kind," murmured Clara, half crying; "but it does seem so dreadful!"

"Of course it do, to a sweet young creatur' like you. But Lor' bless you, mum, there's places I go to reg'lar, as you may say, and where I'm quite like one of the family. The children calls me uncle. 'Crikey, father!' cries one of the little chaps, 'if here ain't Uncle Jiffins come back agen!' and they're quite took aback to find their parents ain't over glad to see me. I suppose there ain't no objection to a pipe in this here room, ma'am?"

"Oh, no, no, no," cried Clara piteously, "you can smoke as much as you like; and there's some of my husband's Turkish tobacco in that jar on the mantlepiece which you can take if you please."

"Thank you, mum. Shag's more in my way; but if you could put your hand upon a little bit of Cavendish, I should take it very kind."

A piece of Cavendish tobacco was found, after some little trouble, and Mr. Jiffins ensconced himself in Augustus Hawthornden's easy chair—a charming chair, in which the captain had been wont to read the papers and ponder somewhat gloomily on financial questions; and Mr. Jiffins being duly established in this room, which was conveniently close to the hall door, and in a manner commanded the whole house, Mrs. Hawthornden and Hannah went back to the drawing-room, where Toodleums, happily unconscious of this domestic revolution, was still slumbering placidly in his bassinet.

Together the mistress and maid sat down to face life with its new responsibilities.

"I'll write to Augustus this very night, Hannah; but my letter can't go till to-morrow—perhaps not even then, as it's Christmas Day; and a letter takes such a time travelling to the Highlands; and then there would be the journey back; and oh, dear! when will Gus come to send that awful old creature away? He doesn't seem unkind, but oh, so dirty! And to think that he should be sitting in Gus's favourite chair, with his head against the antimacassar that I worked with my own hands!"

Happily the brisk little nursemaid was too cheery a creature to be altogether discomfited even by a man in possession. She gave the baby refreshment from a bottle furnished with a wonderful gutta-percha machine, which made the feeding business look very much like laying on gas; and then she reminded her mistress that it was getting late, and shops might be closed in the neighbourhood.

"There's to-morrow's dinner, you see, mum; and then there's the old gent's supper. I suppose I'd better get a bit of cheese?"

"Oh, good gracious me!" cried Clara, "will he want supper?"

"Lor' bless your innocence, mum, of course he will, and breakfast and dinner, and all his meals, and his beer. It's the rule, you see, mum: you finds 'em in everythink."

With this Hannah handed her mistress the baby, and departed.

The inexperienced girl-wife sat staring apathetically at the blackened coals in the pretty steel grate. She felt as some young mother of the antediluvian period may have felt, as she sat with her child in her lap, listening to the rising waters, and waiting for the end of the world.

Hannah came back by-and-by, with bread and cheese and beer for the old man, and a modest little joint of beef for the next day's dinner, and a quarter of a pound of tea, and other small matters, which altogether made a terrible hole in that one pound twelve shillings which alone stood between this household and destitution.

"We shall have to change the half sovereign for his beer tomorrow, mum," said the maiden; "but we shall hold out till the captain comes home, depend upon it."

Mrs. Hawthornden counted the hours that must elapse before the captain could possibly come home, and counted them over again, till her brain grew dizzy. Her only comfort next morning was to think that some of those weary hours were gone.

Hannah waited on Mr. Jiffins, taking his meals to the captain's snug little sanctum, and coming back to her mistress to report the awful havoc he had made with the loaf, or the alarming way he had slashed off slices from the joint.

"And I think if there was oceans of gravy, mum, he'd soak them up; for, let alone smashing his purtaters, he sops it up with his bread."

Oh, what a dreary Christmas Day! Cabs and carriages dashed up to other houses in the pretty suburban street; gaily dressed people went to and from the neighbouring churches; at night music sounded and lights gleamed from many windows, while Clara Hawthornden walked up and down with her fretful baby and thought of what they were doing at home—alas, her home no longer!

Toodleums had been fractious all day, and grew worse towards evening; and while Hannah went for the supper beer he took the opportunity of working himself into a paroxysm of crying that terrified the young mother out of her wits. She was pacing the room, trying in vain to soothe her infant, when the door was softly opened, and Mr. Jiffins appeared. Clara almost dropped the baby at sight of this apparition.

"Let me take him a bit," said Mr. Jiffins. "I'm used to babies, bless 'um."

"Oh, please don't!" cried Clara, as the dreaded intruder advanced his grimy hands; "indeed, indeed he wouldn't come to you."

But, to the mother's utter astonishment, Toodleums, the most particular and capricious of babies, did go to this grubby old man, and, after a few minutes' hushing and dandling and see-sawing in the air, did actually cease to cry.

"Bless their dear little hearts! they all come to *me*," said Mr.

Jiffins complacently. "I've got a grandson just this one's size, and what that little dear do suffer with the wind on his stomach is only beknown to hisself and to me. It ain't temper, bless you, when they skreeks like that—it's wind; and you take my advice, and just let your gal fetch twopenn'orth of essence of peppermint—none of your Daffy for my money—and give him two drops on a lump of sugar melted in a spoonful of warm water, and he'll be quiet as a lamb."

Mr. Jiffins nursed the baby till Hannah came back with the beer and the change for that last half sovereign, which Mrs. Hawthornden had contemplated fondly as she parted with it forever. The girl stared aghast on beholding her charge in the arms of the intruder; but he despatched her to the chemist's for peppermint as coolly as if he had been the infant's favourite grandfather. Mrs. Hawthornden had sunk exhausted into her chair, and looked on with amazement while the man in possession developed a perfect genius for nursing, and entertained Toodleums with a broken tobacco-pipe and a latch-key, as that young gentleman rarely allowed himself to be entertained by the most elaborate inventions of the toy-maker.

"You seem to have a wonderful power over children," murmured Clara at last.

"I'm fond of 'em, ma'am, that's where it is; and they knows it. There's nothing gets over 'em like that—real rightdown fondness of 'em. Now, I'll wager while you was carrying this little chap up and down just now, your mind had wandered like, and you was thinking of your own troubles, and you felt him a drag upon you."

Clara nodded assent.

"To be sure!" exclaimed Mr. Jiffins triumphantly; "and that child knowed it—he knowed it as he hadn't got your whole heart; and you can't do nothing with a child unless you gives him your whole heart. They're the deepest little Garricks out for that, bless 'em!——Ain't you now, ducksy? Yes, o' course; you knows you is."

Toodleums assented to this proposition with a rapturous crow.

"Bein' as it's Christmas night, mum," said Mr. Jiffins by-and-by, when the peppermint had been brought and administered, "and my disposition lively like, perhaps you wouldn't take it as a liberty if I asked leave to eat my bit of supper in here? It is rather lonesome in that there little room, and seems lonesomer being Christmas-time."

What could a helpless young wife and mother say to this startling request? Mr. Jiffins was master of the situation. There was something very dreadful in sitting down to supper with this dirty old man; but Toodleums was hanging on to one of his greasy coat-buttons with the affection of a life-time, and a man thus affected by Toodleums could not be utterly base. So Mrs. Hawthornden murmured a faint assent to the proposed arrangement. The tray was brought, modestly furnished with a piece of cheese, a loaf, a little glass dish of butter, and a jug of ale. Mr. Jiffins surveyed these simple preparations with an approving eye.

"Raw cheese is rather too cold to the palate in this weather," he said thoughtfully; "what would say now, mum, to a rabbit?"

"I am very sorry," faltered Mrs. Hawthornden apologetically, "but we haven't any rabbits in the house."

"Lor' bless you, ma'am, I means toasted cheese. If that good-tempered young woman of yours would get me the mustard-pot and a small saucepan, and then kneel down before the fire and toast a round or two of bread, I'd soon show you what I means by a rabbit."

Hannah ran off to procure these articles, and she was presently employed in toasting cheese under the old man's direction.

"A teaspoonful of mustard, and a good lump of fresh butter, and a tablespoonful of ale, and let it simmer by the side of the fire while you toasts the bread, my dear," said Mr. Jiffins, who had nursed the baby, and looked on approvingly while the handmaid obeyed him.

To poor Clara Hawthornden it seemed like some distempered dream. "If anybody should call!" she thought; and she had to tell herself over and over again that ten o'clock on Christmas night was not a likely hour for callers. She thought of the joyous party in her old home—the girls in white muslin and scarlet sashes, the matrons in their rustling silks: and then of the more stately festival at Strathnairn Castle, and the black oak buffets loaded with gold plate, which her husband had so often described to her; but from these bright pictures her fancy always came back to the old man superintending the simmering cheese.

Both he and Hannah persuaded her presently to taste this delicacy. She had eaten nothing at dinner, for the sense of the old man's presence in the captain's study had weighed upon her like an actual burden. He was not nearly so dreadful seated opposite her with her baby on his knee. Our skeletons are never so hideous when confronted boldly as when hidden away in some dark cupboard. Mrs. Hawthornden tasted the Welsh rarebit. It was really excellent. She remembered having heard Augustus talk of eating such things at Evans'. And presently she found herself eating this toasted cheese with more appetite than anything she had tasted since her husband's departure. Though familiar, Mr. Jiffins was not utterly wanting in reverence. He resigned the baby to Hannah, and insisted on taking his supper at the remotest corner of the table, where there was no tablecloth. The edge of the tablecloth he seemed to consider the line of demarcation; no persuasion could induce him to infringe upon it by the breadth of a hair. But at this uncomfortable corner he ate his supper with a relish that was almost contagious, and talked a good deal in a pleasant chirping manner, as he quaffed his ale. After supper he ventured upon a conundrum, and that being approved, upon another; and Mrs. Hawthornden found herself laughing quite merrily, but still with the sense that it was all a distempered dream. Dreadful as it was to be cheerful in the company of a nursemaid and of a broker's man, it was perhaps better for this lonely little wife than brooding over her woes. She slept quite soundly after the toasted cheese and the conundrums, and awoke next morning to find the cheerful Hannah at her bedside with a neatly arranged little breakfast-tray.

"It was Mr. Jiffins as told me to bring you up your breakfast, ma'am. 'Let her sleep a little late, poor pretty!' he said, 'and take her a cup of tea and a new-laid egg when she wakes'; and—*would you believe it*, mum? the old dear goes and fetches the egg hisself, while I biles the kettle, though he told me it was as much as his employment was worth to step outside our door! And if he hasn't been and hearthstoned the steps before I was up, mum, and swep' the kitchen beautiful—for a handier old man I never did see; and he says, if you could pick a bit of Irish stew for your dinner, he's a rare hand at one."

Mrs. Hawthornden did not care to pick a bit of Irish stew, nor did she affect any dish in the preparation of which the broker's man could be manipulatively engaged; but she fully appreciated his kind wish to help her and her faithful handmaiden, and thanked him prettily for his kindness when she encountered him downstairs. Before long she had still greater reason to thank him; for Toodleums suffered severely in the cutting of an upper tooth, and both nursemaid and mother profited by grandfather Jiffins' experience.

The days went by slowly, but no longer made hideous to Clara Hawthornden by her horror of Jiffins, who, instead of an incubus, had proved himself an elderly angel in the house. Her chief trouble now arose from her husband's silence. The fifth day must soon elapse, and then there would be a sale, and she and her child would be turned out of doors, homeless, shelterless. No, not quite. Here Providence interposed in the humble guise of Jiffins.

"My married daughter's got a room as she lets, and as is now empty; and if they've the heart to turn you out of here, you can go there and welcome," said the dingy benefactor. "There ain't no spring sofys, nor shiny steel grates; but it's that clean you might eat your victuals off the floor; and, if you don't mind a mews, it's respectable."

A mews! Where would not the desolate mother have gone to obtain shelter for her baby?

"Oh, Mr. Jiffins!" she cried, clasping one of those grimy hands, which had once inspired her with such aversion, "what should we do without you?"

What, indeed! The last shilling of that last half sovereign had been spent two days ago, and since then the little household had been sustained by money advanced by Jiffins.

"You'll pay me fast enough one of these odd days, I dessay," said Jiffins, when Clara deprecated this last obligation.

For the first time since she had left her home she wrote to ask a favour of her mother. The boon she demanded was a five-pound note, wherewith to pay and reward Jiffins. Never before had she allowed the home-friends to know that her Augustus left her with one wish ungratified.

The fifth day expired. The hour of doom was near. Strange men in paper caps came to take up the carpets. The dear little china closet, in which Clara had so delighted, when the housemaid would allow her to enter it, was rifled of its contents, and dinner services, tea services, and glass were spread on the dining room table. Bills were stuck on the outside of the house; within, nasty little bits of paper, with numbers on them, were pasted upon every article, even—oh, bitterest drop in this cup of bitterness—on the sacred bassinet of Toodleums, still a martyr to his teeth. Ignominy could go no further; and there were still no tidings of the captain. But for Jiffins and Hannah, Clara Hawthornden must surely have died of this agony.

It was the very morning of the sale. Mr. Absalom was there in all his glory. The auctioneer had arrived. Dingy men with greasy little memorandum-books pervaded the house. Clara sat with Hannah and the baby in the little study, where strange faces peered in upon them every now and then; and intending buyers made heartless remarks about the curtains, and informed the dingy commission agents how high they were disposed to bid for the captain's pet chair. There was no corner of the house sacred to the homeless woman's despair. Clara felt that it would have been almost better to sit in the street. The most unfriendly doorstep would have been a more peaceful resting place than this.

Alas! In this bitter crisis even the faithful Jiffins could no longer protect her. He was sent hither and thither by the higher powers, and could not yet snatch half an hour's respite in which to conduct Mrs. Hawthornden to the humble lodging he had secured for her.

"Oh, Hannah, I wish Mr. Jiffins would take us away from all these dreadful people!" Clara cried piteously. She had ceased to hope for rescue from Augustus. *That* ship had foundered, and Jiffins was the lifeboat of benevolence that must carry her to the shore of safety.

"Oh, Hannah, if he would only take us to his daughter's house in the mews!" she cried; and in the next moment a hansom tore up to the door, a stentorian voice broke out into exclamations of surprise and indignation, interspersed with execrations. A shrill scream burst from the young wife's pale lips.

"Gus!" she cried, while Toodleums set up a sympathetic shriek; "oh, thank God, thank God!" and she must have fallen but for Hannah's supporting arms.

Yes, it was the captain, dressed in black, and with a crape hatband. He distributed his anathemas freely as he strode into the villa. What the dash is the meaning of this dashed business? Take down those dashed bills and turn those dashed people out of the house; and so on. Mr. Absalom advanced politely, and suggested that if the captain would be so kind as to settle that little matter of 326*l.* 17*s.* 6*d.* the sale need not proceed. The captain pulled out a brand-new cheque book and signed his first cheque upon a brand new banking account, which document he handed to Mr. Absalom with an injured air.

"You ought to have known better, Absalom," he said, "after all our past dealing."

"To tell you the truth, captain, it was my experience of the past that made me rather sharp in the present," replied the other politely.

"Come, Clara, don't cry," exclaimed Captain Hawthornden to the poor little woman, who was sobbing on his shoulder. "I didn't get your letter till yesterday afternoon, and have been travelling ever since. I was away with a party in the mountains. And there's been a dreadful piece of work at Strathnairn—my cousin Douglas, Sir John's only son, killed by the explosion of his rifle. No one to blame but himself, poor beg—poor dear fellow! Sir John's awfully cut up, as well he may be; and I'm next heir to the title and estates. Yes, little woman, you'll be Lady Strathnairn before you die; for my uncle will never marry, poor old boy! Very dreadful, ain't it, poor Douglas' death? But of course, uncommonly jolly for us."

"Oh, Gus, how awful for Sir John! But, thank Heaven, you have come back! You can never understand what I have suffered; and if it hadn't been for Jiffins——"

"Jiffins! Who the deuce is Jiffins?"

"The man in possession. He has been so good to us—has lent us money, even; and but for him we must have starved."

"Good Heavens, Clara!" cried the captain, aghast, "you don't mean to say you've degraded yourself by borrowing money from a broker's man?"

"What could I do, dear? You left me without any money, you know," replied the wife innocently.

"You really ought to have known better, Clara," said the captain sternly. "But where is Jiffins? Let me pay this fellow his confounded loan."

"I think you'd better let me pay it, dear. If you'll give me a ten-pound note, I can make it all right."

So Mr. Jiffins received about a thousand per cent. for his loan, which had been little more than a sovereign, and he spent New Year's Day very pleasantly in the bosom of his married daughter's household, No. 7½ Stamford Mews, Blackfriars. But perhaps at some future audit, when such small accounts are balanced before the Great Auditor, Mr. Jiffins may receive even more than a thousand per cent for that little loan.

A Bird in the Snow

by ARMANDO PALACIO VALDÉS

HE WAS BORN BLIND, AND HAD been taught the one thing which the blind generally learn,—music; for this art he was specially gifted. His mother died when he was little more than a child, and his father, who was the first cornetist of a military band, followed her to the grave a few years later. He had a brother in America from whom he had never heard; still, through indirect sources he knew him to be well off, married, and the father of two fine children. To the day of his death the old musician, indignant at his son's ingratitude, would not allow his name to be mentioned in his presence; but the blind boy's affection for his brother remained unchanged. He could not forget that this elder brother had been the support of his childhood, the defence of his weakness against the other boys, and that he had always spoken to him with kindness.

The recollection of Santiago's voice as he entered his room in the morning, shouting, "Hey there, Juanito! Get up, man; don't sleep so!" rang in the blind boy's ears with a more pleasing harmony than could ever be drawn from the keys of a piano or the strings of a violin. Was it probable that such a kind heart had grown cold? Juan could not believe it, and was always striving to justify him. At times the fault was with the mail, or it might be that his brother did not wish to write until he could send them a good deal of money; then again, he fancied that he meant to surprise them by presenting himself some fine day, laden with gold, in the modest *entresol* in which they lived. But he never dared communicate any of these fancies to his father; only when the old man, wrought to an unusual pitch of exasperation, bitterly apostrophized the absent one, he found the courage to say: "You must not despair, father. Santiago is good, and my heart tells me that we shall hear from him one of these days."

The father died, however, without hearing from his son, between a priest, who exhorted him, and the blind boy, who clung convulsively to his hand, as if he meant to detain him in this world by main force. When the old man's body was removed from the house, the boy seemed to have lost his reason, and in a frenzy of grief he struggled with the undertaker's men. Then he was left alone. And what loneliness was his! No father, no mother, no relatives, no friends; he was even deprived of the sunlight, which is the friend of all created things. He was two whole days in his room pacing the floor like a caged wolf, without tasting food. The chamber-maid, assisted by a compassionate neighbor, succeeded in saving him from this slow process of suicide. He was prevailed upon to eat. He spent the rest of his life praying, and working at his music.

His father, shortly before his death, had obtained for him a position as organist in one of the churches of Madrid, with a salary of seventy cents a day. This was scarcely sufficient to meet the running expenses of a house, however modest; so within a fortnight Juan sold all that had constituted the furniture of his humble home, dismissed his servant, and took a room at a boarding-house, for which he paid forty cents a day; the remaining thirty cents covered all his other expenses. He lived thus for several months without leaving his room except to fulfil his obligations. His only walks were from the house to the church, and from the church back again. His grief weighed upon him so heavily that he never opened his lips. He spent the long hours of the day composing a grand requiem Mass for the repose of his father's soul, depending upon the charity of the parish for its execution; and although it would be incorrect to say that he strained his five senses,—on account of his having but four,—it can at least be said that he threw all the energies of his body and soul into his work.

The ministerial crisis overtook him before his task was half finished. I do not remember who came into power, whether the Radicals, Conservatives, or Constitutionals; at any rate, there was some great change. The news reached Juan late, and to his sorrow. The new cabinet soon judged him, in his capacity as an organist, to be a dangerous citizen, and felt that from the heights of the choir, at vespers or in the solemnity of the Mass, with the swell and the roar from all the stops of the organ, he was evincing sentiments of opposition which were truly scandalous. The new ministers were ill disposed, as they declared in Congress through the lips of one of their authorized members, "to tolerate any form of imposition," so they proceeded with praiseworthy energy to place Juan on the retired list, and to find him a substitute whose musical manœuvres might offer a better guarantee,—a man, in a word, who would prove more loyal to the institutions. On being officially informed of this, the blind one experienced no emotion beyond surprise. In the deep recesses of his heart he was pleased, as he was thus left more time in which to work at his Mass. The situation appeared to him in its real light only when his landlady, at the end of the month, came to him for money. He had none to give her, naturally, as his salary had been withdrawn; and he was compelled to pawn his father's watch, after which he resumed his work with perfect serenity and without a thought of the future. But the land-lady came again for money at the end of another month, and he once more pawned a jewel of the scant paternal legacy; this was a small diamond ring. In a few months there was nothing left to pawn. So the landlady, in consideration of his helplessness, kept him two or three days beyond the time and then turned him out, with the self-congratulatory feeling of having acted generously in not claiming his trunk and clothes, from which she might have realized the few cents that he still owed her.

He looked for another lodging, but was unable to rent a piano, which was a sore trial to him; evidently he could not finish his Mass. He knew a shopkeeper who owned a piano and who permitted him to make use of it. But Juan soon noticed that his visits grew more and more inopportune, so he left off going. Shortly, too, he was turned out of his new lodgings, only this time they kept his trunk. Then came a period of misery and anguish,—of that misery of which it is hard to conceive. We know that life has few joys for the homeless and the poor, but if in addition they be blind and alone, surely they have found the limit of human suffering. Juan was tossed about from lodging to lodging, lying in bed while his only shirt was being washed, wandering through the streets of Madrid with torn shoes, his trousers worn to a fringe about his feet, his hair long, and his beard unshaven. Some compassionate fellow-lodger obtained a position for him in a café, from which, however, he was soon turned out, for its frequenters did not relish his music. He never played popular dances or peteneras, no fandangos, not even an occasional polka. His fingers glided over the keys in dreamy ecstasies of Beethoven and Chopin, and the audience found some difficulty in keeping time with their spoons. So out he went again through the byways of the capital. Every now and then some charitable soul, accidentally brought in contact with his misery, assisted him indirectly, for Juan shuddered at the thought of begging. He took his meals in some tavern or other in the lowest quarter of Madrid, ate just enough to keep from starving, and for two cents he was allowed to sleep in a hovel between beggars and evil-doers. Once they stole his trousers while he was asleep, and left him a pair of cotton ones in their stead. This was in November.

Poor Juan, who had always cherished the thought of his brother's return, now in the depths of his misery nursed his chimera with redoubled faith. He had a letter written and sent to Havana. As he had no idea how his brother could be reached, the letter bore no direction. He made all manner of inquiries, but to no effect, and he spent long hours on his knees, hoping that Heaven might send Santiago to his rescue. His only happy moments were those spent in prayer, as he knelt behind a pillar in the far-off corner of some solitary church, breathing the acrid odors of dampness and melting wax, listening to the flickering sputter of the tapers and the faint murmur rising from the lips of the faithful in the nave of the temple. His innocent soul then soared above the cruelties of life and communed with God and the Holy Mother. From his early childhood devotion to the Virgin had been deeply rooted in his heart. As he had never known his mother, he instinctively turned to the mother of God for that tender and loving protection which only a woman can give a child. He had composed a number of hymns and canticles in her honor, and he never fell asleep without pressing his lips to the image of the Carmen, which he wore on his neck.

There came a day, however, when heaven and earth forsook him. Driven from his last shelter, without a crust to save him from starvation, or a cloak to protect him from the cold, he realized with terror that the time had come when he would have to beg. A great struggle took place in his soul. Shame and suffering made a desperate stand against necessity. The profound darkness which surrounded him increased the anguish of the strife; but hunger conquered in the end. He prayed for strength with sobs, and resigned himself to his fate. Still, wishing to disguise his humiliation, he determined to sing in the streets, at night only. His voice was good, and he had a rare knowledge of the art of singing. It occurred to him that he had no means of accompaniment. But he soon found another unfortunate, perhaps a trifle less wretched than himself, who lent him an old and broken guitar. He mended it as best he could, and with a voice hoarse with tears he went out into the street on a frosty December night. His heart beat violently; his knees trembled under him. When he tried to sing in one of the central thoroughfares, he found he could not utter a sound. Suffering and shame seemed to have tied a knot in his throat. He groped about until he had found a wall to lean against.

There he stood for awhile, and when he felt a little calmer he began the tenor's aria from the first act of "Favorita." A blind singer who sang neither couplets nor popular songs soon excited some curiosity among the passers-by, and in a few minutes a crowd had gathered around him. There was a murmur of surprise and admiration at the art with which he overcame the difficulties of the composition, and many a copper was dropped in the hat that dangled from his arm. After this he sang the aria of the fourth act of "Africana." But too many had stopped to listen, and the authorities began to fear that this might be a cause of disturbance; for it is a well-established fact with officials of the police force that people who congregate in the streets to hear a blind man sing are always prompted by motives of rebellion,—it means a peculiar hostility to the institutions; in a word, an attitude thoroughly incompatible with the peace of society and the security of the State. Accordingly, a policeman caught Juan energetically by the arm and said, "Here, here! go straight home now, and don't let me catch you stopping at any more street corners."

"I'm doing no harm!"

"You are blocking the thoroughfare. Come, move on, move on, if you don't want to go to the lock-up."

It is really encouraging to see how careful our authorities are in clearing the streets of blind singers; and I really believe, in spite of all that has been said to the contrary, that if they could keep them equally free from thieves and murderers, they would do so with pleasure. Juan went back to his hovel with a heavy heart, for he was by nature shrinking and timid, and was grieved at having disturbed the peace and given rise to the interference of the executive power. He had made twenty-seven cents. With this he bought something to eat on the following day, and paid rent for the little pile of straw on which he slept. The next night he went out again and sang a few more operatic arias; but the people again crowded around him, and once more a policeman felt himself called upon to interfere, shouting at him to move on. But how could he? If he kept moving on, he would not make a cent. He could not expect the people to follow him. Juan moved on, however, on and on, because he was timid, and the mere thought of infringing the laws, of disturbing even momentarily the peace of his native land, was worse than death to him. So his earnings rapidly decreased. The necessity of moving on, on the one hand, and the fact that his performances had lost the charm of novelty, which in Spain always commands its price, daily deprived him of a few coppers. With what he brought home at night he could scarcely buy enough food to keep him alive. The situation was desperate. The poor boy saw but one luminous point in the clouded horizon of his life, and that was his brother's return to Madrid. Every night as he left his hovel with his guitar swinging from his shoulder he thought, "If Santiago should be in Madrid and hear me sing, he would know me by my voice." And this hope, or rather this chimera, alone gave him the strength to endure life. However, there came again a day in which his anguish knew no limit. On the preceding night he had earned only six coppers. It had been so cold! This was Christmas Eve. When the morning dawned upon the world, it found Madrid wrapped in a sheet of snow six inches thick. It snowed steadily all day long, which was a matter of little consequence to the majority of people, and was even a cause of much rejoicing among æsthetes generally. Those poets in particular who enjoy what is called easy circumstances spent the greater part of the day watching the flakes through the plate-glass of their study windows, meditating upon and elaborating those graceful and ingenious similes that cause the audiences at the theatre to shout, "Bravo, bravo!" or those who read their verses to exclaim, "What a genius that young fellow is!"

Juan's breakfast had been a crust of stale bread and a cup of watery coffee. He could not divert his hunger by contemplating the beauty of the snow,—in the first place, because he was blind, and in the second, because, even had he not been blind, he would have had some difficulty in seeing it through the patched and filthy panes of his hovel. He spent the day huddled in a corner on his straw mattress, evoking scenes of his childhood and caressing the sweet dream of his brother's return. At nightfall he grew very faint, but necessity drove him into the streets to beg. His guitar was gone. He had sold it for sixty cents on a day of similar hardship. The snow fell with the same persistence. His legs trembled as they had when he sang for the first time, but now it was from hunger rather than shame. He groped about as best he could, with great lumps of mud above his ankles. The silence told him that there was scarcely a soul on the street. The carriages rolled noiselessly along, and he once came near being run over. In one of the central thoroughfares he began to sing the first thing that came to his lips. His voice was weak and hoarse. Nobody stopped to listen. "Let us try another street." thought he; and he went down the Avenue of San Jeronimo, walking awkwardly in the snow, with a white coating on his shoulders and water squirting from his shoes. The cold had begun to penetrate into his very bones, and hunger gave him a violent pain. For a moment with the cold and the pain came a feeling of faintness which made him think that he was about to die, and lifting his spirit to the Virgin of the Carmen, his protectress, he exclaimed in his anguish, "Mother, have pity!" And after pronouncing these words he felt relieved and walked, or rather dragged himself, to the Plaza de las Cortes. There he grasped a lamp-post, and under the impression of the Virgin's protection sang Gounod's "Ave Maria." Still nobody stopped to hear him. The people of Madrid were at the theatres, at the cafés, or at home, dancing their little ones on their knees in the glow of the hearth,—in the warmth of their love. The snow continued to fall steadily, copiously, with the evident purpose of furnishing a topic for the local column of the morning paper, where it would be described in a thousand delicate phrases. The occasional passers-by hurried along muffled up to their ears under their umbrellas. The lamp-posts had put on their white night-caps, from under which escaped thin rays of dismal light. The silence was broken only by the vague and distant rumble of carriages and by the light fall of the snowflakes, that sounded like the faint and continuous rustle of silk. The voice of Juan alone vibrated in the stillness of the night, imploring the mother of the unprotected; and his chant seemed a cry of anguish rather than a hymn of praise, a moan of sadness and resignation falling dreary and chill, like snow upon the heart.

And his cry for pity was in vain. In vain he repeated the sweet name of Mary, adjusting it to the modulations of every melody. Heaven and the Virgin were far away, it seemed, and could not hear him. The neighbors of the plaza were near at hand, but they did not choose to hear. Nobody came down to take him in from the cold; no window was thrown open to drop him a copper. The passers-by, pursued, as it were, by the fleet steps of pneumonia, scarcely dared stop. Juan's voice at last died in his throat; he could sing no more. His legs trembled under him; his hands lost their sense of touch. He took a few steps, then sank on the sidewalk at the foot of the grating that surrounds the square. He sat with his elbows on his knees and buried his head in his hands. He felt vaguely that it was the last moment of his life, and he again prayed, imploring the divine pity.

At the end of a few minutes he was conscious of being shaken by the arm, and knew that a man was standing before him. He raised his head, and taking for granted it was the old story about moving on, inquired timidly,—

"Are you an officer?"

"No; I am no officer. What is the matter with you? Get up."

"I don't believe I can, sir."

"Are you very cold?"

"Yes, sir; but it isn't exactly that,—I haven't had anything to eat to-day."

"I will help you, then. Come; up with you."

The man took Juan by both arms and stood him on his feet. He seemed very strong.

"Now lean on me, and let us see if we can find a cab."

"But where are you going to take me?"

"Nowhere where you wouldn't want to go. Are you afraid?"

"No; I feel in my heart that you will help me."

"Come along, then. Let's see how soon I can get you something hot to drink."

"God will reward you for this, sir; the Virgin will reward you. I thought I was going to die there, against that grating."

"Don't talk about dying, man. The question now is to find a cab; if we can only move along fast enough—What is the matter? Are you stumbling?"

"Yes, sir. I think I struck a lamp-post. You see—as I am blind—"

"Are you blind?" asked the stranger, anxiously.

"Yes, sir."

"Since when?"

"I was born blind."

Juan felt his companion's arm tremble in his, and they walked along in silence. Suddenly the man stopped and asked in a voice husky with emotion,—

"What is your name?"

"Juan."

"Juan what?"

"Juan Martinez."

"And your father was Manuel Martinez, wasn't he,—musician of the third artillery band?"

"Yes, sir."

The blind one felt the tight clasp of two powful arms that almost smothered him, and heard a trembling voice exclaim,—

"My God, how horrible, and how happy! I am a criminal, Juan! I am your brother Santiago!"

And the two brothers stood sobbing together in the middle of the street. The snow fell on them lightly. Suddenly Santiago tore himself from his brother's embrace, and began to shout, intermingling his words with interjections,—

"A cab! A cab! Isn't there a cab anywhere around? Curse my luck! Come. Juanillo, try; make an effort, my boy; we are not so very far. But where in the name of sense are all the cabs? Not one has passed us. Ah, I see one coming, thank God! No; the brute is going in the other direction. Here is another. This one is mine. Hello there, driver! Five dollars if you take us flying to Number 13 Castellana."

And taking his brother in his arms as though he had been a mere child, he put him in the cab and jumped in after him. The driver whipped his horse, and off they went, gliding swiftly and noiselessly over the snow. In the mean time Santiago, with his arms still around Juan, told him something of his life. He had been in Costa Rica, not Cuba, and had accumulated a respectable fortune. He had spent many years in the country, beyond mail service and far from any point of communication with Europe. He had written several letters to his father, and had managed to get these on some steamer trading with England, but had never received any answer. In the hope of returning shortly to Spain, he had made no inquiries. He had been in Madrid for four months. He learned from the parish record that his father was dead; but all he could discover concerning Juan was vague and contradictory. Some believed that he had died, while others said that, reduced to the last stages of misery, he went through the streets singing and playing on the guitar. All his efforts to find him had been fruitless; but fortunately Providence had thrown him into his arms. Santiago laughed and cried alternately, showing himself to be the same frank, open-hearted, jovial soul that Juan had loved so in his childhood. The cab finally came to a stop. A manservant opened the door, and Juan was fairly lifted into the house. When the door closed behind him, he breathed a warm atmosphere full of that peculiar aroma of comfort which wealth seems to exhale. His feet sank in the soft carpet. Two servants relieved him of his dripping clothes and brought him clean linen and a warm dressing-gown. In the same room, before a crackling wood fire, he was served a comforting bowl of hot broth, followed by something more substantial, which he was made to take very slowly and with all the precautions which his critical condition required. Then a bottle of old wine was brought up from the cellar. Santiago was too restless to sit still. He came and went, giving orders, interrupting himself every minute to say,—

"How do you feel now, Juan? Are you warm enough? Perhaps you don't care for this wine."

When the meal was over, the two brothers sat silently side by side before the fire. Santiago then inquired of one of the servants if the Señora and the children had already retired. On learning that they had, he said to Juan, beaming with delight,—

"Can you play on the piano?"

"Yes."

"Come into the parlor, then. Let us give them a surprise."

He accordingly led him into an adjoining room and seated him at the piano. He raised the top so as to obtain the greatest possible vibration, threw open the doors, and went through all the manœuvres peculiar to a surprise,—tiptoeing, whispering, speaking in a falsetto, and so much absurd pantomime that Juan could not help laughing as he realized how little his brother had changed.

"Now, Juanillo, play something startling, and play it loud, with all your might."

The blind boy struck up a military march. A quiver ran through the silent house like that which stirs a music-box while it is being wound up. The notes poured from the piano, hurrying, jostling one another, but never losing their triumphant rhythm. Every now and then Santiago exclaimed,—

"Louder, Juanillo! Louder!"

And the blind boy struck the notes with all his spirit and might.

"I see my wife peeping in from behind the curtains. Go on, Juanillo. She is in her nightgown,—he, he! I am pretending not to see her. I have no doubt she thinks I am crazy,—he, he! Go on, Juanillo."

Juan obeyed, although he thought the jest had been carried far enough. He wanted to know his sister-in-law and kiss his nephews.

"Now I can just see Manolita. Hello! Paquito is up too. Didn't I tell you we should surprise them? But I am afraid they will take cold. Stop a minute, Juanito!"

And the infernal clamor was silenced.

"Come, Adela, Manolita, and Paquito, get on your things and come in to see your uncle Juan. This is Juanillo, of whom you have heard me speak so often. I have just found him in the street almost frozen to death. Come, hurry and dress, all of you."

The whole family was soon ready, and rushed in to embrace the blind boy. The wife's voice was soft and harmonious. To Juan it sounded like the voice of the Virgin. He discovered, too, that she was weeping silently at the thought of all his sufferings. She ordered a foot-warmer to be brought in. She wrapped his legs in a cloak and put a soft cushion behind his head. The children stood around his chair, caressing him, and all listened with tears to the accounts of his past misery. Santiago struck his forehead; the children stroked his hands, saying,—

"You will never be hungry again, will you, uncle? Or go out without a cloak and an umbrella? I don't want you to, neither does Manolita, nor mamma, nor papa."

"I wager you will not give him your bed, Paquito," said Santiago, trying to conceal his tears under his affected merriment.

"My bed won't fit him, papa! But he can have the bed in the guests' chamber. It is a great bed, uncle, a big, big bed!"

"I don't believe I care to go to bed," said Juan. "Not just now at any rate, I am so comfortable here."

"That pain has gone, hasn't it, uncle?" whispered Manolita, kissing and stroking his hand.

"Yes, dear, yes,—God bless you! Nothing pains me now. I am happy, very happy! Only I feel sleepy, so sleepy that I can hardly raise my eyelids."

"Never mind us; sleep if you feel like it," said Santiago.

"Yes, uncle, sleep," repeated the children.

And Juan fell asleep,—but he wakened in another world.

The next morning, at dawn, two policemen stumbled against a corpse in the snow. The doctor of the charity hospital pronounced it a case of congealing of the blood.

As one of the officers turned him over, face-upward,—

"Look, Jimenez," said he; "he seems to be laughing."

A Great Tree

by Zona Gale

I never had felt so much like Christmas, said Calliope Marsh, as I did that year.

"I wish't," I says, when it got 'most time, "I wish't I knew somebody to have a Christmas tree with."

"Well, Calliope Marsh," says Mis' Postmaster Sykes, looking surprised-on-purpose, the way she does, "ain't there enough poor and neglected folks in this world to please anybody?"

"I didn't say have a Christmas tree *for,*" I says back at her; "I says have one *with.*"

"I don't know what you mean by that difference," she says, "I'm sure."

"I donno," I says, "as I know either. But there is a difference, somewhere. I'd kind of like to have a tree *with* folks this year."

"Why don't you help on your church tree?" Mis' Sykes ask' me. "They're going to spend quite a little money on theirs this year."

"I hate to box Christmas up in a church," I says.

"Why, Calliope Marsh!" she says, shocked.

I didn't want to hurt her feelings—I ain't never one of those that likes to throw their idees in folks's faces and watch folks jump back. So I tried to talk about something else, but she went right on, trying her best to help me out.

"The ward schools is each going to have a tree this year, I hear," she says. "Why don't you go in on your ward, Calliope, and help out there? They'd be real glad of help, you know."

"I hate to divide Christmas off into wards," I says to her.

"Well, then, go in with a family," she says; "any of us'll be real glad to have you," she adds, generous. "*We* would. Come to ours—we're going to have a great big tree for the children. I've been stringing the pop-corn and cutting the paper for it whenever I got an odd minute. The Holcombs, they're going to have one too—and Mis' Uppers and Mis' Merriman and even the Hubbelthwaits and Abigail Arnold, for her little nieces. I never see a year when everybody was going to celebrate so nice. Come on with one of us, why don't you?"

"Well," I says, "mebbe I will. I'll see. I don't know yet what I will do," I told her. And I went off down the street. What I wanted to say was, "I hate to box Christmas up in a family," but I didn't quite dare—yet.

Friendship Village ain't ever looked much more like Christmas, to my notion, than it did that December. Just the right snow had come—and no more; and just the right cold—and no more. The moon was getting along so's about the night of the twenty-fifth it was going to loom up big and gold and warm over the fields on the flats, where it always comes up in winter like it had just edged around there to get sort of a wide front yard for its big show, where the whole village could have a porch seat.

You know when you live in a village you always know whether the moon is new or to the full or where it is and when it's going to be; but when you live in a city you just look up in the sky some night and say "Oh, that's so, there's the moon," and go right on thinking about something else. Here in the village that December everything was getting ready, deliberate, for a full-moon Christmas, like long ago. The moon and the cold and the snow, and all them public things, was doing their best, together, for our common Christmas. All but us. It seemed like all of us humans was working for it separate.

Tramping along there in the snow that night, I thought over what Mis' Sykes had said, and about all the places she'd mentioned over was going to have Christmas trees. And I looked along to the houses, most of 'em lying right there on Daphne Street, where they were going to have 'em—I could see 'em all, one tree after another, lighted and streaming from house to house all up and down Daphne Street, just the way they were going to look.

And then there was the little back streets, and the houses down on the flats, where there wouldn't be any trees nor much of any Christmas. Of course, as Mis' Sykes had said, the poor and the neglected are always with us—yet; but I didn't want to pounce down on any of 'em with a bag of fruit and a box of animal crackers and set and watch 'em.

That wasn't what I meant by having a Christmas *with* somebody.

"There'd ought to be some place—" I was beginning to

think, when right along where I was, by the Market Square, I come on five or six children, kicking around in the snow. It was 'most dark, but I could just make 'em out: Eddie Newhaven, Arthur Mills, Lily Dorron, and two-three more.

"Hello, folks," I says, "what you doing? Having a carnival?" Because it's on the Market Square that carnivals and some little circuses and things that belongs to everybody is usually celebrated.

Little Arthur Mills spoke up. "No," he says, "we was just playing we's selling a load of Christmas trees."

"Christmas trees," I says. "Why, that's so. This is where they always bring 'em to sell—big load of 'em for everybody, ain't it?"

"They're going to bring an *awful* big load here this time," says Eddie Newhaven—"big enough for everybody in town to have one. Most of the fellows is going to have 'em—us and Ned Backus and the Cartwrights and Joe Tyrril and Lifty—all of 'em."

"My," I says, "what a lot of Christmas trees! Why, if they was set along by the curbstone here on Daphne Street," I says, just to please the children and make a little talk with 'em, "why, the line of 'em would reach all up and down the town," I says. "Wouldn't that be fun?"

Little Lily claps her hands.

"Oh, yes," she cries, "wouldn't that be fun? With popcorn strings all going from one to the other?"

"It would be a grand sight," says I, looking down across the Market Square. There, hanging all gold and quiet, like it didn't think it amounted to much, right over the big cedar-of-Lebanon-looking tree in the Square, was the moon, crooked to a horn.

"Once," says Eddie Newhaven, "when they was selling the Christmas trees here, they kept right on selling 'em after dark. And they stood 'em around here and put a little light in each one. It was awful nice. Wouldn't it be nice if they'd do that all over the Square some time!"

"It would be a grand sight," says I again, "but one that the folks in this town would never have time for. . . ."

While I spoke I was looking down across Market Square again toward the moon hanging over the cedar-of-Lebanon-looking tree.

"There's a pretty good-looking tree there already," I says idle. "What a grand thing it would be lit up," says I, for not much of any reason—only to keep the talk going with the children. Then something went through me from my head to my feet. "Why not light it some time?" I says.

The children set up a little shout—part because they liked it, part because they thought such a thing could never be. I laughed with 'em, and I went on up the street—but all the time something in me kept on saying something, all hurried and as if it meant it. And little ends of ideas, and little jagged edges of other ideas, and plans part raveled out that you thought you could knit up again, and long, sharp motions, a little something like light, kept going through my head and going through it.

Down to the next corner I met Ben Cory, that keeps the livery-stable and sings bass to nearly everybody's funeral and to other public occasions.

"Ben," I says excited, though I hadn't thought anything about this till that minute, "Ben—you getting up any Christmas Eve Christmas carols to sing this year?"

He had a new string of sleigh-bells over his shoulder, and he give it a shift, I recollect, so's they all jingled.

"Well," he says, "I did allow to do it. But I've spoke to one or two, and they donno's they can do it. Some has got to sing to churches earlier in the evening and they donno's they want to tune up all night. And the most has got to be home for family Christmas."

"There ain't," I says, "no manner o' doubt about the folks that'd be glad to listen, is there, provided you had the singers?"

"Oh, sure," he says. "Folks shines up to music consider'ble, Christmas Eve. It—sort of—well, it——"

"Yes," I says, "I know. It does, don't it? Well, Ben Cory, you get your Christmas-carol singers together and a-caroling, and I'll undertake that there sha'n't nothing much stand in the way of their being out on Christmas Eve. Is it a bargain?"

His face lit up, all jolly and hearty.

"Why, sure it's a bargain," he says. "I'll get 'em. I wanted to, only I didn't want to carol 'em any more than they wanted to be caroled. I'll get 'em," he says, and gives his bells a hunch that made 'em ring all up and down Daphne Street—that the moon was looking down at just as if it was public property and not all made up of little private plans with just room enough for us four and no more, or figures to that effect.

I donno if you've ever managed any kind of a revolution?

They's two kinds of revolutions. One breaks off of something that's always been. You pick up the broke piece and try to throw it away to make room for something that's growing out of the other part. And 'most everybody will begin to tell you that the growing piece ain't any good, but that the other part is the kind you have always bought and that you'd better save it and stick it back on. But then they's the other kind of revolution that backs away from something that's always been and looks at it a little farther off than it ever see it before, and says: "Let's us move a little way around and pay attention to this thing from a new spot." And real often, if you put it that way, they's enough people willing to do that, because they know they can go right back afterward and stand in the same old place if they want to.

Well, this last was the kind of a revolution I took charge of that week before Christmas. I got my plans and my ideas and my notions all planned and thought and budded, and then I presented 'em around, abundant.

The very next morning after I'd seen the children I started out, while I had kind of a glow to drape around the difficulties so's I couldn't see 'em. I went first to the store-keepers, seeing Christmas always seems to hinge and hang on what they say and do. And I went to Eppleby Holcomb, because I knew he'd see it like I done—and I wanted the brace of being agreed with, like you do.

Eppleby's store was all decorated up with green cut paper and tassels and turkey-red calico poinsettias, and it looked real nice and tasty. And the store was full of the country trade. The little overhead track that took the bundles had broke down just at the wrong minute, and old rich Mis' Wiswell's felt soles had got stuck half-way, and Eppleby himself was up on top of a counter trying to rescue 'em for her, while she made tart remarks below. When he'd fished 'em out and wrapped 'em up for her,

"Eppleby," I says, "would you be willing to shut up shop on Christmas Eve, or wouldn't you?"

He looked kind of startled. "It's a pretty good night for trade, you know, Calliope?" says he—doubtful.

"Why, yes," I says, "it is. But everybody that's going to give presents to people'll give presents to people. And if the stores ain't open Christmas Eve, folks'll buy 'em when the stores *is* open. Is that sense, or ain't it?"

He knew it was. And when I told him what I'd got hold of, stray places in my head, he says if the rest would shut he'd shut, and be glad of it. Abigail Arnold done the same about her home bakery, and the Gekerjecks, and two-three more. But Silas Sykes, that keeps the post-office store, he was firm.

"If that ain't woman-foolish," he says, "I donno what is. You ain't no more idee of business than so many cats. No, sir. I don't betray the public by cutting 'em off of one evening's shopping like that."

It made a nice little sentence to quote, and I quoted it consider'ble. And the result was, the rest of 'em, that knew Silas, head and heart, finally says, all right, he could keep open if he wanted to, and enjoy himself, and they'd all shut up. I honestly think they kind of appreciated, in a nice, neighborly way, making Silas feel mean—when he'd ought to.

It was a little harder to make the Sunday-school superintendents see the thing that I had in my head. Of course, when a thing has been the way it has been for a good while, you can't really blame people for feeling that it's been the way it ought to be. Feelings seems made that way. Our superintendent has been our superintendent for 'most forty years—ever since the church was built—and of course his thoughts is kind of turned to bone in some places, naturally.

His name is Jerry Bemus, and he keeps a little harness shop next door to the Town Hall that's across from Market Square. When I went in that day he was resting from making harnesses, and he was practising on his cornet. He can make a bugle call real nice—you can often hear it, going up and down

Daphne Street in the morning, and when I'm down doing my trading I always like to hear it—it gives me kind of a nice, old-fashioned feeling, like when Abigail Arnold fries doughnuts in the back of the Home Bakery and we can all smell 'em, out in the road.

"Jerry," I says, "how much is our Sunday-school Christmas tree going to cost us?"

Jerry's got a wooden leg, and he can *not* remember not to try to cross it over the other one. He done that now, and give it up.

"We calc'late about twenty-five dollars," says he, proud.

"What we going to do to celebrate?"

"Well," he says, "have speaking pieces—we got a program of twenty numbers already," says he, pleased. "And a trimmed tree, and an orange, and a bag of nuts and candy for every child," he says.

"All the other churches is going to do the same," I says. "Five trees and five programs and five sets of stuff all around. And all of 'em on Christmas Eve, when you'd think we'd all sort of draw together instead of setting apart, in cliques. Land," I says out, "that first Christmas Eve wouldn't the angels have stopped singing and wept in the sky if they could of seen what we'd do to it!"

"Hush, Calliope," says Jerry Bemus, shocked. "They ain't no need to be sacrilegious, is they?"

"Not a bit," says I; "we've been it so long a'ready, worshiping around in sections like Hottentots. Well, now," I says, "do you honestly think we've all chose the best way to go at Christmas Eve for the children, filling them up with colored stuff and getting their stummicks all upset?"

We had quite a little talk about it, back and forth, Jerry and me. And all of a sudden, while I was trying my best to make him see what I saw, I happened to notice his bugle again.

"There ain't no thrill in none of it," I was saying to him. "Not half so much," I says, "as there is in your bugle. When I hear that go floating up and down the street, I always kind of feel like it was announcing something. To my notion," I says, "it could announce Christmas to this town far better than forty-'leven little separate trimmed-up trees. . . . Why, Jerry," I says out sudden, "listen to what I've thought of. . . ."

A little something had come in my head that minute, unexpected, that fitted itself into the rest of my plan. And it made Jerry say, pretty soon, that he was willing to go with me to see the other superintendents; and we done so that very day. Ain't it funny how big things work out by homely means—by homely means? Sole because the choir-leader in one choir had resigned because the bass in that choir was the bass in that choir, and so they didn't have anybody there to train their Christmas music, and sole because another congregation was hard up and was having to borrow its Christmas celebration money out of the foreign missionary fund—we got 'em to see sense. And then the other two joined in.

The schools were all right from the first, being built, like they are, on a basis of belonging to everybody, same as breathing and one-two other public utilities, and nothing dividing anybody from anybody. And I begun to feel like life and the world was just one great bud, longing to open, so be it could get enough care.

The worst ones to get weaned away from a perfectly selfish way of observing Christ's birthday was the private families. Land, land, I kept saying to myself them days, we all of us act like we was studying kindergarten mathematics. We count up them that's closest to us, and we can't none of us seem to count much above ten.

Not all of 'em was that way, though. Well—if it just happens that you live in any town whatever in the civilized world, I think you'll know about what I had said to me.

On the one hand it went about like this, from Mis' Timothy Toplady and the Holcombs and the Hubbelthwaits and a lot more:

"Well, land knows, it'd save us lots of back-aching work—but—will the children like it?"

"Like it?" I says. "Try 'em. Trust 'em without trying 'em if you want to. I would. Remember," I couldn't help adding, "you like to be with the children a whole lot oftener than they like to be with you. What they like is to be together."

And, "Well, do you honestly think it'll work? I don't see how it can—anything so differ'nt."

And, "Well, they ain't any harm trying it one year, as I can see. That can't break up the holidays, as I know of."

But the other side had figured it out just like the other side of everything always figures.

"Calliope," says Mis' Postmaster Sykes, "are you crazy-headed? What's your idee? Ain't things all right the way they've always been done?"

"Well," says I, conservative, "not all of 'em. Not wholesale, I wouldn't say."

"But you can't go changing things like this," she told me. "What'll become of Christmas?"

"Christmas," I says, "don't need you or me, Mis' Sykes, to be its guardians. All Christmas needs is for us to get out of its way, and leave it express what it means."

"But the *home* Christmas," she says, 'most like a wail. "Would you do away with that?"

Then I sort of turned on her. I couldn't help it.

"Whose home?" I says stern. "If it's your home you mean, or any of the thousands of others like it where Christmas is kept, then you know, and they all know, that nothing on earth can take away the Christmas feeling and the Christmas joy as long as you want it to be there. But if it's the homes you mean—and there's thousands of 'em—where no Christmas ever comes, you surely ain't arguing to keep them the way they've been kept?"

But she continued to shake her head.

"You can do as you like, of course," she said, "and so can everybody else. It's their privilege. But as for me, I shall trim my little tree here by our own fireside. And here we shall celebrate Christmas—Jeddie and Nora and father and me."

"Why can't you do *both?*" I says. "I wouldn't have you give up your fireside end of things for anything on earth. But why can't you do both?"

Mis' Sykes didn't rightly seem to know—at least she didn't say. But she give me to understand that her mind run right along in the self-same groove it had had made for it, cozy.

Somehow, the longer I live, the less sense I seem to have. There's some things I've learned from twenty-five to thirty times in my life, and yet I can't seem to remember them no more than I can remember whether it's sulphite or sulphate of soda that I take for my quinsy. And one of these is about taking things casual.

That night, for instance, when I come round the corner on

to Daphne Street at half-past seven on Christmas Eve, I thought I was going to have to waste a minute or two standing just where the bill-board makes a shadow for the arc-light, trying to get used to the idea of what we were doing—used to it in my throat. But there wasn't much time to spend that way, being there were things to do between then and eight o'clock, when we'd told 'em all to be there. So I ran along and tried not to think about it—except the work part. 'Most always, the work part of anything'll steady you.

The great cedar-of-Lebanon-looking tree, standing down there on the edge of the Market Square and acting as if it had been left from some long-ago forest, on purpose, had been hung round with lines and lines of strung popcorn—the kind that no Christmas tree would be a Christmas tree without, because so many, many folks has set up stringing it nights of Christmas week, after the children was in bed, and has kept it, careful, in a box, so's it'd do for next year. We had all that from the churches—Methodist and Presbyterian and Episcopal and Baptist and Catholic pop-corn, and you couldn't tell 'em apart at all when you got 'em on the tree. The festoons showed ghostly-white in the dark and the folks showed ghostly-black, hurrying back and forth doing the last things.

And the folks was coming—you could hear 'em all along Daphne Street, tripping on the bad place that hadn't been mended because it was right under the arc-light, and coming over the hollow-sounding place by Graham's drug-store, and coming from the little side streets and the dark back streets and the streets down on the flats. Some of 'em had Christmas trees waiting at home—the load had been there on the Market Square, just like we had let it be there for years without seeing that the Market Square had any other Christmas uses—and a good many had bought trees. But a good many more had decided not to have any—only just to hang up stockings; and to let the great big common Christmas tree stand for what it stood for, gathering most of that little garland of Daphne Street trees up into its living heart.

Over by the bandstand I come on them I'd been looking for—Eddie Newhaven and Arthur Mills and Lily Dorron and Sarah and Mollie and the Cartwrights and Lifty and six-eight more.

"Hello, folks," I says. "What you down here for? Why ain't you home?"

They answered all together:

"For the big tree!"

"Are you, now?" I says—just to keep on a-talking to 'em. "Whose tree?"

I love to remember the way they answered. It was Eddie Newhaven that said it.

"Why, all of us's!" he said.

All of us's! I like to say it over when they get to saying "mine" and "theirs" too hard where I am.

When it was eight o'clock and there was enough gathered on the Square, they done the thing that was going to be done, only nobody had known how well they were going to do it. They touched the button, and from the bottom branch to the tip-top little cone, the big old tree came alight, just like it knew what it was all about and like it had come out of the ground long ago for this reason—only we'd never known. Two hundred little electric lights there were, colored, and paid for private, though I done my best to get the town to pay for 'em, like it ought to for its own tree; but they was paid for private—yet.

It made a little *oh!* come in the crowd and run round, it was so big and beautiful, standing there against the stars like it knew well enough that it was onc of 'em, whether we knew it or not. And coming up across the flats, big and gold and low, was the moon, most full, like *it* belonged, too.

"And glory shone around," I says to myself—and I stood there feeling the glory, outside and in. Not my little celebration, and your little celebration, and their little celebration, private, that was costing each of us more than it ought to—but our celebration, paying attention to the message that Christ paid attention to.

I was so full of it that I didn't half see Ben Cory and his carolers come racing out of the dark. They was all fixed up in funny pointed hoods and in cloaks and carrying long staves with everybody's barn-yard lanterns tied on the end of 'em, and they run out in a line down to the tree, and they took hold of hands and danced around it, singing to their voices' top a funny old tune, one of them tunes that, whether you've ever heard it before or not, kind of makes things in you that's older than you are yourself wake up and remember, real plain.

And Jerry Bemus shouted out at 'em: "Sing it again—sing it again!" and pounded his wooden leg with his cane. "Sing it again, I tell you. I ain't heard anybody sing that for goin' on forty years." And everybody laughed, and they sung it again for him, and some more songs that had come out of the old country that a little bit of it was living inside everybody that was there. And while they were singing, it came to me all of a sudden about another night, 'most three hundred years before, when on American soil that lonesome English heart, up there in Boston, had dreamed ahead to a time when Christmas would come here. . . .

"But faith unrolls the future scrolls;
Christmas shall not die,
Nor men of English blood and speech
Forget their ancestry—"

or any other blood, or any other speech that has in it the spirit of what Christ come to teach. And that's all of us. And it felt to me as if now we were only just beginning to take out our little single, lonely tapers and carry them to light a great tree.

Then, just after the carols died down, the thing happened that we'd planned to happen: Over on one side the choirs of all the churches, that I guess had never sung together in their lives before, though they'd been singing steadily about the self-same things since they was born choirs, begun to sing—

Silent night, holy night.

Think of it—down there on the Market Square that had never had anything sung on it before except carnival tunes and circus tunes. All up and down Daphne Street it must of sounded, only there was hardly anybody far off to hear it, the most of 'em being right there with all of us. They sung it without anybody playing it for 'em and they sung it from first to last.

And then they slipped into another song that isn't a Christmas carol exactly, nor not any song that comes in the book under "Christmas," but something that comes in just as natural as if it was another name for what Christmas was—"Nearer, my God, to thee," and "Lead, Kindly Light," and some more. And after a bar or two of the first one, the voices all around begun kind of mumbling and humming and carrying the tunes along in their throats without anybody in particular starting 'em there, and then they all just naturally burst out and sung too.

And so I donno who done it—whether the choirs had planned it that way, or whether they just thought of it then, or whether somebody in the crowd struck it up unbeknownst to himself, or whether the song begun to sing itself; but it come from somewhere, strong and clear and real—a song that the children has been learning in school and has been teaching the town for a year or two now, sung to the tune of "Wacht am Rhein":

The crest and crowning of all good—
Life's common goal—is brotherhood.

And then everybody sung. Because that's a piece you can't sing alone. You can *not* sing it alone. All over the Market Square they took it up, and folks that couldn't sing, and me that can't sing a note except when there's nobody around that would recognize me if they ever saw me again—we all sung together, there in the dark, with the tree in the midst.

And we seemed long and long away from the time when the leader in one of them singing choirs had left the other choir because the bass in the other choir was the bass in the other choir. And it was like the Way Things Are had suddenly spoke for a minute, there in the singing choirs come out of their separate lofts, and in all the singing folks. And in all of us—all of us.

Then up hopped Eppleby Holcomb on to a box in front of the tree, and he calls out:

"Merry Christmas! Merry Christmas—on the first annual outdoor Christmas-tree celebration of Friendship Village!"

When he said that I felt—well, it don't make any difference to anybody how I felt; but what I done was to turn and make for the edge of the crowd just as fast as I could. And just then there come what Eppleby's words was the signal for. And out on the little flagstaff balcony of the Town Hall Jerry Bemus stepped with his bugle, and he blew it shrill and clear, so that it sounded all over the town, once, twice, three times, a bugle-call to say it was Christmas. We couldn't wait till twelve o'clock—we are all in bed long before that time in Friendship Village, holiday or not.

But the bugle-call said it was Christmas just the same. Think of it . . . the bugle that used to say it was war. And the same minute the big tree went out, all still and quiet, but to be lit again next year and to stay a living thing in between.

When I stepped on to Daphne Street, who should I come face to face with but Mis' Postmaster Sykes. I was feeling so glorified over, that I never thought of its being strange that she was there. But she spoke up, just the same as if I'd said: "Why, I thought you wasn't coming near."

"The children was bound to come," she says, "so I had to bring 'em."

"Yes," I thought to myself, "the children know. They know."

And I even couldn't feel bad when I passed the post-office store and see Silas sitting in there all sole alone—the only lit store in the street. I knew he'd be on the Market Square the next year.

They went singing through all the streets that night, Ben Cory and his carolers. "Silent night, holy night" come from my front gate when I was 'most asleep. It was like the whole town was being sung to by something that didn't show. And when the time comes that this something speaks clear all the time,—well, it ain't a very far-off time, you know.

A Christmas Present for a Lady

BY MYRA KELLY

IT WAS THE WEEK BEFORE Christmas, and the First-Reader Class had, almost to a man, decided on the gifts to be lavished on "Teacher." She was quite unprepared for any such observance on the part of her small adherents, for her first study of the roll-book had shown her that its numerous Jacobs, Isidores, and Rachels belonged to a class to which Christmas Day was much as other days. And so she went serenely on her way, all unconscious of the swift and strict relation between her manner and her chances. She was, for instance, the only person in the room who did not know that her criticism of Isidore Belchatosky's hands and face cost her a tall "three for ten cents" candlestick and a plump box of candy.

But Morris Mogilewsky, whose love for Teacher was far greater than the combined loves of all the other children, had as yet no present to bestow. That his "kind feeling" should be without proof when the lesser loves of Isidore Wishnewsky, Sadie Gonorowsky, and Bertha Binderwitz were taking the tangible but surprising forms which were daily exhibited to his confidential gaze, was more than he could bear. The knowledge saddened all his hours and was the more maddening because it could in no wise be shared by Teacher, who noticed his altered bearing and tried with all sorts of artful beguilements to make him happy and at ease. But her efforts served only to increase his unhappiness and his love. And he loved her! Oh, how he loved her! Since first his dreading eyes had clung for a breath's space to her "like man's shoes" and had then crept timidly upward past a black skirt, a "from silk" apron, a red "jumper," and "from gold" chain to her "light face," she had been mistress of his heart of hearts. That was more than three months ago. And well he remembered the day!

His mother had washed him horribly, and had taken him into the big, red school-house, so familiar from the outside, but so full of unknown terrors within. After his dusty little shoes had stumbled over the threshold he had passed from ordeal to ordeal until at last he was torn in mute and white-faced despair from his mother's skirts.

He was then dragged through long halls and up tall stairs by a large boy, who spoke to him disdainfully as "greenie," and cautioned him as to the laying down softly and taking up gently of those poor dusty shoes, so that his spirit was quite broken and his nerves were all unstrung when he was pushed into a room full of bright sunshine and of children who laughed at his frightened little face. The sunshine smote his timid eyes, the laughter smote his timid heart, and he turned to flee. But the door was shut, the large boy gone, and despair took him for its own.

Down upon the floor he dropped, and wailed, and wept, and kicked. It was then that he heard, for the first time the voice which now he loved. A hand was forced between his aching body and the floor, and the voice said:

"Why, my dear little chap, you mustn't cry like that. What's the matter?"

The hand was gentle and the question kind, and these, combined with a faint perfume suggestive of drug stores and barber shops—but nicer than either—made him uncover his hot little face. Kneeling beside him was a lady, and he forced his eyes to that perilous ascent from shoes to skirt, from skirt to jumper, from jumper to face, they trailed in dread uncertainty, but at the face they stopped. They had found—rest.

Morris allowed himself to be gathered into the lady's arms and held upon her knee, and when his sobs no longer rent the very foundations of his pink and wide-spread tie, he answered her question in a voice as soft as his eyes, and as gently sad.

"I ain't so big, und I don't know where is my mamma."

So, having cast his troubles on the shoulders of the lady, he had added his throbbing head to the burden, and from that safe retreat had enjoyed his first day at school immensely.

Thereafter he had been the first to arrive every morning, and the last to leave every afternoon; and under the care of Teacher, his liege lady, he had grown in wisdom and love and happiness. But the greatest of these was love. And now, when the other boys and girls were planning surprises and gifts of price for Teacher, his hands were as empty as his heart was full. Appeal to his mother met with denial prompt and energetic.

"For what you go und make, over Christmas, presents? You

ain't no Krisht; you should better have no kind feelings over Krishts, neither; your papa could to have a mad."

"Teacher ain't no Krisht," said Morris stoutly; "all the other fellows buys her presents, und I'm loving mit her too; it's polite I gives her presents the while I'm got such a kind feeling over her."

"Well, we ain't got no money for buy nothings," said Mrs. Mogilewsky. "No money, und your papa, he has all times a scare he shouldn't to get no more, the while the boss"—and here followed incomprehensible, but depressing, financial details, until the end of the interview found Morris and his mother sobbing and rocking in one another's arms. So Morris was helpless, his mother poor, and Teacher all unknowing.

And the great day, the Friday before Christmas came, and the school was, for the first half hour, quite mad. Doors opened suddenly and softly to admit small persons, clad in wondrous ways and bearing wondrous parcels. Room 18, generally so placid and so peaceful, was a howling wilderness full of brightly coloured, quickly changing groups of children, all whispering, all gurgling and all hiding queer bundles. A newcomer invariably caused a diversion; the assembled multitude, athirst for novelty, fell upon him and clamoured for a glimpse of his bundle and a statement of its price.

Teacher watched in dumb amaze. What could be the matter with the children, she wondered. They could not have guessed the shrouded something in the corner to be a Christmas-tree. What made them behave so queerly, and why did they look so strange? They seemed to have grown stout in a single night, and Teacher, as she noted this, marvelled greatly. The explanation was simple, though it came in alarming form. The sounds of revelry were pierced by a long, shrill yell, and a pair of agitated legs sprang suddenly into view between two desks. Teacher, rushing to the rescue, noted that the legs formed the unsteady stem of an upturned mushroom of brown flannel and green braid, which she recognized as the outward seeming of her cherished Bertha Binderwitz; and yet, when the desks were forced to disgorge their prey, the legs restored to their normal position were found to support a fat child—and Bertha was best described as "skinny"—in a dress of the Stuart tartan tastefully trimmed with purple. Investigation proved that Bertha's accumulative taste in dress was an established custom. In nearly all cases the glory of holiday attire was hung upon the solid foundation of every day clothes as bunting is hung upon a building. The habit was economical of time, and produced a charming embonpoint.

Teacher, too, was more beautiful than ever. Her dress was blue, and "very long down, like a lady," with bands of silk and scraps of lace distributed with the eye of art. In her hair she wore a bow of what Sadie Gonorowsky, whose father "worked by fancy goods," described as black "from plush ribbon—costs ten cents."

Isidore Belchatosky, relenting, was the first to lay tribute before Teacher. He came forward with a sweet smile and a tall candlestick—the candy had gone to its long home—and Teacher, for a moment, could not be made to understand that all that length of bluish-white china was really hers "for keeps."

"It's to-morrow holiday," Isidore assured her; "and we gives you presents, the while we have a kind feeling. Candlesticks could to cost twenty-five cents."

"It's a lie. Three for ten," said a voice in the background, but Teacher hastened to respond to Isidore's test of her credulity:

"Indeed, they could. This candlestick could have cost fifty cents, and it's just what I want. It is very good of you to bring me a present."

"You're welcome," said Isidore, retiring; and then, the ice being broken, the First-Reader Class in a body rose to cast its gifts on Teacher's desk, and its arms around Teacher's neck.

Nathan Horowitz presented a small cup and saucer; Isidore Applebaum bestowed a large calendar for the year before last; Sadie Gonorowsky brought a basket containing a bottle of perfume, a thimble, and a bright silk handkerchief; Sarah Schrodsky offered a penwiper and a yellow celluloid collar-button; and Eva Kidansky gave an elaborate nasal douche, under the pleasing delusion that it was an atomizer.

Once more sounds of grief reached Teacher's ears. Rushing again to the rescue, she threw open the door and came upon Woe personified. Eva Gonorowsky, her hair in wildest disarray, her stocking fouled, ungartered, and down-gyved to her ankle, appeared before her teacher. She bore all the marks of Hamlet's excitement, and many more, including a tear-stained little face and a gilt saucer clasped to a panting breast.

"Eva, my dearest Eva, what's happened to you *now?*" asked Teacher, for the list of ill-chances which had befallen this one of her charges was very long. And Eva's wail was that a boy, a very big boy, had stolen her golden cup "what I had for you by present," and had left her only the saucer and her undying love to bestow.

Before Eva's sobs had quite yielded to Teacher's arts, Jacob Spitsky pressed forward with a tortoise-shell comb of terrifying aspect and hungry teeth, and an air showing forth a determination to adjust it in its destined place. Teacher meekly bowed her head; Jacob forced his offering into her long-suffering hair, and then retired with the information, "Costs fifteen cents, Teacher," and the courteous phrase—by etiquette prescribed—"Wish you health to wear it." He was plainly a hero, and was heard remarking to less favoured admirers that "Teacher's hair is awful softy, and smells off of perfumery."

Here a big boy, a very big boy, entered hastily. He did not belong to Room 18, but he had long known Teacher. He had brought her a present; he wished her a Merry Christmas. The present, when produced, proved to be a pretty gold cup, and Eva Gonorowsky, with renewed emotion, recognized the boy as her assailant and the cup as her property. Teacher was dreadfully embarrassed; the boy not at all so. His policy was simple and entire denial, and in this he persevered, even after Eva's saucer had unmistakably proclaimed its relationship to the cup.

Meanwhile the rush of presentation went steadily on. Other cups and saucers came in wild profusion. The desk was covered with them, and their wrappings of purple tissue paper required a monitor's whole attention. The soap, too, became urgently perceptible. It was of all sizes, shapes and colours, but of uniform and dreadful power of perfume. Teacher's eyes filled with tears—of gratitude—as each new piece or box was pressed against her nose, and Teacher's mind was full of wonder as to what she could ever do with all of it. Bottles of perfume vied with one another and with the all-pervading soap until the air was heavy and breathing grew laborious. But pride swelled the hearts of the assembled multitude. No other Teacher had so many helps to the toilet. None other was so beloved.

Teacher's aspect was quite changed, and the "blue long down like a lady dress" was almost hidden by the offerings she had received. Jacob's comb had two massive and bejewelled rivals in the "softy hair." The front of the dress, where aching or despondent heads were wont to rest, glittered with campaign buttons of American celebrities, beginning with James G. Blaine and extending into modern history as far as Patrick Divver, Admiral Dewey, and Captain Dreyfus. Outside the blue belt was a white one, nearly clean, and bearing in "sure 'nough golden words" the curt, but stirring, invitation, "Remember the Maine." Around the neck were three chaplets of beads, wrought by chubby fingers and embodying much love, while the waist-line was further adorned by tiny and beribboned aprons. Truly, it was a day of triumph.

When the waste-paper basket had been twice filled with wrappings and twice emptied; when order was emerging out of chaos; when the Christmas-tree had been disclosed and its treasures distributed, a timid hand was laid on Teacher's knee and a plaintive voice whispered, "Say, Teacher, I got something for you;" and Teacher turned quickly to see Morris, her dearest boy charge, with his poor little body showing quite plainly between his shirt-waist buttons and through the gashes he called pockets. This was his ordinary costume, and the funds of the house of Mogilewsky were evidently unequal to an outer layer of finery.

"Now, Morris dear," said Teacher, "you shouldn't have troubled to get me a present; you know you and I are such good friends that—"

"Teacher, yiss ma'an," Morris interrupted, in a bewitching and rising inflection of his soft and plaintive voice. "I know you got a kind feeling by me, and I couldn't to tell even how I got a kind feeling by you. Only it's about that kind feeling I should give you a present. I didn't"—with a glance at the crowded desk—"I didn't to have no soap nor no perfumery, and my mamma she couldn't to buy none by the store; but, Teacher, I'm got something awful nice for you by present."

"And what is it, deary?" asked the already rich and gifted young person. "What is my new present?"

"Teacher, it's like this: I don't know; I ain't so big like I could to know"—and, truly, God pity him! he was passing small—"it ain't for boys—it's for ladies. Over yesterday on the night comes my papa to my house, und he gives my mamma the present. Sooner she looks on it, sooner she has a awful glad; in her eyes stands tears, und she says, like that—out of Jewish—'Thanks,' un' she kisses my papa a kiss. Und my papa, *how* he is polite! he says—out of Jewish too—"You're welcome, all right,' un' he kisses my mamma a kiss. So my momma, she sets und looks on the present, und all the time she looks she has a glad over it. Und I didn't to have no soap, so you could to have the present."

"But did your mother say I might?"

"Teacher, no ma'an; she didn't say like that, und she didn't to say *not* like that. She didn't to know. But it's for ladies, un' I didn't to have no soap. You could to look on it. It ain't for boys."

And here Morris opened a hot little hand and disclosed a tightly folded pinkish paper. As Teacher read it he watched her with eager, furtive eyes, dry and bright, until hers grew suddenly moist, when he promptly followed suit. As she looked down at him, he made his moan once more:

"It's for ladies, und I didn't to have no soap."

"But, Morris, dear," cried Teacher unsteadily, laughing a little, and yet not far from tears, "this is ever so much nicer than soap—a thousand times better than perfume; and you're quite right, it is for ladies, and I never had one in all my life before. I am so very thankful."

"You're welcome, all right. That's how my papa says; it's polite," said Morris proudly. And proudly he took his place among the very little boys, and loudly he joined in the ensuing song. For the rest of that exciting day he was a shining point of virtue in the rest of that confused class. And at three o'clock he was at Teacher's desk again, carrying on the conversation as if there had been no interruption.

"Und my mamma," he said insinuatingly—"she kisses my papa a kiss."

"Well?" said Teacher.

"Well," said Morris, "you ain't never kissed me a kiss, und I seen how you kissed Eva Gonorowsky. I'm loving mit you too. Why don't you never kiss me a kiss?"

"Perhaps," suggested Teacher mischievously, "perhaps it ain't for boys."

But a glance at her "light face," with its crown of surprising combs, reassured him.

"Teacher, yiss ma'an; it's for boys," he cried as he felt her arms about him, and saw that in her eyes, too, "stands tears."

"It's polite you kisses me a kiss over that for ladies' present."

Late that night Teacher sat in her pretty room—for she was, unofficially, a greatly pampered young person—and reviewed her treasures. She saw that they were very numerous, very touching, very whimsical, and very precious. But above all the rest she cherished a frayed and pinkish paper, rather crumpled and a little soiled. For it held the love of a man and a woman and a little child, and the magic of a home, for Morris Mogilewsky's Christmas present for ladies was the receipt for a month's rent for a room on the top floor of a Monroe Street tenement.

The Golden Wassail

by Ida M. H. Starr

Down in the still country, on tidewater, there is a house so old that on its walls are written the autographs of a hundred and more winters. Its ancient shutters that, possibly in a spirit of jest, had been painted bright red long ago, were faded to the colour of eyes that weep and close with the pain of more tears. In olden times it had two wings, one reaching to the sunrise and the other to the golden west. They had been of twin-like proportions, but a destroyer of beauty had torn off the gentle curves of the east wing and put in its place a bastard. Long years went by, and the sun looked ashamed when he stole into the bed of the bastard. About the house were a forsaken garden and trees ancient as the mansion itself.

The old house shut its eyes tighter year by year. Friendly

lichens softened to gray its red brick walls, and merciful vines crept noiselessly up to its heart and covered its desolation.

Then it was that we found the still country, the tidewater, the old house, the ancient trees, and the forsaken garden, and loved them with a great love. We banished the bastard, made a memory picture of the west wing before it fell to earth too weary to gaze longer at the stars through its ruinous roof, and then nothing remained but an old house with its merciful vines, and its tear-stained eyes fast closed—an old house in the still country where naught changes but night and day. Its past was an interwoven fabric of truth and fancy; its soul was the substance of dreams. None walked through its halls or stood by my side in the desolate garden but told some tale, of haunted chambers or of water sprites seen on May nights dancing in the marsh. It was whispered that on Candlemas Day, if one hid in the thicket at the end of the lane, where no one goes alone by night, there might be seen a woman with great lonely eyes, standing there, reaching out her hands in the direction of the house. And again and again I have heard stories of a lordly cavalier, periwigged, wearing a three-cornered hat and a coat of fine cloth with lace and ruffles, who wanders about in the garden beneath the ancient trees he is said to have planted long ago. He it was, they say, who built the house.

And so I slept in the old house nights of unbroken rest. Dearly as I love to drop into an abyss of dreams, I felt disappointed. I should have heard phantom steps in the hall; something should have happened, but nothing did for a long time. After completing the restoration which the old house seemed to wish, when night came on and I went to rest, I would lie a long time with wide-open eyes, just listening, for what I cannot tell you. Those who would suddenly meet me with candle in hand out in the hall can testify that I would ask, "Have you just come upstairs? I thought someone was in the hall."

About that time, in order to make some repairs on the fireplace in the west drawing room, we were obliged to lift out the old mantel from the hearth over which it had presided for more than a century. It was an affair of state. I stood guard to see that no harm befell. When, with protesting creaks, it was finally pried out from the broad brick breasting, I found back there, amidst dust and soot, a tiny box containing a rusty key. It was no sooner in my hand than I ran up to my room and shut the door, jealously hiding the box, for I felt that at last things were as they should be—an old house, a deserted garden, and a hidden key.

The key lay on my lap. I took it up and scrutinized it. In the days when this key was used, people needed secret drawers and secret panels. Had I been all this time near some mystery that this key might reveal?

Where was the lock that waited for this mysterious key? Many a sunset found me searching through the house of a hundred windows, through haunted chambers, down long passages and up circuitous stairs, all to no purpose, until one night I came to a little closet in the lower hall. After the lights were out, I stole down with a candle and into the closet. It tapered off to a point under the stairs, so I dropped down on my hands and knees and held the candle nearer the wall. The closet was panelled with the same care that characterized all the other Colonial work in the house. I saw no place for a key as I felt along, but as I came to the panel near the extreme end of the closet something rattled. I had brought a screw driver, and with it gently loosened the panel. It moved to one side, and in its framework I found a little wooden door let into the wall, and in this a keyhole. One second more, and the rusty key turned the lock, the door opened, and then——

I let the candle throw its warm, heartening glow into the precious mystery I saw there, and heard the clock strike from the stair landing directly above my head; and still I sat looking at the pile of things that somehow I could not bear to touch. There were a book, a bundle of letters, some shoe buckles, and a pair of spurs.

Then followed night after night when I would creep down to the closet and lose all thought of to-day in the old book. Its cover was of green calfskin, the hue of a smoky emerald, and its surface was as smooth as satin. It was tied together with lacings of leather. Its leaves were as yellow as gold, but the ink was as black as if wet but the night before. It was the plantation book of the estate dating back to 1738, and, oh, what it revealed of the old house and its masters! Besides plantation accounts, prices of slaves bought and sold, and itemized shopping lists sent to England, there were pages of household recipes of all kinds of country cookery, for the curing of hams and bacon, and the making of wines and simples.

In the bundle of letters I found this one:

> Christmas Day.
> Year of Our Lord 1765.
> MAJOR JONATHAN WOODRUFF,
>
> HONORED SIR:
>
> It becomes my painful duty to announce to you the death of Sir Richard, the builder of this House,

upon the eve of the most worshipful Birthday of our Lord. He was in the act of mixing the Wassail when suddenly dropping into a chair, he said,

"Gentlemen, my last toast—May this House of Hope be ever a haven of refuge and good will to me. I shall return at midnight on Christmas Eve to mix the Wassail."

With that he spake no more. There passes from life a lover of all gentle arts, viz. the making of gardens, brewing of simples, and with all a loyal follower of the Crown—a most noble gentleman.

Obediently your servant,
William Hunt *(Overseer)*.

"Sir Richard—a most noble gentleman," I said, "the Cavalier who wanders in the garden beneath the old trees, for whom I have been watching all these days. Is it he or is it some other one? And is his coming only on Christmas Eve?"

And in the old Green Book I found this:

For the brewing of the Wassail let there be added to some goodly Ale, ½ ounce of Ginger made fine, likewise Nutmeg and a pinch of Cinnamon and ½ pound of dull Sugar. Heat and stir but not to boil. Then to this add a good portion more of Ale and Malaga Wine, the zest of a Lemon and then six cored apples roasted by the fire. Let each one place an apple in his cup and pour thereon the Hot Wassail which must be served from a Silver Bowl.

It is difficult to understand the influences that gradually mould our lives; how much more difficult the power that calls us to face suddenly about and leave forever a certain manner of living, which seems as fixed as character itself, and walk forward in an opposite direction, knowing that we can never again face the other way. We cannot fathom these mysteries. They come only at rare intervals. One came to me the night I read the old Green Book for the first time. I faced about that night. My new direction was indicated only step by step. Sometimes there seemed the pressure of a hand pushing me on, and back of the hand a voice whispering.

Slowly I began to walk along a quiet, pleasant way. I sought hours of contemplation; I forgot that there was a great, throbbing world outside. I forgot that I lived in an age when domestic virtues were fast becoming a lost art. I opened the old Green Book and read how the housewives of old made ready for the feasts of the year, and the voice said—or did I think it out myself?—"Why not do the same?" Ah, those December days when, bundled to the ears, I would start out to my neighbour's house, under no pressure of haste, to spend the day and incidentally add to my store of famous Maryland recipes. Who but the Mistress of Hope should bake the cakes, make the mincemeat, and mix the plum pudding? No, none should assume that prerogative. This was the prelude to the first Christmas festival after reading the Green Book, this work with my own hands.

On the day of our Christmas baking it happened curiously that, as I was about to turn the fruit cake into the big pan, I felt a pressure at my elbow. I looked around, but no one was near me. Aunt Sally was over the stove, S'lina chopping apples, Greensbury seeding raisins in the pantry.

"That's queer," I said. Then, in broad daylight, I stopped to listen. It was with the same sensation that I had stood looking about in the old hall many a time at night. Then I laughed and said, "Why, Aunt Sally, I've forgotten the sherry. Glad I thought of it in time."

At last, all the cakes were baked, and the mincemeat was stowed away with Christmas dainties. Hope hams, sugar cured and smoked with sassafras leaves from the shore, were hanging with sides of bacon in the west cellar.

While I was in the midst of holiday decorations the day before Christmas, I suddenly dropped everything and walked down to the kitchen.

"Aunt Sally," I said, "peel, core, and roast me some fine apples."

"How many, miss?"

"I wish I knew, Sally. Really, I don't know how many. I might need quite a lot. Whatever you do, roast plenty."

"Yas, miss. When does you want dem?"

"To-night, Christmas Eve."

Then I returned to the festooning of holly, absorbed in the thought of other things.

It was Christmas Eve. The lights from the tree had been blown out, the children had flown off to bed early, the guests were busy over certain mysteries in their various rooms, and I was sitting quite alone in the library. From a secret hiding place again I took out that old letter and the Green Book and read:

> I shall return at midnight on Christmas Eve to mix the Wassail.

Had he been coming year after year to an empty, desolate board? Would he come if I really made things ready? Why not try? It could do no harm.

I read the recipe over. It called for cinnamon, nutmeg, ale, Malaga wine, apples, lemons, and sugar. Some occult power brought me to my feet. On tiptoe I stole up to the third story and opened my grandmother's chest, where, as fresh as if her hands had but just laid it there, I found her linen and the cloth-of-gold embroidered for her in Venice. I took it out, closed the lid reverently, and flew downstairs to the dining room. By the light of a candle I spread the Venetian cloth, and at the head of the table placed the great china punch bowl, the one merry with dancing Cupids. Then, to the right of the bowl, I placed a silver ladle and decanters for old wine, and near by an antique silver bowl. As the house was growing cold, I flung on my long, red cloak; then I went down into the wine cellar and found some cobwebby Malaga wine and some ale, and I stopped in the pantry for everything the ancient wassail demanded. I put Aunt Sally's roasted apples into the silver bowl, and from Grandmother's cupboard I took out the tall crystal glasses, themselves rich in remembrance.

Then, when all was ready and the clock pointed to half after eleven, I began to light the candles. Oh, I lighted so many, on table, sideboard, and mantel, and as each one sent its heart of flame up into the room, I trembled as one does when awaiting an unknown guest. Minute by minute the place became more and more wonderful, for, in the great stillness of the holy night, there came over me the impelling sense that I must wait and listen. Only a few minutes lacked of midnight. Something I wished to say stuck in my throat.

I had placed two chairs at the table. Summoning all my

courage and standing close to the door with my hand on the knob, I said, as loud as I dared: "Sir Richard, I am waiting for you to mix the wassail. Will you come? Everything is ready."

Heaven only knows what I expected, but as my words fell from my lips I heard the click of spurs on the stairway. The sound came nearer; it reached the arcade, and then my hand fell from the door handle, for it was turning. The door opened with a swing, then closed. The draft blew out all the candles save those on the table. I saw nothing at all, but I heard a most contagious laugh.

"A right Merrie Christmas to the Mistress of Hope," said a courteous voice.

"Merrie Christmas," I replied, faintly.

Then the silver ladle began to move slowly toward the punch bowl and the decanter gradually tipped up, and the wine flowed into the bowl.

"Thou dost not perceive me?" spoke a voice that smoothed all the fear from my soul.

"No, I don't. Where are you?"

"I am here. I am at the head of the table. Thou hast summoned me. I have come to mix the wassail. I have been in attendance upon thee ever since thine advent into this house, but I must needs await until Christmas to make myself known. A Christmas cake without good wine has no flavour. Thou didst forget, fair mistress?"

"Sir, I did. Was it you that reminded me?"

"It was I."

"I'm very glad. It wouldn't have been good without it, would it? I wish I could see you. How can I?"

"Prithee be seated at thine accustomed place. Thou art weary."

"I am. It's Christmas, you know."

"That I know full well. 'Tis sad to be aweary this glad, festal day; but thou art turning into pleasant ways. As each Yule comes, from this day forth, thou shalt be less and less distraught. I shall help thee."

There was much comfort in the voice, so I dropped into my chair.

"Now, my dear mistress, I shall extinguish the tapers and we shall see if I can open thine eyes."

"But they are open now, sir."

"I mean thine other eyes."

With a puff, out went every candle, and as the light vanished I heard the gurgling of more wine into the china bowl, and the stirring of the great ladle; and like the afterglow of a white, wintry day there spread from the depths of my punch bowl a rosy light that grew brighter each second, and as it increased gradually there emerged from behind the bowl the figure of a tall, stately man, with eyes that laughed when the lips were silent.

"Sir, are you Lord Baltimore?" I gasped under my breath, as I instinctively sprang to my feet and curtsied low.

"No, not he."

"Pray who are you, then?"

"The builder of this House."

"Oh, my dear, dear sir!" I cried. "Then you are Sir Richard. Are you also the Cavalier? I've been looking for him so long. They told me he would come to the yew and to the holly on Christmas Eve, but I've been hoping there might be other days he would pass the trees he planted, because, when we love things, we must watch over them, and I've waited out there all this fall. When I found William Hunt's letter in which Sir Richard said he would return on Christmas Eve to mix the wassail, I made ready, but I was almost afraid to hope."

"Then, why, madam, did'st thou prepare?"

"I can't tell you exactly, only somebody seemed to be telling me that I must."

"I told thee, madam."

"Why did you tell me to do so?"

Then the laugh in his eyes stole to his lips.

"I pray thee knit not thy brow. I have heard thy laugh in yonder garden. With each laugh our trees have grown. I say 'our trees,' for that which man leaves to adorn this earth becomes the heritage for those who follow after. If thou wilt but laugh, I can help thee much. Who would eat of Christmas cake without the zest of a good wine?"

"I didn't dream that the Cavalier would notice such things as cake-baking."

"It was but to awaken thee. Thou shouldst know that, if I can advise thee in trifles, how much more could I in great affairs. I was overjoyed to behold the roof whole again on my old home. I straightway returned to these halls. Thou art the first in half a century to carry on my labour. Thou hast been learning of me day by day."

"I learning of you, Sir Richard? How did you ever teach me?"

"In mine own way. Thou art a good child."

I put my head down on the table and let the flood of tears pour from my eyes. "Child—child—am I anybody's child? If he would only say that once again," I said under my breath. "I didn't suppose mothers could ever be anybody's children."

"Ah, that they can, but thou should'st not weep. This night is all for jollity. Listen; they are coming. They have been bidden."

At that all the glass pendants in the arcade began to tinkle, as they do when the wind blows in the summer. Then the door flew open and I jumped to my feet. The Cavalier with glowing eyes called out "Merrie Christmas," and ladled from the flaming bowl goblet after goblet of glittering wassail and passed the golden fluid around the room, which was filled and yet was empty. I heard the flash of silken robes, the clicking of spurs, and laughing and dancing and the kissing of lips.

"I can't see them, but I hear them. Who are they?"

"They are those who brought the daffodils years ago, the lilacs, the magnolias, the jasmine, the crêpe myrtles. Those of the silken frocks and the low voices, they are the lovers of flowers. The rollicking ones were my companions; they built mansions and brought the holly, box, and yew; they all watch with me in the gardens and along the countryside, and they are come to be glad with us this Yule night. Come, take the cup; they are drinking to thee. The souls of the adorners of this earth who crowd about whenever thou walkest in gardens are wishing thee well. Drink, drink the wassail."

"Why cannot I see them as I do you, most noble Cavalier?"

"This is the day of my earthly death; therefore I can make myself visible to those who wait."

"I'm glad it happened on Christmas. It's such a splendid day to be coming home."

"Come, let us join the dance. Wilt thou step the minuet, fair mistress?"

Like a country lass, I lifted my eyes to the beautiful Cavalier and said timidly, "Yes, I love the dance, but"—my eyes fell to the simple folds of my frock —"I'm not gay enough for your company. My dress, you see how it is."

"And yet thou shalt dance with me this very night and withal in festive attire. Wait—drink more of the wassail."

He took the silver ladle and with it dipped into the rosy bowl. Then there poured forth into my goblet that which overflowed and spread over and about my body. First a gauzy veil spangled with silver such as is flung in whirling cobwebs between the two old rose bushes in the garden to the June sunrise, and then there tumbled from out my goblet flowers, flowers, so fast that my eyes were dazzled.

"Oh, my flowers," I cried. "My children, I thought you were gone."

I tried to catch them for kisses, but they slipped from my hands to the hem of my silver robe. Columbine bells tinkled about my feet, violets and daffodils rose flowering to my waist, and my bodice was from the petals of lilies. Then, with my delight so great I could scarcely speak, the Cavalier lifted from the bowl a green mantle, elusive and shining as if it were the heart of ethereal iris.

"Oh, what can I say? You have made me so beautiful, oh, so beautiful with these flowers."

"Not I, sweet mistress, thou hast made thine own garments."

"When could I have done so, dear sir?"

"The day thou first loved this garden, the robe was fashioned. This is the hour for the bringing of gifts. When wilt thou offer thine to the Earth Mother?"

"Oh, dear sir, I have none prepared for her."

"Thou dost not clearly understand. Thy gift hath been prepared, but it is hidden by being so close to thee. Alas for him who brings no gift to Mother Earth. Now let us go. They await us for the dance."

"I'm afraid I cannot step the minuet, but I can try." With a laugh like a mellow flute, he took my hand, and suddenly there came a sound that caused me to lift my head and breathe fast.

"Thine eyes glistened; wherefore, my child?"

"Oh, most noble Cavalier, don't you hear it, the music, the

music of my garden? When it sounds, I must always follow after, and if you do not bid it cease, I shall have to go, and then we couldn't dance the minuet."

With that he took my hand.

"Come, we shall go together. For two centuries I have answered that call, and am never weary. We shall dance the minuet together, for it is the glad Yuletide. We shall dance it under the holly."

Then the music grew more distinct; its themes were the scent of magnolias, the night plaint of the mocking bird, the lap of waves on our brimful river, the ascending and descending scale of the haunting dirge that sweeps from the tulip tree to the heart of the yew when the earth grows cold. Think of it, you who love gardens; you will understand. The Cavalier understood, for he held fast my hand, and in the other he took a branch of the holly which grew up from the midst of the golden wassail; this he lifted aloft and my feet felt as blithe as my heart as I stepped into the night. There, beyond the bowling green, the holly of Old England was transformed from sober shade to dazzling light as if sifted over with star dust. Each glossy bough was hung with a shining light, and the light spread far beyond to where the lilies were sleeping.

I cannot say how long we danced, nor how we discoursed in our intervals of rest, but the night was short; that I know. At the first glimpse of dawn, the Cavalier said, " 'Tis another Christmas morning. I leave you in trust."

"Oh, you will not be going! I know so little what to do in my garden yet; I am but just learning the sound of its voice."

" 'Tis enough for one lifetime. Be content with thy first lesson."

I looked up into his face, but the face was not there. I felt his hand still within mine.

"Where are you? I can't see you, I only feel your hand. You are going—going away. It's the music you're following. Tell it to stop. You must stay."

"I am here as I shall always remain. Thou alone art changing. Thou art going along pleasant ways."

"No, no, I'm just the same."

"Thine eyes are closing."

"No, no, I'm just the same."

"Closing———"

"But I will, I must keep them open."

"The time—is—not—ripe."

The words grew less and less distinct, the lights upon the holly faded, I felt for my green mantle; it, too, was gone, and my flowery robe likewise, and in its place the familiar folds of my long red cloak.

I called. No sound came to my ears. No light but a still, early morn met my eyes, but my heart was full of a great joy, for I then began to understand what the Cavalier meant when he said, "Thy gift is hidden by being so close to thee."

I ran quickly across the lawn and stood a moment to look at the Christmas daybreak creeping in crimson flood over the still country, the tidewater, the ancient trees, and the old house. Then I spoke.

"Earth Mother, I know now what he meant. The gift is ready for you. It is poor and pitiful in its wee beginning, but it is yours, yours every bit of it, and it is out there on the other side of the yew tree. Take it, my garden, it is my soul; take it into your beautiful hands, I give it all to you."

The Child Who Had Everything But—

by John Kendrick Bangs

I

I knew it was coming long before it got there. Every symptom was in sight. I had grown fidgety, and sat fearful of something overpoweringly impending. Strange noises filled the house. Things generally, according to their nature, severally creaked, soughed and moaned. There was a ghost on the way. That was perfectly clear to an expert in uncanny visitations of my wide experience, and I heartily wished it were not. There was a time when I welcomed such visitors with open arms, because there was a decided demand for them in the literary market, and I had been able to turn a great variety of spooks into anywhere from three thousand to five thousand words apiece at five cents a word, but now the age had grown too sceptical to swallow ghostly reminiscence with any degree of satisfaction. People had grown tired of hearing about Visions, and desired that their tales should reek with the scent of gasoline, quiver with the superfervid fever of tangential loves, and crash with moral thunderbolts aimed against malefactors of great achievement and high social and commercial standing. Wherefore it seemed an egregious waste of time for me to dally with a spook, or with anything else, for that matter, that had no strictly utilitarian value to one so professionally pressed as I was, and especially at a moment like that—it was Christmas morning and the hour was twenty-eight minutes after two—when I was so busy preparing my Ode to June, and trying to work out the details of a midsummer romance in time for the market for such productions early in the coming January.

And right in the midst of all this pressure there rose up these beastly symptoms of an impending visitation. At first I strove to fight them off, but as the minutes passed they became so obsessively intrusive that I could not concentrate upon the work in hand, and I resolved to have it over with.

"Oh, well," said I, striking a few impatient chords upon my typewriting machine, "if you insist upon coming, come, and let's have done with it."

I roared this out, addressing the dim depths of the adjoining apartment, whence had risen the first dank apprehension of the uncanny something that had come to pester me.

"This is my busy night," I went on, when nothing happened in response to my summons, "and I give you fair warning that, however psychic I may be now, I've got too much to do to stay so much longer. If you're going to haunt, haunt!"

It was in response to this appeal that the thing first manifested itself to the eye. It took the shape first of a very slight veil of green fog, which shortly began to swirl slowly from the darkness of the other room through the intervening portières into my den. Once within, it increased the vigor of its swirl, until almost before I knew it there was spinning immediately before my desk something in the nature of a misty maelstrom, buzzing around like a pin-wheel in action.

"Very pretty—very pretty indeed," said I, a trifle sarcastically, refusing to be impressed, "but I don't care for pyrotechnics. I suppose," I added flippantly, "that you are what might be called a mince-pyrotechnic, eh?"

Whether it was the quality of my jest, or some other inward pang due to its gyratory behavior, that caused it I know not, but as I spoke a deep groan issued from the centre of the whirling mist, and then out of its indeterminateness there was resolved the hazy figure of an angel—only, she was an intensely modern angel. She wore a hobble-skirt instead of the usual flowing robes of ladies of the supernal order, and her halo, instead of hovering over her head as used to be the correct manner of wearing these hard-won adornments, had perforce become a mere golden fillet binding together the great mass of finger-curls and other distinctly yellow capillary attractions that stretched out from the back of her cerebellum for two or three feet, like a monumental psyche-knot. I could hardly restrain a shudder as I realized the theatric quality of the lady's appearance, and I honestly dreaded the possible consequences of her visit. We live in a tolerably censorious age, and I did not care to be seen in the company of such a peroxidized vision as she appeared to be.

"I am afraid, madam," said I, shrinking back against the wall as she approached—"I am very much afraid that you have got into the wrong house. Mr. Slatherberry, the theatrical manager, lives next door."

She paid no attention to this observation, but, holding out

a compelling hand, bade me come along with her, her voice having about it all the musical charm of an oboe suffering from bronchitis.

"Not in a year of Sundays I won't!" I retorted. "I am a respectable man, a steady church-goer, a trustee for several philanthropic institutions, and a Sunday-School teacher. I don't wish to be impolite, but really, madam, rich as I am in reputation, I am too poor to be seen in public with you."

"I am a spirit," she began.

"I'll take your word for it," I interjected, and I could see that she told the truth, for she was entirely diaphanous, so much so indeed that one could perceive the piano in the other room with perfect clarity through her intervening shadiness. "It is, however, the unfortunate fact that I have sworn off spirits."

"None the less," she returned, her eye flashing and her hand held forth peremptorily, "you must come. It is your predestined doom."

My next remark I am not wholly clear about, but, as I remember it, it sounded something like "I'll be doomed if I do!" whereupon she threatened me.

"It is useless to resist," she said. "If you decline to come voluntarily, I shall hypnotize you and force you to follow me. We have need of you."

"But, my dear lady," I pleaded, "please have some regard for my position. I never did any of you spirits any harm. I've treated every visitor from the spirit-land with the most distinguished consideration, and I feel that you owe it to me to be regardful of my good name. Suppose you take a look at yourself in yonder looking-glass, and then say if you think it fair to compel a decent, law-abiding man, of domestic inclinations like myself, to be seen in public with—well, with such a looking head of hair as that of yours."

My visitor laughed heartily.

"Oh, if that's all," she said, most amiably, "we can arrange matters in a jiffy. Your wife possesses a hooded mackintosh, does she not? I think I saw something of the kind hanging on the hat-rack as I floated in. I will wear that if it will make you feel any easier."

"It certainly would," said I; "but see here—can't you scare up some other cavalier to escort you to the haven of your desires?"

She fixed a sternly steady eye upon me for a moment.

"Aren't you the man who wrote the lines,

> The World's a green and gladsome ball,
> And Love's the Ruler of it all,
> And Life's the chance vouchsafed to me
> For Deeds and Gifts of Sympathy?

Didn't you write that?" she demanded.

"I did, madam," said I, "and I meant every word of it, but what of it? Is that any reason why I should be seen on a public highway with a lady-ghost of your especial kind?"

"Enough of your objections," she retorted firmly. "You are the person for whom I have been sent. We have a case needing your immediate attention. The only question is, will you come pleasantly and of your own free will, or must I resort to extreme measures?"

These words were spoken with such determination that I realized that further resistance was useless, and I yielded.

"All right," said I. "On your way. I'll follow."

"Good!" she cried, her face wreathing with a pleasant little nile-green smile. "Get the mackintosh, and we'll be off. There's no time to lose," she added, as the clock in the tower on the square boomed out the hour of three.

"What is this anyhow?" I demanded, as I helped her on with the mackintosh and saw that the hood covered every vestige of that awful coiffure. "Another case of Scrooge?"

"Sort of," she replied as, hooking her arm in mine, she led me forth into the night.

II

We passed over to Fifth Avenue, and proceeded uptown at a pace which reminded me of the active gait of my youth. My footsteps had grown unwontedly light, and we covered the first ten blocks in about three minutes.

"We don't seem to be headed for the slums," I panted.

"Indeed, we are not," she retorted. "There is no need of carrying coals to Newcastle on this occasion. This isn't a slum case. It's far more acute than that."

A tear came forth from her eye and trickled down over the mackintosh.

"It is a peculiarity of modern effort on behalf of suffering humanity," she went on, "that it is concentrated upon the relief of the misery of the so-called *sub*merged, to the utter neglect of the often more poignant needs of the *e*merged. We have workers by the thousand in the slums, doing all that can be done, and successfully too, to relieve the unhappy condition of the poor, but nobody ever seems to think of the sorrows of the starving hundreds on upper Fifth Avenue."

"See here, madam," said I, stopping suddenly short under a lamp-post in front of the Public Library, "I want to tell you right now that if you think you are going to take me into any of the homes of the hopelessly rich at this hour of the morning, you are the most mightily mistaken creature that ever wore a psyche-knot. Why, great heavens, my dear lady, suppose the owner of the house were to wake up and demand to know what I was doing there at this time of night? What could I say?"

"You have gone on slumming parties, haven't you?" she demanded coldly.

"Often," said I. "But that's different."

"Why?" she asked, with a simplicity that baffled me. "Is it any worse for you to intrude upon the home of a Fifth Avenue millionaire than it is to go unasked into the small, squalid tenement of some poor sweatshop worker on the East Side?"

"Oh, but it's different," I protested. "I go there to see if there is anything I can do to relieve the unhappy condition of the persons who live in the slums."

"No doubt," said she. "I'll take your word for it, but is that any reason why you should neglect the sufferers who live in these marble palaces?"

As she spoke, she hooked hold of my arm once more, and in a moment we were climbing the front door steps of a palatial residence. The house showed a dark and forbidding front at that hour in the morning despite its marble splendors, and I was glad to note that the massive grille doors of wrought iron were heavily barred.

"It's useless, you see. We're locked out," I ventured.

"Indeed?" she retorted, with a sarcastic smile, as she seized my hand in her icy grip and literally pulled me after her through the marble front of the dwelling. "What have we to do with bolts and bars?"

"I don't know," said I ruefully, "but I have a notion that if I don't bolt I'll get the bars all right."

I could see them coming, and they were headed straight for me.

"All you have to do is to follow me," she went on, as we floated upward for two flights, paying but little attention to the treasures of art that lined the walls, and finally passed into a superbly lighted salon, more daintily beautiful than anything of the kind I had ever seen before.

"Jove!" I ejaculated, standing amazed in the presence of such luxury and beauty. "I did not realize that with all her treasures New York held anything quite so fine as this. What is it, a music-room?"

"It is the nursery," said my companion. "Look about you and see for yourself."

I did as I was bidden, and such an array of toys as that inspection revealed! Truly it looked as if the toy-market in all sections of the world had been levied upon for tribute. Had all the famous toy emporiums of Nuremberg itself been transported thither bodily, there could not have been playthings in greater variety than there greeted my eye. From the most insignificant of tin-soldiers to the most intricate of mechanical toys for the delectation of the youthful mind, nothing that I could think of was missing.

The tin-soldiers as ever had a fascination for me, and in an instant I was down upon the floor, ranging them in their serried ranks, while the face of my companion wreathed with an indulgent smile.

"You'll do," said she, as I loaded a little spring-cannon with a stub of a lead-pencil and bowled over half a regiment with one well-directed shot.

"These are the finest tin-soldiers I ever saw!" I cried with enthusiasm.

"Only they're not tin," said she. "Solid silver, every man-jack of them—except the officers—they're made of platinum."

"And will you look at that little electric railroad!" I cried, my eye ranging to the other end of the salon. "Stations, switches, danger-signals, cars of all kinds, and even miniature Pullmans, with real little berths that can be let up and down—who is the lucky kid who's getting all these beautiful things?"

"Sh!" she whispered, putting her finger to her lips. "He is coming—go on and play. Pretend you don't see him until he speaks to you."

As she spoke, a door at the far end of the apartment swung gently open, and a little boy tiptoed softly in. He was a golden-haired little chap, and I fell in love with his soft, dreamy eyes the moment my own rested upon them. I could not help glancing up furtively to see his joy over the discovery of all these wondrous possessions, but alas, to my surprise, there was only an unemotional stare in his eyes as they swept the aggregation of childish treasures. Then, on a sudden, he saw me, squatting on the floor, setting up again the army of silver warriors.

"How do you do?" he said gently, but with just a touch of weariness in his sad little voice.

"Good morning, and a Merry Christmas to you, sir," I replied.

"What are you doing?" he asked, drawing near, and watching me with a good deal of seeming curiosity.

"I am playing with your soldiers," said I. "I hope you don't mind?"

"Oh, no indeed," he replied; "but what do you mean by that? What is playing?"

I could hardly believe my ears.

"What is what?" said I.

"You said you were playing, sir," said he, "and I don't know exactly what you mean."

"Why," said I, scratching my head hard in a mad quest for a definition, for I couldn't for the life of me think of the answer to his question offhand, any more than I could define one of the elements. "Playing is—why, it's playing, laddie. Don't you know what it is to play?"

"Oh, yes," said he. "It's what you do on the piano—I've been taught to play on the piano, sir."

"Oh, but this is different," said I. "This kind is fun—it's what most little boys do with their toys."

"You mean—breaking them?" said he.

"No, indeed," said I. "It's getting all the fun there is out of them."

"I think I should like to do that," said he, with a fixed gaze upon the soldiers. "Can a little fellow like me learn to play that way?"

"Well, rather, kiddie," said I, reaching out and taking him by the hand. "Sit down here on the floor alongside of me, and I'll show you."

"Oh, no," said he, drawing back; "I—I can't sit on the floor. I'd catch cold."

"Now, who under the canopy told you that?" I demanded, somewhat impatiently, I fear.

"My governesses and both my nurses, sir," said he. "You see, there are drafts—"

"Well, there won't be any drafts this time," said I. "Just you sit down here, and we'll have a game of marbles—ever play marbles with your father?"

"No, sir," he replied. "He's always too busy, and neither of my nurses has ever known how."

"But your mother comes up here and plays games with you sometimes, doesn't she?" I asked.

"Mother is busy, too," said the child. "Besides, she wouldn't care for a game which you had to sit on the floor to—"

I sprang to my feet and lifted him bodily in my arms, and, after squatting him over by the fireplace where if there were any drafts at all they would be as harmless as a summer breeze, I took up a similar position on the other side of the room, and initiated him into the mystery of miggles as well as I could, considering that all his marbles were real agates.

"You don't happen to have a china-alley anywhere, do you?" I asked.

"No, sir," he answered. "We only have china plates—"

"Never mind," I interrupted. "We can get along very nicely with these."

And then for half an hour, despite the rich quality of our paraphernalia, that little boy and I indulged in a glorious game of real plebeian miggs, and it was a joy to see how quickly his stiff little fingers relaxed and adapted themselves to the uses of his eye, which was as accurate as it was deeply blue. So expert did he become that in a short while he had completely cleaned me out, giving joyous little cries of delight with every hit, and then we turned our attention to the soldiers.

"I want some playing now," he said gleefully, as I informed him that he had beaten me out of my boots at one of my best games. "Show me what you were doing with those soldiers when I came in."

"All right," said I, obeying with alacrity. "First, we'll have a parade."

I started a great talking-machine standing in one corner of the room off on a spirited military march, and inside of ten minutes, with his assistance, I had all the troops out and to all intents and purposes bravely swinging by to the martial music of Sousa.

"How's that?" said I, when we had got the whole corps arranged to our satisfaction.

"Fine!" he cried, jumping up and down upon the floor and clapping his hands with glee. "I've got lots more of these stored away in my toy-closet," he went on, "but I never knew that you could do such things as this with them."

"But what did you think they were for?" I asked.

"Why—just to—to keep," he said hesitatingly.

"Wait a minute," said I, wheeling a couple of cannon off to a distance of a yard from the passing troops. "I'll show you something else you can do with them."

I loaded both cannon to the muzzle with dried pease, and showed him how to shoot.

"Now," said I, *"fire!"*

He snapped the spring, and the dried pease flew out like death-dealing shells in war. In a moment the platinum commander of the forces, and about thirty-seven solid silver warriors, lay flat on their backs. It needed only a little red ink on the carpet to reproduce in miniature a scene of great carnage, but I shall never forget the expression of mingled joy and regret on his countenance as those creatures went down.

"Don't you like it, son?" I asked.

"I don't know," he said, with an anxious glance at the prostrate warriors. "They aren't deaded, are they?"

"Of course not," said I, restoring the presumably defunct troopers to life by setting them up again. "The only thing that'll dead a soldier like these is to step on him. Try the other gun."

Thus reassured, he did as I bade him, and again the proud paraders went down, this time amid shouts of glee. And so we passed an all too fleeting two hours, that little boy and I. Through the whole list of his famous toys we went, and as well as I could I taught him the delicious uses of each and all of them, until finally he seemed to grow weary, and so, drawing up a big arm-chair before the fire and taking his tired little body into my lap, with his tousled head cuddled up close over the spot where my heart is alleged to be, I started to read a story to him out of one of the many beautiful books that had been provided for him by his generous parents. But I had not gone far when I saw that his attention was wandering.

"Perhaps you'd rather have me tell you a story instead of reading it," said I.

"What's to tell a story?" he asked, fixing his blue eyes gravely upon mine.

"Great Scott, kiddie!" said I, "didn't anybody ever tell you a story?"

"No, sir," he replied sleepily; "I get read to every afternoon by my governess, but nobody ever told me a story."

"Well, just you listen to this," said I, giving him a hearty squeeze. "Once upon a time there was a little boy," I began, "and he lived in a beautiful house not far from the Park, and his daddy—"

"What's a daddy?" asked the child, looking up into my face.

"Why, a daddy is a little boy's father," I explained. "You've got a daddy—"

"Oh, yes," he said. "If a daddy is a father, I've got one. I saw him yesterday," he added.

"Oh, did you?" said I. "And what did he say to you?"

"He said he was glad to see me and hoped I was a good boy,"

said the child. "He seemed very glad when I told him I hoped so, too, and he gave me all these things here—he and my mother."

"That was very nice of them," said I huskily.

"And they're both coming up some time to-day or to-morrow to see if I like them," said the lad.

"And what are you going to say?" I asked, with difficulty getting the words out over a most unaccountable lump that had arisen in my throat.

"I'm going to tell them," he began, as his eyes closed sleepily, "that I like them all very, very much."

"And which one of them all do you like the best?" said I.

He snuggled up closer in my arms, and, raising his little head a trifle higher, he kissed me on the tip end of my chin, and murmured softly as he dropped off to sleep,

"You!"

III

"Good night," said my spectral visitor as she left me, once more bending over my desk, whither I had been retransported without my knowledge, for I must have fallen asleep, too, with that little boy in my arms. "You have done a good night's work."

"Have I?" said I, rubbing my eyes to see if I were really awake. "But tell me—who was that little kiddie anyhow?"

"He?" she answered with a smile. "Why, he is the Child Who Has Everything But—"

And then she vanished from my sight.

"Everything but what?" I cried, starting up and peering into the darkness into which she had disappeared.

But there was no response, and I was left alone to guess the answer to my question.

Not If I Know It

by ANTHONY TROLLOPE

"NOT IF I KNOW IT." It was an ill-natured answer to give, made in the tone that was used, by a brother-in-law to a brother-in-law, in the hearing of the sister of the one and wife of the other,—made, too, on Christmas Eve, when the married couple had come as visitors to the house of him who made it! There was no joke in the words, and the man who had uttered them had gone for the night. There was to be no other farewell spoken indicative of the brightness of the coming day. "Not if I know it!" and the door was slammed behind him. The words were very harsh in the ears even of a loving sister.

"He was always a cur," said the husband.

"No; not so. George has his ill-humours and his little periods of bad temper; but he was not always a cur. Don't say so of him, Wilfred."

"He always was so to me. He wanted you to marry that fellow Cross because he had a lot of money."

"But I didn't," said the wife, who now had been three years married to Wilfred Horton.

"I cannot understand that you and he should have been children of the same parents. Just the use of his name, and there would be no risk."

"I suppose he thinks that there might have been risk," said the wife. "He cannot know you as I do."

"Had he asked me I would have given him mine without thinking of it. Though he knows that I am a busy man, I have never asked him to lend me a shilling. I never will."

"Wilfred!"

"All right, old girl—I am going to bed; and you will see that I shall treat him to-morrow just as though he had refused me nothing. But I shall think that he is a cur." And Wilfred Horton prepared to leave the room.

"Wilfred!"

"Well, Mary, out with it."

"Curs are curs——"

"Because other curs make them so; that is what you are going to say."

"No, dear, no; I will never call you a cur, because I know well that you are not one. There is nothing like a cur about you." Then she took him in her arms and kissed him. "But if there be any signs of ill-humour in a man, the way to increase it is to think much of it. Men are curs because other men think them so; women are angels sometimes, just because some loving husband like you tells them that they are. How can a woman not have something good about her when everything she does is taken to be good? I could be as cross as George is if only I were called cross. I don't suppose you want the use of his name so very badly."

"But I have condescended to ask for it. And then to be answered with that jeering pride! I wouldn't have his name to a paper now, though you and I were starving for the want of it. As it is, it doesn't much signify. I suppose you won't be long before you come." So saying, he took his departure.

She followed him, and went through the house till she came to her brother's apartments. He was a bachelor, and was living all alone when he was in the country at Hallam Hall. It was a large, rambling house, in which there had been of custom many visitors at Christmas time. But Mrs. Wade, the widow, had died during the past year, and there was nobody there now but the owner of the house, and his sister, and his sister's husband. She followed him to his rooms, and found him sitting alone, with a pipe in his mouth, and as she entered she saw that preparations had been made for the comfort of more than one person. "If there be anything that I hate," said George Wade, "it is to be asked for the use of my name. I would sooner lend money to a fellow at once,—or give it to him."

"There is no question about money, George."

"Oh, isn't there? I never knew a man's name wanted when there was no question about money."

"I suppose there is a question—in some remote degree." Here George Wade shook his head. "In some remote degree," she went on repeating her words. "Surely you know him well enough not to be afraid of him."

"I know no man well enough not to be afraid of him where my name is concerned."

"You need not have refused him so crossly, just on Christmas Eve."

"I don't know much about Christmas where money is wanted."

" 'Not if I know it!' you said."

"I simply meant that I did not wish to do it. Wilfred expects that everybody should answer him with such constrained courtesy! What I said was as good a way of answering him as any other; and if he didn't like it—he must lump it."

"Is that the message that you send him?" she asked.

"I don't send it as a message at all. If he wants a message you may tell him that I'm extremely sorry, but that it's against my principles. You are not going to quarrel with me as well as he?"

"Indeed, no," she said, as she prepared to leave him for the night. "I should be very unhappy to quarrel with either of you." Then she went.

"He is the most punctilious fellow living at this moment, I believe," said George Wade, as he walked alone up and down the room. There were certain regrets which did make the moment bitter to him. His brother-in-law had on the whole treated him well,—had been liberal to him in all those matters in which one brother comes in contact with another. He had never asked him for a shilling, or even for the use of his name. His sister was passionately devoted to her husband. In fact, he knew Wilfred Horton to be a fine fellow. He told himself that he had not meant to be especially uncourteous, but that he had been at the moment startled by the expression of Horton's wishes. But looking back over his own conduct, he could remember that in the course of their intimacy he himself had been occasionally rough to his brother-in-law, and he could remember that his brother-in-law had not liked it. "After all what does it mean, 'Not if I know it?' It is just a form of saying that I had rather not." Nevertheless, Wilfred Horton could not persuade himself to go to bed in a good humour with George Wade.

"I think I shall get back to London to-morrow," said Mr. Horton, speaking to his wife from beneath the bedclothes, as soon as she had entered the room.

"To-morrow?"

"It is not that I cannot bear his insolence, but that I should have to show by my face that I had made a request, and had been refused. You need not come."

"On Christmas Day?"

"Well, yes. You cannot understand the sort of flutter I am in. 'Not if I know it!' The insolence of the phrase in answering such a request! The suspicion that it showed! If he had told me that he had any feeling about it, I would have deposited the money in his hands. There is a train in the morning. You can stay here and go to church with him, while I run up to town."

"That you two should part like that on Christmas Day; you two dear ones! Wilfred, it will break my heart." Then he turned round and endeavoured to make himself comfortable among the bedclothes. "Wilfred, say that you will not go out of this to-morrow.

"Oh, very well! You have only to speak and I obey. If you could only manage to make your brother more civil for the one day it would be an improvement."

"I think he will be civil. I have been speaking to him, and he seems to be sorry that he should have annoyed you."

"Well, yes; he did annoy me. 'Not if I know it!' in answer to such a request! As if I had asked him for five thousand pounds! I wouldn't have asked him or any man alive for five thousand pence. Coming down to his house at Christmastime, and to be suspected of such a thing!" Then he prepared himself steadily to sleep, and she, before she stretched herself by his side, prayed that God's mercy might obliterate the wrath between these men, whom she loved so well, before the morrow's sun should have come and gone.

The bells sounded merry from Hallam Church tower on the following morning, and told to each of the inhabitants of the old hall a tale that was varied according to the minds of the three inhabitants whom we know. With her it was all hope, but hope accompanied by that despondency which is apt to afflict the weak in the presence of those that are stronger. With her husband it was anger,—but mitigated anger. He seemed, as he came into his wife's room while dressing, to be aware that there was something which should be abandoned, but which still it did his heart some good to nourish. With George Wade there was more of Christian feeling, but of Christian feeling which it was disagreeable to entertain. "How on earth is a man to get on with his relatives, if he cannot speak a word above his breath?" But still he would have been very willing that those words should have been left unsaid.

Any observer might have seen that the three persons as they sat down to breakfast were each under some little constraint. The lady was more than ordinarily courteous, or even affectionate, in her manner. This was natural on Christmas Day, but her too apparent anxiety was hardly natural. Her husband accosted his brother-in-law with almost loud good humour. "Well, George, a merry Christmas, and many of them. My word;—how hard it froze last night! You won't get any hunting for the next fortnight. I hope old Burnaby won't spin us a long yarn."

George Wade simply kissed his sister, and shook hands with his brother-in-law. But he shook hands with more apparent zeal than he would have done but for the quarrel, and when he pressed Wilfred Horton to eat some devilled turkey, he did it with more ardour than was usual with him. "Mrs. Jones is generally very successful with devilled turkey." Then, as he passed round the table behind his sister's back, she put out her hand to touch him, and as though to thank him for his goodness. But any one could see that it was not quite natural.

The two men as they left the house for church, were thinking of the request that had been made yesterday, and which had been refused. "Not if I know it!" said George Wade to himself. "There is nothing so unnatural in that, that a fellow should think so much of it. I didn't mean to do it. Of course, if he had said that he wanted it particularly I should have done it."

"Not if I know it!" said Wilfred Horton. "There was an insolence about it. I only came to him just because he was my brother-in-law. Jones, or Smith, or Walker would have done it without a word." Then the three walked into church, and took their places in the front seat, just under Dr. Burnaby's reading-desk.

We will not attempt to describe the minds of the three as the Psalms were sung, and as the prayers were said. A twinge did cross the minds of the two men as the coming of the Prince of Peace was foretold to them; and a stronger hope did sink into the heart of her whose happiness depended so much on the manner in which they two stood with one another. And when Dr. Burnaby found time, in the fifteen minutes which he gave to his sermon, to tell his hearers why the Prophet had specially spoken of Christ as the Prince of Peace, and to describe what the blessings were, hitherto unknown, which had come upon the world since a desire for peace had filled the minds of men, a feeling did come on the hearts of both of them,—to one that the words had better not have been spoken, and to the other that they had better have been forgiven. Then came the Sacrament, more powerful with its thoughts than its words, and the two men as they left the church were ready to forgive each other—if they only knew how.

There was something a little sheep-faced about the two men as they walked up together across the grounds to the old hall,—something sheep-faced which Mrs. Horton fully understood, and which made her feel for the moment triumphant over them. It is always so with a woman when she knows that she has for the moment got the better of a man. How much more so when she has conquered two? She hovered about among them as though they were dear human beings subject to the power of some beneficent angel. The three sat down to lunch, and Dr. Burnaby could not but have been gratified had he heard the things that were said of him. "I tell you, you know," said George, "that Burnaby is a right good fellow, and awfully clever. There isn't a man or woman in the parish that he doesn't know how to get to the inside of."

"And he knows what to do when he gets there," said Mrs. Horton, who remembered with affection the gracious old parson as he had blessed her at her wedding.

"No; I couldn't let him do it for me." It was thus Horton spoke to his wife as they were walking together about the gardens. "Dear Wilfred, you ought to forgive him."

"I have forgiven him. There!" And he made a sign as of blowing his anger away to the winds. "I do forgive him. I will think no more about it. It is as though the words had never been spoken,—though they were very unkind. 'Not if I know it!' All the same, they don't leave a sting behind."

"But they do."

"Nothing of the kind. I shall drink prosperity to the old

house and a loving wife to the master just as cheerily by and by as though the words had never been spoken."

"But there will not be peace,—not the peace of which Dr. Burnaby told us. It must be as though it had really—really never been uttered. George has not spoken to me about it, not to-day, but if he asks, you will let him do it?"

"He will never ask—unless at your instigation."

"I will not speak to him," she answered,—"not without telling you. I would never go behind your back. But whether he does it or not, I feel that it is in his heart to do it." Then the brother came up and joined them in their walk, and told them of all the little plans he had in hand in reference to the garden. "You must wait till *she* comes, for that, George," said his sister.

"Oh, yes; there must always be a she when another she is talking. But what will you say if I tell you there is to be a she?"

"Oh, George!"

"Your nose is going to be put out of joint, as far as Hallam Hall is concerned." Then he told them all his love story, and so the afternoon was allowed to wear itself away till the dinner hour had nearly come.

"Just come in here, Wilfred," he said to his brother-in-law when his sister had gone up to dress. "I have something I want to say to you before dinner."

"All right," said Wilfred. And as he got up to follow the master of the house, he told himself that after all his wife would prove herself too many for him.

"I don't know the least in the world what it was you were asking me to do yesterday."

"It was a matter of no consequence," said Wilfred, not able to avoid assuming an air of renewed injury.

"But I do know that I was cross," said George Wade.

"After that," said Wilfred, "everything is smooth between us. No man can expect anything more straightforward. I was a little hurt, but I know that I was a fool. Every man has a right to have his own ideas as to the use of his name."

"But that will not suffice," said George.

"Oh! yes it will."

"Not for me," repeated George. "I have brought myself to ask your pardon for refusing, and you should bring yourself to accept my offer to do it."

"It was nothing. It was only because you were my brother-in-law, and therefore the nearest to me. The Turco-Egyptian New Waterworks Company simply requires somebody to assert that I am worth ten thousands pounds."

"Let me do it, Wilfred," said George Wade. "Nobody can know your circumstances better than I do. I have begged your pardon, and I think that you ought now in return to accept this at my hand."

"All right," said Wilfred Horton. "I will accept it at your hand." And then he went away to dress. What took place up in the dressingroom need not here be told. But when Mrs. Horton came down to dinner the smile upon her face was a truer index of her heart than it had been in the morning.

"I have been very sorry for what took place last night," said George afterwards in the drawing-room, feeling himself obliged, as it were, to make full confession and restitution before the assembled multitude,—which consisted, however, of his brother-in-law and his sister. "I have asked pardon, and have begged Wilfred to show his grace by accepting from me what I had before declined. I hope that he will not refuse me."

"Not if I know it," said Wilfred Horton.

The Colonel's Awakening

by Paul Laurence Dunbar

It was the morning before Christmas. The cold winter sunlight fell brightly through the window into a small room where an old man was sitting. The room, now bare and cheerless, still retained evidences of having once been the abode of refinement and luxury. It was the one open chamber of many in a great rambling old Virginia house, which in its time had been one of the proudest in the county. But it had been in the path of the hurricane of war, and had been shorn of its glory as a tree is stripped of its foliage. Now, like the bare tree, dismantled, it remained, and this one old man, with the aristocratic face, clung to it like the last leaf.

He did not turn his head when an ancient serving-man came in and began laying the things for breakfast. After a while the servant spoke: "I got a monst'ous fine breakfus' fu' you dis mo'nin', Mas' Estridge. I got fresh aigs, an' beat biscuits, an' Lize done fried you a young chicken dat'll sholy mek yo' mouf worter."

"Thank you, Ike, thank you," was the dignified response. "Lize is a likely girl, and she's improving in her cooking greatly."

"Yes, Mas' Estridge, she sho is a mighty fine ooman."

"And you're not a bad servant yourself, Ike," the old man went on, with an air of youthful playfulness that ill accorded with his aged face. "I expect some day you'll be coming around asking me to let you marry Lize, eh! What have you got to say to that?"

"I reckon dat's right, mastah, I reckon dat's mighty nigh right."

"Well, we shall see about it when the time comes; we shall see about it."

"Lawd, how long!" mumbled the old servant to himself as he went on about his work. "Ain't Mas' Bob nevah gwine to git his almanec straight? He been gwine on dis way fu' ovah twenty yeahs now. He cain't git it thoo' his haid dat time been a-passin'. Hyeah I done been ma'ied to Lize fu' lo dese many yeahs, an' we've got ma'ied chillum, but he still think I's a-cou'tin' huh."

To Colonel Robert Estridge time had not passed and conditions had not changed for a generation. He was still the gallant aristocrat he had been when the war broke out,—a little past the age to enlist himself, but able and glad to give two sons to the cause of the South. They had gone out, light-hearted and gay, and brave in their military trappings and suits of gray. The father had watched them away with moist eyes and a swelling bosom. After that the tide of war had surged on and on, had even rolled to his very gates, and the widowed man watched and waited for it to bring his boys back to him. One of them came. They brought him back from the valley of the Shenandoah, and laid him in the old orchard out there behind the house. Then all the love of the father was concentrated upon the one remaining son, and his calendar could know but one day and that the one on which his Bob, his namesake and his youngest, should return to him. But one day there came to him the news that his boy had fallen in the front of a terrific fight, and in the haste of retreat he had been buried with the unknown dead. Into that trench, among the unknown, Colonel Robert Estridge had laid his heart, and there it had stayed. Time stopped, and his faculties wandered. He lived always in the dear past. The present and future were not. He did not even know when the fortunes of war brought an opposing host to his very doors. He was unconscious of it all when they devoured his substance like a plague of locusts. It was all a blank to him when the old manor house was fired and he was like to lose his possessions and his life. When his servants left him he did not know, but sat and gave orders to the one faithful retainer as though he were ordering the old host of blacks. And so for more than a generation he had lived.

"Hope you gwine to enjoy yo' Christmas Eve breakfus', Mas' Estridge," said the old servant.

"Christmas Eve. Christmas Eve? Yes, yes, so it is. Tomorrow is Christmas Day, and I'm afraid I have been rather sluggish in getting things ready for the celebration. I reckon the darkies have already begun to jubilate and to shirk in consequence, and I won't be able to get a thing done decently for a week."

"Don't you bother 'bout none o' de res', Mas' Estridge;

you kin 'pend on me—I ain't gwine to shu'k even ef 't is Christmas."

"That's right, Ike. I can depend upon you. You're always faithful. Just you get things done up right for me, and I'll give you that broadcloth suit of mine. It's most as good as new."

"Thanky, Mas' Bob, thanky." The old Negro said it as fervently as if he had not worn out that old broadcloth a dozen years ago.

"It's late and we've got to hurry if we want things prepared in time. Tell Lize that I want her to let herself out on that dinner. Your Mas' Bob and Mas' Stanton are going to be home tomorrow, and I want to show them that their father's house hasn't lost any of the qualities that have made it famous in Virginia for a hundred years. Ike, there ain't anything in this world for making men out of boys like making them feel the debt they owe to their name and family."

"Yes, suh, Mas' Bob an' Mas' Stant' sholy is mighty fine men.'

"There ain't two finer in the whole country, sir,—no, sir, not in all Virginia, and that of necessity means the whole country. Now, Ike, I want you to get out some of that wine up in the second cellar, and when I say some I mean plenty. It ain't seen the light for years, but it shall gurgle into the glasses tomorrow in honor of my sons' homecoming. Good wine makes good blood, and who should drink good wine if not an Estridge of Virginia, sir, eh, Ike?"

The wine had gone to make good cheer when a Federal regiment had lighted its camp fires on the Estridge lawn, but old Ike had heard it too often before and knew his business too well to give any sign.

"I want you to take some things up to Miss Clarinda Randolph tomorrow, too, and I've got a silver snuffbox for

Thomas Daniels. I can't make many presents this year. I've got to devote my money to the interest of your young masters."

There was a catch in the Negro's voice as he replied, "Yes, Mas' Estridge, dey needs it mos', dey needs it mos'."

The old Colonel's spell of talking seldom lasted long, and now he fell to eating in silence; but his face was the face of one in a dream. Ike waited on him until he had done, and then, clearing the things away, slipped out, leaving him to sit and muse in his chair by the window.

"Look hyeah, Lize," said the old servant, as he entered his wife's cabin a little later. "Pleggoned ef I didn't come purt' nigh brekin' down dis mo'nin'."

"Wha's de mattah wif you, Ike?"

"Jes' a-listenin' to ol' Mas' a-sittin' dah a-talkin' lak it was de ol' times,—a-sendin' messages to ol' Miss Randolph, dat's been daid too long to talk about, an' to Mas' Tom Daniels, dat went acrost de wateh ruther'n tek de oaf o' 'legiance."

"Oomph," said the old lady, wiping her eyes on her cotton apron.

"Den he expectin' Mas' Bob an' Mas' Stant' home tomorrer. 'Clah to goodness, when he say dat I lak to hollahed right out."

"Den you would 'a' fixed it, wouldn't you? Set down an' eat yo' breakfus', Ike, an' don't you nevah let on when Mas' Estridge talkin', you jes' go 'long 'bout yo' wuk an' keep yo' mouf shet, 'ca'se ef evah he wake up now he gwine to die right straight off."

"Lawd he'p him not to wake up den, 'ca'se he ol', but we needs him. I do' know whut I'd do ef I didn't have Mas' Bob to wuk fu'. You got ol' Miss Randolph's present ready fu' him?"

"Co'se I has. I done made him somep'n' diffunt dis yeah."

"Made him somep'n' diffunt—whut you say, Lize?" exclaimed the old man, laying his knife and fork on his plate and looking up at his wife with wide-open eyes. "You ain't gwine change afteh all dese yeahs?"

"Yes. I jes' pintly had to. It's been de same thing now fu' mo' 'n twenty yeahs."

"Whut you done made fu' him?"

"I's made him a comfo't to go roun' his naik."

"But, Lize, ol' Miss Cla'indy allus sont him gloves knit wif huh own han'. Ain't you feared Mas' Estridge gwine to 'spect?"

"No, he ain't gwine to 'spect. He don't tek no notice o' nuffin', an' he jes' pintly had to have dat comfo't fu' his naik, 'ca'se he boun' to go out in de col' sometime er ruther an' he got plenty gloves."

"I's feared," said the old man, sententiously, "I's mighty feared. I wouldn't have Mastah know we been doin' fu' him an' a-sendin' him dese presents all dis time fu' nuffin' in de worl'. It 'u'd hu't him mighty bad."

"He ain't foun' out all dese yeahs, an' he ain't gwine fin' out now." The old man shook his head dubiously, and ate the rest of his meal in silence.

It was a beautiful Christmas morning as he wended his way across the lawn to his old master's room, bearing the tray of breakfast things and "ol' Miss Randolph's present,"—a heavy home-made scarf. The air was full of frosty brightness. Ike was happy, for the frost had turned the persimmons. The 'possums had gorged themselves, and he had one of the fattest of them for his Christmas dinner. Colonel Estridge was sitting in his old place by the window. He crumbled an old yellow envelope in his hand as Ike came in and set the things down. It looked like the letter which had brought the news of young Robert Estridge's loss, but it could not be, for the old man sitting there had forgotten that and was expecting the son home on that day.

Ike took the comforter to his master, and began in the old way: "Miss Cla'iny Randolph mek huh comperments to you, Mas' Bob, an' say—" But his master had turned and was looking him square in the face, and something in the look checked his flow of words. Colonel Estridge did not extend his hand to take the gift. "Clarinda Randolph," he said, "always sends me gloves." His tone was not angry, but it was cold and sorrowful. "Lay it down," he went on more kindly and pointing to the comforter, "and you may go now. I will get whatever I want from the table." Ike did not dare to demur. He slipped away, embarrassed and distressed.

"Wha' 'd I tell you?" he asked Lize, as soon as he reached the cabin. "I believe he done woke up." But the old woman could only mourn and wring her hands.

"Well, nevah min'," said Ike, after his first moment of sad triumph was over. "I guess it wasn't the comfo't nohow, 'ca'se I seed him wif a letteh when I went in, but I didn't 'spicion nuffin' tell he look at me an' talk jes' ez sensible ez me er you."

It was not until dinner-time that Ike found courage to go back to his master's room, and then he did not find him sitting in his accustomed place, nor was he on the porch or in the hall.

Growing alarmed, the old servant searched high and low for him, until he came to the door of a long-disused room. A bundle of keys hung from the keyhole.

"Hyeah's whah he got dat letteh," said Ike. "I reckon he come to put it back." But even as he spoke, his eyes bulged with apprehension. He opened the door further, and went in.

And there at last his search was ended. Colonel Estridge was on his knees before an old oak chest. On the floor about him were scattered pair on pair of home-knit gloves. He was very still. His head had fallen forward on the edge of the chest. Ike went up to him and touched his shoulder. There was no motion in response. The black man lifted his master's head. The face was pale and cold and lifeless. In the stiffening hand was clenched a pair of gloves,—the last Miss Randolph had ever really knit for him. The servant lifted up the lifeless form, and laid it upon the bed. When Lize came she would have wept and made loud lamentations, but Ike checked her. "Keep still," he said. "Pray if you want to, but don't hollah. We ought to be proud, Lize." His shoulders were thrown back and his head was up. "Mas' Bob's in glory. Dis is Virginia's Christmas gif' to Gawd!"

Christmas Every Day

by William Dean Howells

THE LITTLE GIRL CAME INTO her papa's study, as she always did Saturday morning before breakfast, and asked for a story. He tried to beg off that morning, for he was very busy, but she would not let him. So he began:

"Well, once there was a little pig—"

She stopped him at the word. She said she had heard little pig-stories till she was perfectly sick of them.

"Well, what kind of story *shall* I tell, then?"

"About Christmas. It's getting to be the season."

"Well!" Her papa roused himself. "Then I'll tell you about the little girl that wanted it Christmas every day in the year. How would you like that?"

"First-rate!" said the little girl; and she nestled into comfortable shape in his lap, ready for listening.

"Very well, then, this little pig—Oh, what are you pounding me for?"

"Because you said little pig instead of little girl."

"I should like to know what's the difference between a little pig and a little girl that wanted it Christmas every day!"

"Papa!" said the little girl warningly. At this her papa began to tell the story.

Once there was a little girl who liked Christmas so much that she wanted it to be Christmas every day in the year, and as soon as Thanksgiving was over she began to send postcards to the old Christmas Fairy to ask if she mightn't have it. But the old Fairy never answered, and after a while the little girl found out that the Fairy wouldn't notice anything but real letters sealed outside with a monogram—or your initial, anyway. So, then, she began to send letters, and just the day before Christmas, she got a letter from the Fairy, saying she might have it Christmas every day for a year, and then they would see about having it longer.

The little girl was excited already, preparing for the old-fashioned, once-a-year Christmas that was coming the next day. So she resolved to keep the Fairy's promise to herself and surprise everybody with it as it kept coming true, but then it slipped out of her mind altogether.

She had a splendid Christmas. She went to bed early, so as to let Santa Claus fill the stockings, and in the morning she was up the first of anybody and found hers all lumpy with packages of candy, and oranges and grapes, and rubber balls, and all kinds of small presents. Then she waited until the rest of the family was up, and she burst into the library to look at the large presents laid out on the library table—books, and boxes of stationery, and dolls, and little stoves, and dozens of handkerchiefs, and inkstands, and skates, and photograph frames, and boxes of watercolors, and dolls' houses—and the big Christmas tree, lighted and standing in the middle.

She had a splendid Christmas all day. She ate so much candy that she did not want any breakfast, and the whole forenoon the presents kept pouring in that had not been delivered the night before, and she went round giving the presents she had got for other people, and came home and ate turkey and cranberry for dinner, and plum pudding and nuts and raisins and oranges, and then went out and coasted, and came in with a stomachache crying, and her papa said he would see if his house was turned into that sort of fool's paradise another year, and they had a light supper, and pretty early everybody went to bed cross.

The little girl slept very heavily and very late, but she was wakened at last by the other children dancing around her bed with their stockings full of presents in their hands. "Christmas! Christmas! Christmas!" they all shouted.

"Nonsense! It was Christmas yesterday," said the little girl, rubbing her eyes sleepily.

Her brothers and sisters just laughed. "We don't know about that. It's Christmas today, anyway. You come into the library and see."

Then all at once it flashed on the little girl that the Fairy was keeping her promise, and her year of Christmases was beginning. She was dreadfully sleepy, but she sprang up and darted into the library. There it was again! Books, and boxes of stationery, and dolls, and so on.

There was the Christmas tree blazing away, and the family picking out their presents, and her father looking perfectly puzzled, and her mother ready to cry. "I'm sure I don't see how I'm to dispose of all these things," said her mother, and her father said it seemed to him they had had something just like it the day before, but he supposed he must have dreamed it. This struck the little girl as the best kind of a joke, and so she ate so much candy she didn't want any breakfast, and went round carrying presents, and had turkey and cranberry for dinner, and then went out and coasted, and came in with a stomachache, crying.

Now, the next day, it was the same thing over again, but everybody getting crosser, and at the end of a week's time so many people had lost their tempers that you could pick up lost tempers anywhere, they perfectly strewed the ground. Even when people tried to recover their tempers they usually got somebody else's, and it made the most dreadful mix.

The little girl began to get frightened, keeping the secret all to herself, she wanted to tell her mother, but she didn't dare to, and she was ashamed to ask the Fairy to take back her gift, it seemed ungrateful and ill-bred. So it went on and on, and it was Christmas on St. Valentine's Day and Washington's Birthday, just the same as any day, and it didn't skip even the First of April, though everything was counterfeit that day, and that was some little relief.

After a while turkeys got to be awfully scarce, selling for about a thousand dollars apiece. They got to passing off almost anything for turkeys—even half-grown hummingbirds. And cranberries—well they asked a diamond apiece for cranberries. All the woods and orchards were cut down for Christmas trees. After a while they had to make Christmas trees out of rags. But there were plenty of rags, because people got so poor, buying presents for one another, that they couldn't get any new clothes, and they just wore their old ones to tatters. They got so poor that everybody had to go to the poorhouse, except the confectioners, and the storekeepers, and the book-sellers, and they all got so rich and proud that they would hardly wait upon a person when he came to buy. It was perfectly shameful!

After it had gone on about three or four months, the little girl, whenever she came into the room in the morning and saw those great ugly, lumpy stockings dangling at the fireplace, and the disgusting presents around everywhere, used to sit down and burst out crying. In six months she was perfectly exhausted, she couldn't even cry anymore.

And how it was on the Fourth of July! On the Fourth of July, the first boy in the United States woke up and found out that his firecrackers and toy pistol and two-dollar collection of fireworks were nothing but sugar and candy painted up to look like fireworks. Before ten o'clock every boy in the United States discovered that his July Fourth things had turned into Christmas things and was so mad. The Fourth of July orations all turned into Christmas carols, and when anybody tried to read the Declaration of Independence, instead of saying, "When in the course of human events it becomes necessary," he was sure to sing, "God rest you merry gentlemen." It was perfectly awful.

About the beginning of October the little girl took to sitting down on dolls wherever she found them—she hated the sight of them so, and by Thanksgiving she just slammed her presents across the room. By that time people didn't carry presents around nicely anymore. They flung them over the fence or through the window, and, instead of taking great pains to write "For dear Papa," or "Mama" or "Brother," or "Sister," they used to write, "Take it, you horrid old thing!" and then go and bang it against the front door.

Nearly everybody had built barns to hold their presents, but pretty soon the barns overflowed, and then they used to let them lie out in the rain, or anywhere. Sometimes the police used to come and tell them to shovel their presents off the sidewalk or they would arrest them.

Before Thanksgiving came it had leaked out who had caused all these Christmases. The little girl had suffered so much that she had talked about it in her sleep, and after that hardly anybody would play with her, because if it had not been for her greediness it wouldn't have happened. And now, when it came Thanksgiving, and she wanted them to go to church, and have turkey, and show their gratitude, they said that all the turkeys had been eaten for her old Christmas dinners and if she would stop the Christmases, they would see about the gratitude. And the very next day the little girl began sending letters to the Christmas Fairy, and then telegrams, to stop it. But it didn't do any good, and then she got to calling at the Fairy's house, but the girl that came to the door always said, "Not at home," or "Engaged," or something like that, and so it went on till it came to the old once-a-year Christmas Eve. The little girl fell asleep, and when she woke up in the morning—

"She found it was all nothing but a dream," suggested the little girl.

"No indeed!" said her papa. "It was all every bit true!"

"What *did* she find out, then?"

"Why, that it wasn't Christmas at last, and wasn't ever going to be, anymore. Now it's time for breakfast."

The little girl held her papa fast around the neck.

"You shan't go if you're going to leave it so!"

"How do you want it left?"

"Christmas once a year."

"All right," said her papa, and he went on again.

Well, with no Christmas ever again, there was the greatest rejoicing all over the country. People met together everywhere and kissed and cried for joy. Carts went around and gathered up all the candy and raisins and nuts, and dumped them into the river, and it made the fish perfectly sick. And the whole United States, as far out as Alaska, was one blaze of bonfires, where the children were burning up their presents of all kinds. They had the greatest time!

The little girl went to thank the old Fairy because she had stopped its being Christmas, and she said she hoped the Fairy would keep her promise and see that Christmas never, never came again. Then the Fairy frowned, and said that now the little girl was behaving just as greedily as ever, and she'd better look out. This made the little girl think it all over carefully again, and she said she would be willing to have it Christmas about once in a thousand years, and then she said a hundred, and then she said ten, and at last she got down to one. Then the Fairy said that was the good old way that had pleased people ever since Christmas began, and she was agreed. Then the little girl said, "What're your shoes made of?" And the Fairy said, "Leather." And the little girl said, "Bargain's done forever," and skipped off, and hippity-hopped the whole way home, she was so glad.

"How will that do?" asked the papa.

"First-rate!" said the little girl, but she hated to have the story stop, and was rather sober. However, her mama put her head in at the door and asked her papa:

"Are you never coming to breakfast? What have you been telling that child?"

"Oh, just a tale with a moral."

The little girl caught him around the neck again.

"*We* know! Don't you tell *what,* papa! Don't you tell *what!*"

The Adventures of a Christmas Turkey

BY MARK LEMON

SOME FEW YEARS AGO I met with a great sorrow, and as the hunting season was at an end, and I could not resort to my usual remedy for vexation, I turned sulky, and went alone to an out of the way seaside place on the coast of Sussex. It was a small ship-building town, and one fine July afternoon I was lying on the beach listening idly to the hammers and mallets of the shipwrights "closing rivets up" or caulking the sides of some storm-worn collier. The noise of a wandering circus band occasionally mingled with the sounds of industry, but were all sufficiently distant to make the quiet murmuring of the sea more distinct and soothing. Between me and the town were oyster-beds, fed by one or two creeks which were filled and emptied by the tides, and a tract of coarse brown grass which had grown up between the shingle long deserted by the sea. I had stolen away, as I have said, from a great grief, and sat looking upon the deep green waters, ever upheaving and falling as from the action of some mighty heart, that, like my own, was full to silence. I had strange dreams that day, lying lonely on the beach—dreams of other dreams which had made up much of my life which had passed, and, perhaps, of the life which is left to me. After a time some schoolboys came shouting and laughing across the brown grass to the seaside, and soon made playfellows of the waves, as though the restless waters had never wrecked mighty ships and drowned hosts of men, or torn down rocks, and cliffs, and solid masonry. The play ended, I was again alone, looking upon the sea, recalling the time when I had had such sport, and wondering if any of that merry group would ever sit, as I then sat, thankful for the silence and the solitude of the quiet shore. The solitude and silence were thus disturbed:

"If ever I catch you near those oyster-beds again, I'll rope's end you till you're as blue-lined as a sailor's shirt."

The speaker was evidently in earnest, and close behind me. He was a fiery-faced, white-headed old gentleman, of a nautical build, and the boy he held by the collar, and whom he was thus addressing, was seaborn also, as his suit of tar and canvas certified.

"I wasn't anigh 'em!" cried the boy. "I see another boy mucking [loitering] about there, but it wasn't me. You let me goa!" And the lad struggled like a dog-fish.

"I know that it was you," said Captain Crump (I afterwards learned the speaker's name); "and those periwinkles I found you boiling in your mother's teakettle came out of my beds, I've no doubt."

"They wasn't my winkles," replied the boy; "I never eats

them; they always terrifies [annoys] me so when I does. You let me goa, or I'll kick your bad leg, I will."

Captain Crump gave his captive another hearty shake and a tap on the head with his walking-cane (the boy's skull must have been as strong as a cocoanut-shell not to have cracked with the blow), receiving a sharp kick in exchange, and the belligerents parted company.

The boy put a few yards between himself and the enemy, wiped his streaming eyes with the back of his hand, and, mounting a pile of shingle, bawled out:

"Captain Crump! Hallo, Captain Crump! how did you like your Christmas turkee?"

There was nothing particularly uncivil in the inquiry that I could discover, but it hit Captain Crump in a tender part, and set him gesticulating like an insane windmill—if you will allow me such a figure of speech.

That the Captain was mentally expressing a great deal no one could doubt who saw his distended eyes and cheeks, the latter being as red as his nose in its normal state, and nothing incombustible could be redder than that useful and prominent feature of Captain Crump's physiognomy. There is nothing new or remarkable in a red nose, I am aware. In fact, to mention such a distinction is commonplace; but Captain Crump, owner of the oyster and periwinkle beds, was a commonplace character, and he had a red nose.

The boy scampered away over the brown grass like a human plover (the *oyster-catcher*, perhaps), occasionally pausing to utter his cry of "Christmas turkee!" until he could no longer be heard, but only seen, evidently screaming in defiance of Captain Crump.

I do not know what there was in my appearance to justify

the confidence, but the irritated gentleman stopped at the place where I was lying, and without any preface began the explanation of his late extraordinary display of temper and annoyance; and, to my surprise, I confess, I learned that the oysters and periwinkles had nothing to do with the matter.

I was glad to leave my own sad thoughts for a while, and therefore encouraged my new acquaintance to be communicative; and what he told me as we walked over the brown grass to Littletown, and what I gathered from the landlady of the Ship Torbay in the course of the ensuing evening, I will tell to you if you will listen to me.

On the extreme right of Littletown, looking towards the sea, stands a neat one-storied cottage, distinguished by a high flagstaff, from which, on high days and holidays, floats the union-jack or the Maltese cross, and on other days a man-o'-war's whip flouts any breeze that may be stirring. On one side of a neatly-kept garden, ornamented here and there with flint boulders and bordered with large shingle, is a wire inclosure containing a number of hencoops, formerly belonging to an Indiaman wrecked upon the coast in the year 18—. A variety of poultry strut, scratch, and peck away their lives within, being carefully, tenderly, and daily fed by Mrs. Crump, the kindly, good-natured spouse of Captain Crump, who is the proprietor of the aforesaid cottage, flagpost, flags, garden, boulders, shingle, hencoops, and poultry. An old ship's gun formerly stood at the foot of the flagpost; but, being discharged on some occasion of public rejoicing, it proved to have been cracked, and burst into a hundred pieces, fortunately doing no other damage than destroying all the front windows of Crump Cottage, and throwing Mrs. Crump's pet parrot into a fit of convulsions. The bird moulted, in consequence, all but its head feathers, and looked very like a late Vice-Chancellor in his bathing-dress and with his wig on.

On the extreme left of Littletown stood another villa of more urban pretensions, "verandahed, and stuccoed, and cockneyfied," according to Captain Crump, but made "snug and comfortable," according to the opinion of its owners, Mr. and Mrs. Macgrey; and I have no doubt but their estimate was the just one. Mr. Alexander Macgrey had made his own way in the world. From carrying a pedlar's pack, he had secured a small competency in a City warehouse, and, having no children to keep him in harness to the end of his days, had wisely written the word "Content" at the bottom of his last year's balance-sheet and come to settle at his wife's birthplace, Littletown. Captain William Crump was also a Littletownian, and, as a matter of course, had known Mrs. Macgrey when they were boy and girl together; but for some unguessed-at reason, Captain Crump resisted all approaches to intimacy on the part of the Macgreys—almost treating the gentleman with open rudeness. The ladies were more amiable, and never failed to recognise each other at church, or in the very small market-place, which boasted of one butcher's stall and a greengrocer's barrow, and now and then ventured to give each other the state of the weather when they passed in the street. The gentlemen bowed, sometimes; although one would have supposed that, being so nearly on an equality in point of station and education, they would have been glad of each other's society, as Littletown was only inhabited by boatbuilders, ship-chandlers, and their like.

Except John Bishopp, general shopkeeper, who added the cultivation of a few acres of land to the vending of the multifarious articles of his commercial establishment; he lived midway between the Crumps and the Macgreys and made his money out of both. John Bishopp was a jolly sort of man that everybody liked, and, as his business took him about the country a good deal, the management of the shop was principally left to Mrs. Bishopp, who was a good woman enough, as times go, although a bit of a shrew. John kept her in pretty fair order, and when he stayed rather later than he ought to have done over his pipe and alepot, he received (what he called) "his supper of carp-pie" with good humour, but always expected to hear no more of his delinquencies in the morning. A very wise regulation that of John Bishopp, and young couples would do well to adopt it. What say you, dear grandmamma, who have had some patching and botching of the matrimonial yoke to do in your time?

Captain William Crump was, as you may have imagined, a Captain by courtesy only. He had amassed money in many ways during some thirty years' service in the merchant navy, and had retired to Littletown to spend the evening of his busy life. He had rather a warm temper, which he kept well supplied with fuel in the form of three-quarter grog, although he never drank to excess, if you accepted his own notion of temperance. He had many odd opinions, whims, and prejudices, but was not a bad fellow, take him for all in all. One of his whims led to the incidents of this story, and with that we have, therefore, only to do at present. It was this: Having found it impossible to procure in Littletown a turkey for his Christmas dinner, 18—, he had determined before the next coming of that festive season to rear one for his own consumption, and had therefore added to Mrs. Crump's ornithological collection a fine young bird to be reared, fattened, and sacrificed at the Christmastide ensuing. It wrung the tender soul of Mrs.

Crump to know that the pretty creature she tended daily and which came at last to feed from her hand like her other favourites was doomed to a culinary end; but her duty as a wife overcame her feelings as a philanthropist, and she saw with a melancholy pleasure the satisfactory progress of the condemned. One November night, however, by some unknown and undiscovered means the thriving bird broke its leg, and so serious was the fracture that amputation became necessary, to the great grief of Mrs. Crump and the exceeding wrath of her irritable husband. The turkey soon suffered in flesh from the absence of its lost member, and would probably have been unworthy its high destiny had not Captain Crump—handy as most sailors are—made it a wooden leg, which was so cleverly contrived that motion again became easy, and plumpness was restored long before the day of execution, which had been fixed for December the 22nd. On the morning of that day Mrs. Crump shut herself up in the bedroom, whilst Captain Crump and his man Jabez proceeded to execution in the stable, and it was some satisfaction to the sensitive lady to know that the victim made a most exemplary end, and died weighing 14 lb. 6 oz. As the Captain kept no quadruped except a cat, the turkey was suspended to the hook which usually supports the stable-lantern, and Crump and Jabez were both engaged in silent contemplation of the noble bird, when a gipsy-looking man approached, laden with branches of holly and mistletoe for sale. Now, one of Captain Crump's prejudices was a thorough hatred of the whole Bohemian race, declaring them to be, without exception, rogues and vagabonds of the worst kind; and it is believed he would have willingly subscribed to have chartered the *Great Eastern* and freighted her with all the tribes of Cooper, Lee, and Bonnys, provided the owners would have undertaken to have scuttled the Leviathan in the deepest depths of the Atlantic.

"Buy any holly and mistletoe?" asked the gipsy, "capital lot here, your honour, cheap."

"No!" roared Crump from the stable, whilst Jabez winked at the man and motioned him to be gone.

"Holly werry scarce, your honour," continued the gipsy, "and mistletoe hard to be got. Brought this ten mile, or more. You shall have it cheap."

"No!" again shouted Crump. "Do you think I'll encourage such scamps as you in destroying honest gentlemen's plantations in the dead of the night? No, you vagabond!"

"Easy, mister!" said the gipsy. "I've travelled this country these thirty years, and I couldn't do that if I stole holly or anything else. I bought it at C——in open market, and ain't ashamed who sees me selling it."

Captain Crump's rejoinder contained several adjectives of an exceptional character, and cannot be recorded in these pages.

The gipsy had been used to hard words all his life; so, gathering up the holly and mistletoe which he had spread out for Captain Crump's inspection, said, mildly enough, "No harm done, master, as I see. A poor chap must try to turn an honest penny or starve, which you don't seem likely to do this Christmas. That's an uncommon fine turkey!"

"What's that to you, you——" etc., etc., replied Crump.

"Oh, nothing; I'm sure of that. It's long afore you'd ask me to take my Christmas dinner at your expense," said the gipsy, leaning against the stable-door. "But it is an uncommon fine turkey, I'll pound it, whoever has the luck to eat it."

Now Captain Crump, like many seagoing people, had a strong

dash of the superstitious in his composition, and he felt an unpleasant sensation as the gipsy spoke, although the words were simple enough. Before he could make any reply the man had said, "Good day, master," and walked away towards Littletown.

In a few minutes the gipsy was forgotten, and Mrs. Crump and the maid-servant were summoned to inspect and admire their future Christmas dinner; and it was a sad evidence of the selfishness of human nature when Mrs. Crump forgot all the past and asked, without a tremor in her voice, "whether it was to be boiled or roasted?"

Jabez did not sleep on the premises, and he was allowed to go home earlier than usual in order that he might ascertain who in Littletown were likely to have sausages, and to bespeak the quantity requisite for the proper adornment of the sacrifice. He had been gone some time, and the evening was closing in, when Captain Crump proceeded to shut the stable-door, and discovered to his annoyance that Jabez had taken the key with him. The ears of Jabez must have burned finely if warm words spoken behind his back could have quickened their circulation. Not that there was any real cause for anger, as Mrs. Crump had a duplicate key to the lock, and all was made secure for the night. "Fast bind, fast find," said the Captain, as he heard the bolt shoot home. And with that satisfactory conclusion he went to bed as the kitchen clock struck ten.

He awoke in the morning and found that adages are not always to be relied on, for the stable-door was still locked, but the turkey was gone; and Jahez vowed he had not seen the key since the day before.

Of course everyone suspects that the gipsy took away the key and then stole the turkey. It might have been so, for he was hiding something under some litter in an old hovel a good mile or more away from Littletown about twelve o'clock that very night.

Another of Captain Crump's prejudices was an objection to being laughed at, and he dreaded his loss becoming known to anyone—the Macgreys in particular—and therefore he all but swore the family to silence. Moreover, Crump had gone about the world with his eyes open, and he wisely concluded that if his lost dinner was to be cooked in Littletown he should smell it out the sooner by allowing the marauder to become bold from a false feeling of security. So Captain Crump and Jabez prowled about Littletown with still tongues, but with most observant eyes and noses.

December the twenty-third, and John Bishopp was tucking himself up snugly in his chaise-cart before his own shop-door preparatory to starting for C——, where he had business. It was a fresh frosty morning, with a briskish wind blowing about the curls and cap border of Mrs. Bishopp, who stood in the doorway to see all right and to give her husband a few words of advice at parting.

"Now, don't you be late, John," said Mrs. Bishopp. "Recollect tomorrow's Christmas Eve, and there's more than I can do, mind that."

"All right, my dear," replied John Bishopp.

"Mind it is all right," said his wife; "and don't you get keeping Christmas before it comes. I haven't forgot——"

Nor had John, evidently, for, with a wink and smile, he drove off at once, not thinking it necessary to wait for any more of Mrs. Bishopp's reminiscences.

Before that good helpmate could make up her mind to go indoors and cease looking after her husband, the gipsy had approached her with his Christmas ware.

"Buy a little holly, ma'am?" said the man; "berries uncommon scarce this Christmas."

"No. Go along, my man," answered Mrs. Bishopp. "I have no money to spare for such nonsense."

"I'll sell it you cheap, missus," continued the man, "and a bunch of mistletoe as well, though I don't think you need wait for that to have your share of the kissing."

"What do you mean by that, you impudent fellow?" said Mrs. Bishopp; "a dirty tramp like you talking in that way to me! If I could see the police I'd give you in charge, I would," and the insulted lady retired into her citadel and closed her castle-gate with a bang.

The gipsy scratched his head as though surprised at the reception of his compliment, and then muttered to himself,

"I should like to take the starch out of you, my lady; and if I only knew how, I'd do it. Why, she bristled up like a hotchy-witchy!* She'd make a first-rate romany** for the fiery old sea-cock at the flag-post yonder." And then bawling, "Any holly? Buy any holly or mistletoe?" at last found a customer in Mrs. Macgrey, who always gave Christmas a welcome after the manner of her ancestors.

The gipsy made so good a bargain that, as the December day closed in, he was found, clean shaven and tidily dressed, seated in the taproom of the Fox Inn, not far from the old hovel he had visited the night before. He was well known in those parts as a tinker, hawker, and higgler, and was a welcome visitor at most of the publics, as he could sing a score of songs, play on a tin whistle, and do many hanky-panky tricks with cards, to the

* Hedgehog.
** Wife or companion.

wonder and amusement of the rustic frequenters of such places. He was a merry fellow always, and, though no one would have cared to stand bail for his honesty, none could prove him to have been dishonest. Ah! I know what you are about to say. What was he hiding in the old hovel? It is thought to be cant nowadays to say that such a man as the gipsy, was as honest, according to his lights, as many a well-to-do gentleman who never had the one-thousandth part of the temptations to go wrong that our poor Bohemian has had crossing his path since he was old enough to beg a penny by the roadside. Hunger, cold, hard words, and hard thoughts of him have invited him at times to evil; and now and then he had listened to the tempter and gone a mile or two on the broad way that leads to perdition. And the recording angel has had, haply, to write down many kindly actions of the gipsy's life and many a wrong resisted; so let us not sit in judgment upon him.

Still, you ask, and rightly, what did he hide in the old hovel?

Why, Captain Crump's Christmas turkey, to be sure, prompted thereto by an irresistible desire to revenge himself on the fiery old skipper. And there gipsy was at the Fox Inn, waiting until the young moon should have made her short journey in the heavens, to recover the hidden turkey and replace it in Captain Crump's stable before the morning. It was a foolish and dangerous jest, and might have stopped the gipsy's rambles for many a long month.

Two jolly-faced men in a chaise-cart are approaching the Fox Inn. Both speak somewhat thickly, and roll against each other now and then, or sway about with the motion of the cart. The driver is John Bishopp, and the other the host of the Fox Inn, whom John picked up in the morning on his way to C——. John had been repelling his friend's repeated invitation to alight when they should get to the Fox, and his resistance had been growing weaker and weaker ever since the bright windows of the inn had shown themselves, contrasting their ruddy glow with the cold grey of the winter's night. As John pulled up at the door, the last hearty chorus to one of the gipsy's songs came pealing from within, and drove away all the little good resolution remaining to the Littletown trader. The ostler was roused up, the horse led into an adjoining shed, and ordered "a bit of wet hay and a horsecloth," as Mr. Bishopp would stay only five minutes. When the ostler was again roused up from his sleep in the shed, beside the horse and the chaise-cart, he could have sworn he had been dozing an hour. John Bishopp and his friend, mine host of the Fox, were soon at their ease in the little bar-parlour, toasting each other a "Merry Christmas" in some steaming mixture, and listening to

The Tinker's Song

'Tis I am the tinker, Joe,
And where is there one like me,
If your saucepans are only so, so,
And your kettles won't boil for tea?
In my tent there is never a table,
Our furniture's rather queer,
But I eats of the best when I'm able,
Or puts up with bacon and beer!
Oh, there's nothing like tinkering!

I envy no king or churchwarden
As spouts at the parish boards,
And I'm sure I'd not give a farden

To sit in the House of Lords!
Though my tent has got many a flaw,
Where the wind when it likes may pass,
In the winter I sleep upon straw,
And in summer I sleeps on the grass.
Oh, there's nothing like tinkering!

The two cronies would have sat out the night had not the mistress of the inn stopped the supplies and sent out the gipsy to order Mr. Bishopp's horse. A quarter of an hour passed before the chaise came to the door, the ostler having been very hard to wake, at least so said the gipsy. The parting between John Bishopp and his crony was somewhat tedious and tautological, and the combined efforts of the ostler, the host, and the gipsy were required to place John comfortably in his chaise-cart. Once up, he was "all right," and as the horse had travelled the same road a hundred times before there was no doubt of a safe journey to John Bishopp.

Leaving the topers at the Fox to finish their orgy and go home as they list, we will stop at John Bishopp's shop, as the boy is putting up the shutters and the master has driven to the door. The "carp-pie" would be very hot and highly seasoned that night, for it was too evident to Mrs. Bishopp how her husband had been employing the later hours of the day. John contented himself by standing, or rather wobbling, at the head of the horse, and merely remarking, "Whoa!" at certain intervals, whilst Mrs. Bishopp, her assistant, and the maid unloaded the cart, placing the various packages on the counter.

"Now, Mr. Bishopp, let Tom take the horse to the stable, if you please; and if you are able to walk come into the shop, and don't let the neighbours see the state you're in. Now, Mr.

Bishopp." And the angry woman's voice might have been heard all over Littletown and miles out at sea.

John, with much "backing and filling," managed to make the doorway, and then, with great judgment, brought up alongside the counter, and made himself fast with his hands, whilst Mrs. Bishopp overhauled the cargo and required John to check it.

"Six pounds of black tea," said Mrs. Bishopp.

"Ri-i-ght," replied John.

"Twelve pounds of candles."

"Ri-i-ght, my dear."

"A gross of lucifers."

"Cor-rect, 'Lizabeth."

"Two sides of bacon."

"Streaky—ri-i-ght."

"Four Dutch cheeses."

"Four's the lot."

"And a turkey," said Mrs. Bishopp, adding, "whatever you bought that for I *don't* know."

Nor John either. "A tur-ur-key?" he asked, opening both his eyes until they seemed like the two lenses of an opera-glass. "I haven't bought a turkey, Mrs. B-ishopp."

"You don't know what you *have* bought, it strikes me," said the justly-angered wife. "Here's a turkey sure enough, and, as I live, it's got a wooden leg."

John tried to obtain a nearer view of the bird, but, lurching (to preserve our nautical metaphors) a good deal in the endeavour, put his larboard fin into the treacle-jar which had been left on the counter. Tom, the shop lad, and Susan, the maid, were quite justified in laughing aloud, although it made Mrs. Bishopp more angry.

John could not bring his confused mind to recognise this turkey. He tried to recall the day's proceedings, the persons he had met, and the subjects of his conversation, and he always stopped at the second glass "hot without sugar" in the little bar-parlour of the Fox Inn.

The mystery is soon explained. When the gipsy heard that Mr. Bishopp had arrived at the Fox, and was disposed to remain there, certain collections of Mrs. Bishopp's hard words came back to him, and the spirit of mischief whispered in his ear to send Captain Crump's turkey as a present to his enemy, nothing doubting but Fortune would manufacture some small tribulation out of it, and so revenge him for the morning's indignity.

It was with this intent that the gipsy had offered his services to call the ostler, but before arousing the sleeper the turkey was taken from the old hovel and deposited in John Bishopp's cart. Consequently the morning brought no clearer knowledge to John Bishopp as to his possession of the wooden-legged stranger, and he was half inclined to drive to the Fox and make some inquiries, but his own fear of ridicule and Mrs. Bishopp forbade it.

Mrs. Macgrey, we have seen, was an observer of old Christmas customs, and in the course of making her preparation for the next day, called at the multifarious establishment of John Bishopp, little thinking that she should there find hanging at the back of the shop one of the desires of her hospitable heart—a Christmas turkey.

"What a beauty! What a weight! What a rarity in Littletown! Was it very dear?"

Now, Mrs. Bishopp, as soon as she awoke that morning, had questioned John upon the purchase of the turkey, but, as I have said, he could remember nothing about it. John's money was right enough, except a shilling or so; still, he might have bought it on credit, and a demand for payment would certainly arrive from some quarter or the other. The careful tradeswoman, therefore, made sure of a market, and Mrs. Macgrey went home the happy possessor (as she believed) of the only turkey in Littletown.

For two days Crump Cottage had been anything but an Agapemone. Captain Crump kept his anger at his loss bottled up when abroad, but drew the cork the moment he arrived at home. Jabez generally received the first bumper of wrath, and the remainder was very fairly distributed between Mrs. Crump and the maid-servant. Not the least tidings had reached Crump of his lost dinner, and to-morrow was Christmas Day. So incensed and so incoherent was he at last, that he threatened to hang Jabez up as a stable lantern and put Mrs. Crump in a hen-coop. Jabez liked his place and liked his old master also, despite his fiery temper, and so he made no remonstrance, but walked down quietly to Littletown, determined to make some private inquiries. It so chanced that John Bishopp was the first person Jabez met, and, as John stood very high in his opinion, Jabez resolved to confide the secret to him. As he unbosomed himself John Bishopp changed red and purple (being the only colours he was capable of displaying), and, as he said to his wife, "felt as though one was pouring cold water down his back," which was not a pleasant sensation on a frosty December day. John wisely kept silent, however, as visions of the magistrate's bench and the county gaol presented themselves. He, John Bishopp, was, without doubt, a receiver of stolen goods, and how to account for the possession he knew not! So, promising Jabez not to mention what he had told him, except to his wife, and faithfully intending to keep his word, for his own sake, John Bishopp hurried home as fast as he could.

Mrs. Bishopp was somewhat startled at her husband's haggard appearance, but consoled herself with the hope that it was the proper consequence of his yesterday's irregularity. She was not left long in doubt; for John beckoned her into their little parlour and closed the door when she had entered.

"Elizabeth," said John, in a hoarse whisper, "where's that turkey?"

"Sold to Mrs. Macgrey, I'm thankful to say," replied the wife. John fairly reeled at the intelligence, and sat down flop in the old leather chair by the fire.

It was some time before he could repeat, in answer to his wife's inquiries, the story he had heard from Jabez, and its effect was nearly as terrible upon the wife as upon the husband.

"Oh, John, John, this comes of your love of drinking! Stolen? And from Captain Crump! Our good name's gone for ever": and Mrs. Bishopp, believing what she said, set up a tremendous bellowing. The sight of his wife's sorrow roused up John.

"No, my dear, not so bad as that. It's an awkward job, for certain, but our character's too good to be hurt by it. At worst it will only be a row with old Crump, should he ever hear the truth on't."

John Bishopp, why not have gone, like a man, and told the tale to Captain Crump, and not allowed him to learn the truth from his stable-door?

Yes, from his stable-door; for on opening it on December the 24th he found on the inside what follows, written in chalk:

> if you wants to no ware your turke is arsk missus bishup.

Captain Crump nearly committed apoplexy, so irate was he on reading the above, for it was now evident that someone had access to his stable whenever he pleased, and might, for aught that he knew to the contrary, pay nocturnal visits to his larder and wine-cellar. However, when he had cooled down a little, he determined to take the door's advice, and, as he did want to know where his turkey was, he would ask Mrs. Bishopp—and he did.

Mrs. Bishopp was only a woman, and an ignorant one into the bargain. She had therefore that disregard for the truth which usually distinguishes such persons when they are in a position of difficulty, and resolutely resolved to screen herself and her husband the moment she saw Captain Crump enter the shop, guessing his errand.

"Mrs. Bishopp," said Crump emphatically, and without pausing to sit down, "have you a turkey?"

"A turkey! Captain Crump?" replied Mrs. Bishopp, smiling. "La, bless you, sir, turkeys ain't for people in our state of life."

"No, I know that," said Crump; "but I've lost one that I've been rearing these ten months, and some —— has stolen it."

"Not me, I beg to say, Captain Crump," observed Mrs. Bishopp, with a toss of her head.

"I don't say you have," answered Crump; "but some one chalked on my stable-door, 'If you want to know where your turkey is, ask Mrs. Bishopp!' "

"And now you have done so, and got your answer, Captain Crump, perhaps you'll inquire elsewhere," said Mrs. Bishopp, affecting to be hurt and indignant; and, as Crump had no further evidence to offer, he was about to depart, when a servant-girl opened the door and said, without entering the shop:

"Did you know our turkey's got a wooden leg?"

Captain Crump had always been a man of action and decision, and he proved eminently so on the present occasion; for, before Mrs. Bishopp could utter a word in reply, Crump had fixed the maidservant's head between the shop-door and the post, and was furiously demanding who she was, where she came from, and whence she had got a turkey. The cries of the girl were the only answers to his inquiries; and, Mrs. Bishopp having succeeded in releasing the unfortunate domestic, the affrighted creature ran with all speed to her master's house, followed at a much diminished rate by Captain Crump.

Could he believe his eyes! Yes, she enters the house of the man he dislikes most in Littletown, if not in the universe. If that turkey is his turkey, what a Christmas dinner of revenge he will have! Thirty years—well, presently.

Captain Crump hastened home, and informed his wife of the discovery he had made, put on his best coat, and posted off, despite the earnest remonstrances of Mrs. Crump, to the police-office, and there obtained the assistance of the stolid young man who paraded the streets of Littletown as guardian of the peace.

Captain Crump knocked at Mr. Macgrey's with an emphasis that declared him to be master of the situation; and the consternation of the maid may be imagined when, on opening the door, she discovered her assailant of the morning, and instantly rushed into the back garden. Captain Crump and the officer did not stand for the ceremony of an introduction, but proceeded at once to the kitchen, and there, sure enough, was the abducted turkey, partly plucked of its feathers, but retaining still its wooden leg.

The stupid policeman, acting under the directions of the captain, seized the bird, and then entered the parlour where

Mr. and Mrs. Macgrey were seated, perfectly unconscious of their perilous position.

Captain Crump's lips quivered, and his ruby nose glowed like a hot coal, as he delivered himself as follows: "Officer, the turkey which you hold in your hands is my property. You know where you found it; and I give that man into custody as a thief or a receiver."

The effect of this speech may be imagined. Mr. Macgrey, ordinarily a peaceful man, was for knocking the speaker down with the poker; but his wife's better discretion interposed and she attempted to account for their possession of the turkey.

Captain Crump was obduracy itself. He would hear of no explanation from anyone, and kept iterating, each time with increasing energy, "Officer, do your duty!" And there is little doubt but that the stupid policeman would have dragged off Mr. Macgrey had not Mrs. Crump arrived at the scene of action, and, by a counter command, delayed that unpleasant operation.

Captain Crump was not the man to be mollified by uxorial intervention; and the stupid policeman stood like the traditional donkey between two bundles of hay, not knowing whom to obey. At last Mrs. Macgrey said, in her softest tones:

"William! William Crump!"

Crump started as though a voice from the spirit-world had spoken.

"William!" repeated Mrs. Macgrey, "is there to be no forgiveness between us? I know the cause of this violence, and am ashamed of you, William."

Mrs. Crump began to bridle a little at this.

"Thirty years ago, when we were almost boy and girl in this place, we thought we were in love with each other."

Mrs. Crump gave a short angry cough.

"In that time, when we walked hand-in-hand on yonder seashore, the moon and the sea the only witnesses to the loving words then spoken——"

Mrs. Crump said, "Well, I'm sure!" and Mr. Macgrey blew his nose pettishly.

"At that time, William, could we have believed that you would seek to bring sorrow and disgrace to me—me, your once loved Mary?"

The stupid policeman being ordered out of the room by general consent walked, from force of habit, straight to the kitchen.

"Answer me, William. Is all forgotten? Can you do this cruel thing?" said Mrs. Macgrey, laying her hand gracefully on Crump's shoulder.

Crump tried to reply, but found he had a great ball in his throat, and so he could only point at Mr. Macgrey and then at the fourth finger of his own left hand.

"True, I have married another; so have you," said Mrs. Macgrey.

"Well, I'm glad you've remembered that at last," said Mrs. Crump, fairly nettled. "I thought such a trifling circumstance had escaped your recollection."

"So did I," grunted Macgrey.

"Are you all angry with me?" asked the candid Mrs. Macgrey, quite theatrically. "Had I married him, Mrs. Crump, you would not have been the happy woman I know you to be—and deserve to be."

"Alexander," she paused until Mr. Macgrey raised his eyes from the carpet at which he had been intently gazing, "did I not give you the preference—if that was a gift worth having?"

"William, William Crump, I gave you the chance of marrying a worthier woman than myself. Take her to your heart and own I speak the truth."

Crump had nothing for it but to open his arms and press his lawful wife to his full-frilled bosom.

Alexander Macgrey accepted a similar invitation from his Mary, silently wishing, however, that this *confessio amoris* had not been necessary.

As a matter of course, the two ladies next embraced each other, and the two gentlemen, for the first time in their lives, shook hands, vowing a lifelong friendship; and it was arranged that the turkey, which had so nearly brought discord among them, should furnish forth their Christmas dinner. The story of the turkey oozed out by degrees, and the gipsy has not been seen in Littletown for some time, whilst John Bishopp is reported to have turned his fright to such good account that he has never been more than properly jolly ever since. The only ill consequence that has remained is, the opportunity afforded to a few of the worst boys in Littletown to tease Captain Crump by impertinent inquiries about his last Christmas dinner.

The Christmas Heretic

by J. Edgar Park

Our street, like your street, might have been considered humdrum and ordinary. The usual folks lived in the usual houses. We got up about the same time and went to work about the same time and went to bed about half past ten—or our neighbors knew the reason why.

But there is a fantastic world just a millionth of an inch below the surface of the regular world. The only thing you really know about life is—that you never can tell. A new personality may drop into the most ordinary street and disturb the even surface with strange impossibilities. That is what happened on our street.

We were all away the day the Joneses moved in. Have you ever heard of anyone's moving on Thanksgiving Day? We never had. When we got home from Grandfather's the next morning we were astonished to see burlap and excelsior around the doors of No. 17. The draperies were up in the parlor. They must have got settled very quickly.

As I passed on my way to work, the remover's man, who evidently had stayed after the vans had left and who looked as if he had been working all night, was gathering up the remains of a broken chair or two that lay at the gate. He was very angry and tired, and was communicating some of his wrath to our genial street cleaner, Tony, who was always on hand to make friends with everybody.

"I'll never move for him again!" he was saying as I passed. "Of all the bad-tempered cusses I ever met, he is the absolute limit, scolding and fussing all day. I never did hear such language, over a few broken chairs and crockery and such like!"

Just then a man, whom I afterward discovered to be Mr. Jones, came down the steps radiant with smiles and good humor, and placing a bill in the hands of the astonished man said, "That's for yourself! And a thousand thanks for all your care and work!" It was a strange sight, the disgruntled man just halted in his imprecations, gazing at a bill whose proportions evidently astounded him, and Mr. Jones with hearty hand outstretched to say good-by. Then the corner of the house hid them from my view, an incredible tableau.

Few people could win their way into the esteem of their neighbors as quickly as did Mr. Jones. He was the friend of every child on the street before he had been with us a week. Inside a month every boy in the vicinity had been allowed to work the wireless he had fitted up in his attic. His predecessor had been so bothered by children's riding their bicycles over his walks—for there was a lovely turn around the house—that he had put up a bit of barbed wire and a notice: "Children Keep Off. Police Take Notice." Mr. Jones took down the wire and taught one of our little girls how to ride round, coasting the last part of the way. He used the notice to fill up a cross drain so that the children could ride more smoothly. Our new neighbor proved to be an artist in the planning of the most satisfactory surprises. He always had an extra ticket for a ball game, an extra seat or two in his car when going for a ride.

Yet Mr. Jones was not to be explained simply as a kind-hearted man. There were complications. The remarks of the furniture remover lingered in my mind as an inexplicable mystery. And on Christmas Day I was reminded of that curious scene at his gate.

This newcomer had become such a favorite with us all that we vied with one another as to who should have the pleasure of entertaining him on Christmas Day. We found that he had had six invitations from our street alone. I will not conceal the fact that in three of these houses there were marriageable daughters—for Mr. Jones was a bachelor; but I think he would have been invited anyway. Each of us felt sure our new neighbor would come to us, for to each of us he had become so special and personal a friend that it had not struck us that he could seem so much a part of any other family as he did of ours. All the invitations he refused. We were surprised, and I confess the idea occurred to me that perhaps he was preparing some special surprise for the children on that day.

The children in our house were all up on Christmas morning at crack of dawn and rushed down at once to investigate the contents of their stockings. Mildred was overjoyed with her presents; but after going all over them twice she returned to her stocking again. Something troubled the child, I could see. Finding it really empty, she turned to her brother George and asked, "Did you get a present from Mr. Jones, George?" "No, that's funny, I didn't," he said. Somehow, Mr. Jones seemed to our children such a familiar friend that they had expected to be remembered by him. They had had great fun in preparing the little gifts they had dropped into his letter box, the evening before.

After the stocking presents had been admired and exhibited, it was still a long time till breakfast, and Mildred suggested they go out for a spin on their wheels, for it was sunny, snowless and mild. In ten minutes Mildred was back again, with indignant tears on her cheeks, and George scared and sobbing. They could hardly tell their story for emotion. They had been having a lovely time cycling about that beautiful turn around Mr. Jones's house. Mildred confessed that she had been going so fast that her wheel had gone off the asphalt walk onto the lawn; but she had often had the same experience before when Mr. Jones was teaching her.

This time, however, the window had opened and Mr. Jones had put his head out and had scolded them both terribly. How in the world, he said, could he keep a lawn looking like anything with all the kids in the street riding their wheels all over the grass. Give people an inch and they'll take an ell! If people cannot train their children to behave properly he wished they'd keep them at home! These were some of the remarks Mildred and George remembered and told us amid their sobs. I was incredulous till I looked out the window and saw Mr. Jones in his dressing gown, struggling with a tangle of barbed wire. He had put the notice back just where the Browns had had it, and was now fixing up the wire again. Some neighbors' boys, who went to his house for some fun with the wireless later, were, to their astonishment and indignation, thrown out, on the ground that they had dirtied the stair carpets with their muddy boots and had several times come in without permission at all.

The only explanation that we could find for Mr. Jones's behavior that evening at our Neighborhood Club Christmas Dance was that he must have been under the influence of liquor.

Miss Farquerson left early, in tears. When I was going away after a heated political discussion into which he had drawn me unawares, and in which he had told me just what he thought of our popular local representative, I heard his voice, loud and rasping, informing Mrs. Francis Nosegood, "You folks in this neighborhood live in a puddle and think it is the world!"

It seemed, that evening, as we all retired for the night, that in no home in the street could Mr. Jones ever be forgiven. And yet, as I have indicated, his charm and goodness of heart, which asserted themselves again next morning, were so genuine that, in my mind at least, the experience of Christmas Day, like the remarks of the furniture remover, sank into the background of my consciousness as an inexplicable mystery. Next morning he took the wire and the notice down again and he re-won the affection of Mildred and George by a series of remarkably adroit and flattering attentions and kindnesses.

Mrs. Francis Nosegood, however, did not seem able to forgive him. She was the lady who lived in the big house at the corner. She had decided opinions. We were all familiar with her simple philosophy of life. People were either good or bad. Most people were at heart bad. They pretended to be good and often were able to deceive others for a time. But, sooner or later, to a shrewd observer like Mrs. Nosegood, they gave themselves away. Mr. Jones had given himself away. It remained for Mrs. Nosegood to follow up the clue and prove that his remark about the mud puddle was no mere accidental observation but a clear symptom of deep-seated moral depravity. It became her duty to expose his hypocrisy.

She despised us all for allowing Mr. Jones to "bribe" us into liking him again by what she called his "puny charities." Having nothing to do, she was immediately hot upon the scent of his past. We saw her coming out of the real-estate office with a triumphant air; she had a confidential interview with the mail carrier; she happened to pass just as Mr. Jones's housekeeper was going out shopping, and walked down town with her. Soon she began to wear an air of secret and invincible power whenever she haughtily acknowledged his greeting.

Meanwhile, Mr. Jones, seemingly in quiet unconsciousness of his new enemy, continued to act the part of Providence in our street, kind to just and unjust, naughty and good alike, with a sort of omnipotent casualness. He visited and entertained us all till he was to each of us a personal friend.

In a month or so Mrs. Nosegood left for a short visit in Manchester, New Hampshire. It seems the real-estate man had told her he understood Mr. Jones had moved here from that city. Mr. Jones, however, heard of her destination without any apparent uneasiness. She was gone for the better part of a week and returned triumphant. The next evening she called on us immediately after dinner. Her suspicions had been confirmed. On the twenty-ninth of February she had made her great discovery,—that Mr. Jones had lived in the outskirts of Manchester with an old aunt who had brought him up since childhood. His violent bursts of temper had become notorious among the neighbors, and it was generally understood that relations between him and his wealthy old aunt were very unhappy at times, owing to these sudden fits of ungovernable rage. One day, the old aunt, who had been shopping all the afternoon, returned home in the best of health. According to his story, she was on her way upstairs when he heard her fall. Rushing up from the cellar where he was, he said, sorting apples, he found her lying in the hallway—dead. There was great indignation among the neighbors when this story became known; an inquiry was instituted and much testimony was heard; he was committed for trial, but in the end the jury disagreed and he was acquitted. Popular indignation, however, ran so high that he had to leave Manchester and, till Mrs. Nosegood's arrival, his whereabouts had been unknown. Mrs. Nosegood had talked on that day with many of the neighbors and had found that in Manchester Mr. Jones had evinced no special interest in children or neighbors. It was evident, she pointed out, that these traits were simply assumed here, as she had suspected all along, as a mere hypocritical screen.

The subject of her investigations happened to drop in before she left, and she took occasion to say to him in the most pointed manner, "I met some of your old acquaintances, Mr. Jones, in Manchester, these last few days."

"Well, well," he said, beaming on her in the most unconscious way in the world. "I didn't know I had any friends up there. Who were they, may I ask?"

"I met the Thompsons and the Blythes," she answered. As she afterward told us, these were the two nearest neighbors to the house where Mr. Jones had lived.

She spoke with such a meaning stare that he seemed disconcerted and passed it off with "Well, I hope they gave a good account of me, anyway!" Then he gaily changed the subject, and in a few moments Mrs. Nosegood, almost speechless with indignation, went away.

With incredible ingenuity Mrs. Nosegood now began to dig the pit beneath the unsuspecting feet of Mr. Jones. When Mr. Jones was absent her arguments were so cogent that we were almost convinced; but I confess all of them faded into thin air in the genial and kindly presence of that gentleman himself. All summer long Mrs. Nosegood sat in the window behind the curtain and watched the Jones house whenever Mr. Jones was at home. She went away for a well-earned vacation only after she had seen him off for his.

In the fall, a chemical laboratory in one of the upper rooms of the Jones house was added to the wireless equipment—as a further attraction to the boys of the neighborhood. Mr. Jones was a scientific expert of some kind in a large manufacturing concern and, according to the boys, was experimenting till late into the night with certain rare and deadly chemicals. This gave Mrs. Nosegood her next clue. It was now clear that the rich old aunt had been poisoned.

Thanksgiving Day came, the first anniversary of Mr. Jones's arrival. As usual, we went away the evening before to Grandfather's farm. When we returned the morning after Thanksgiving Day we heard of strange doings in our absence. It seemed that Mr. Jones had chosen that day in which to do his "spring cleaning." He had got two Polish girls to assist his housekeeper, and through the open windows could be heard the storming, growling voice of Mr. Jones, scolding and complaining at the poor women as they worked. This went on, the neighbors said, all day, till at six o'clock he let the girls go.

At the Thanksgiving reception at the Neighborhood Club, on the evening of Thanksgiving Day, he had insisted on relating to the whole company his troubles—the clumsy women, the way they had disarranged his books and instruments with bottomless stupidity. He vented his spleen on the whole company, complaining on the general incapacity of every one.

At this, Miss Farquerson, the pretty one from the house opposite, being a college girl and knowing her own mind, could stand it no longer, and told him just what she thought of him. The girl's genuine wrath became her very well. He stopped and looked at her fixedly for a moment, and then said, "Bah! The more I see of people the more thankful I am that my special investigation at this time is the various uses of arsenic!"

At this word, they told us, Mrs. Nosegood looked around triumphantly. Within a week she was back in Manchester, New

Hampshire. She told the Thompsons and the Blythes of her further evidence. They put their heads together, and with the consent of the new tenant of the Jones house they made a thorough investigation of the house from cellar to attic. There were no results; but the apple closet in the cellar was locked and the key in the pocket of the owner, who happened to be away from home. The Blythes promised to investigate that closet as soon as he returned. Mrs. Nosegood came back to her armchair at the window, from which she kept track of every movement of Mr. Jones. He was friendly with every household on the street except her own and Miss Farquerson's, whom he apparently had never forgiven for her frank speech on Thanksgiving Day. Mrs. Nosegood rejoiced in this and missed no opportunity to bestow favors on that young lady, especially in the presence of Mr. Jones.

Christmas Day came again. Christmas trees or Christmas turkeys came to every door on the street except that of Mr. Jones. Early in the morning of Christmas Day he apparently came down and closed his dog outside his door and let him howl horribly there the rest of the hours of darkness, keeping all his neighbors awake. He made his housekeeper wash after breakfast and hung the entire wash out with his own hands, not, as usually, in the screened place behind the house, but on a rope tied between two trees on the front lawn. He then brought out his ash barrels, which the city teams were to call for next day, and put them in a row—he must have been saving them for the purpose for weeks—on the sidewalk in front of his house. Thus he effectively spoiled the looks of the street and gave a black eye to the whole neighborhood. He then resurrected from somewhere a horrible gramophone and, placing it at an open window, ground out on it over and over again the cheapest and most exasperating records he could find. At dinner hour he came out of the house, kicked the dog into howling again, and, making deep-track short cuts over all our lawns and flower beds, disappeared for a walk—thus giving Mrs. Nosegood a chance to go down from her watchtower for her dinner.

The usual Christmas Festival was held at our little Neighborhood Club that evening. We were all with Mrs. Nosegood now, heartily angry with Mr. Jones; we avoided him when he arrived. Mrs. Nosegood came in late and, beckoning to me, told me in tremendous excitement that she had just had a telegram from Manchester, New Hampshire, absolutely establishing Mr. Jones's guilt. He had poisoned his wealthy aunt with arsenic. She had a telegram from the Blythes saying that they had just discovered, under a barrel of rotten apples in the cellar closet, four papers full of a white powder and labeled "Arsenic."

Around the supper table we usually had speeches and toasts of a friendly and amusing nature. The laughter after one of these had died down when I discovered, to my astonishment, Mr. Jones upon his feet. He was about to make a speech. Mrs. Nosegood clutched at her telegram and looked at him with triumphant disdain.

"Friends," he began, "this is a great day in my life, and I am going to ask you to permit me to tell you a little about myself, if it will not bore you." There being no particular dissent, if no great enthusiasm, Mr. Jones continued: "It may surprise you to know that I lived, before arriving here, in Manchester, New Hampshire."

At this, Mrs. Nosegood, unable to contain herself any longer, leapt to her feet and with blazing eye cried out: "Mr. Jones, it may surprise you to know that we know a great deal more about you than you think. I have here in my hand a telegram establishing your guilt. Mr. Jones, your aunt did not die as a result of falling downstairs. She died as a result of arsenic poisoning and you were the murderer." With this she handed the telegram to Mr. Jones.

He read it twice and laid it down, with calmness, at his plate. "I have been guilty, very guilty in this matter, I confess," he said, "but to-night I am going to make a full confession to you all."

The old spell of his friendly courtesy seemed to be weaving itself around us once more. Mrs. Nosegood appealed to Miss Farquerson that he be not heard. But Miss Farquerson quietly answered, "I think it only fair to hear his side of the case, if he has one."

Mr. Jones, with simplicity, continued: "It evidently does not surprise you to know that before I came here I lived in Manchester, New Hampshire. The people among whom I lived were ordinary people; that is to say, they acted as if it were natural to be selfish, and as if there must be a special reason or a special occasion for any act of public spirit or good will. So, while living all the year as selfish lookers-after-themselves, they were terrible sentimentalists about Christmas and Thanksgiving. On these days they dabbled in a little amateurish way at those concerns which ought to have been the main business of their lives—true friendliness and neighborliness.

"After a while I found two homes in Manchester where there were friends who agreed with my point of view, and in the process of time we came to live in three houses next one another—the Thompsons, the Blythes, and I. We formed a club founded upon our principles, and I should like to read you the constitution of that club." He took up a small piece of paper and read:

Principles of the Three Hundred and Sixty-Three Club

1. Every one ought to be generous and thankful every day in the year.

2. Nobody can be generous and thankful every day in the year.
3. Therefore, be it enacted, that we, the members of this club, do observe as solemn festivals two days in every year, (a) The National Day of Grumbling and Growling, and (b) Devilmas Day. Into the first of these we shall try to concentrate all the necessary grumbling and growling which has to be indulged in by any decent man who is human. On it we shall try to locate those tasks (like moving or house cleaning) which cannot be accomplished by any one not a hypocrite, without tension, strain, and profanity. And on Devilmas Day we shall try to work off all the year's accumulated meanness which, even in the best of lives, must accumulate, and even by the best of men must somehow be worked off, if insanity is to be dodged. The rest of the three hundred and sixty-three days of the year we shall observe as Thanksgiving and Christmas Days.

"We lived for some years to our own great satisfaction and, I fear, to the utter mystification of our neighbors, in obedience to these principles. Then business changes made it necessary for me to move away.

"Last year I observed Devilmas Day, as you may remember, on the 25th of December by working off some of my accumulated irritation at the rudeness and carelessness of some of your children. This, together with my extremely irritated remark to Mrs. Nosegood, made me sure that a woman of her type would try to prove, from my past, her theory about me.

"My last action last Devilmas Day was to write to my friends, the Thompsons and Blythes, in Manchester, to tell them that an old woman named Nosegood would be there soon to look up my record. I told them to tell her I was suspected of killing my aunt. My aunt really never existed. I should not be so queer, perhaps, if I were not an only child of two only children.

"This telegram which I hold shows me that my friends in Manchester, true to their vows, are celebrating Devilmas Day in their own jovial fashion. My friends, I call you to witness that my celebration of these festivals has been just a concentration at my house of things that do happen elsewhere in our street all through the year."

We hung our heads, as one of us was guilty of premature ash barrels, one of an occasional public wash, and another of the nocturnal howling dog.

"My friends," he continued, "I was wrong. I am here to confess it heartily and to ask your pardon. Once a man ceases being a mere observer and becomes really entangled in life, he needs far more of an outlet for growling and devilment than I had supposed. I hereby renounce my previous plan and return with the rest of you to the method of trying to be as nice as possible two days in the year."

Turning to Mrs. Nosegood he continued: "It may astonish you to learn that right here under your eyes and without your knowledge has taken place one of the most thrilling of modern dramas. A would-be onlooker in your street has been entangled in life by love; or, to put the matter in a more conventional way, Miss Farquerson and I have the honor to announce—"

When, after a few moments, Doctor Brown returned to the table and said that Mrs. Nosegood had recovered so far that he thought it was all right to send her home in the station hack, Mr. Jones came round and took the place she had so suddenly vacated beside Miss Farquerson.

Innocents' Day

by F. M. Mayor

THE ALARUM WOKE MISS PERRIN at half-past six. It was Christmas Day, and she was going to early service. She opened her window, peered into the darkness, heard the rain dripping, and went sadly back to bed. She could not go out in the wet, she must think of her health, not because it was precious to someone, but because she was poor, and nearly sixty, and knew by experience nothing is more expensive than bronchitis.

At 8 o'clock dawn broke, and dull light struggled through the window of her bed sitting-room at the Residential Hostel for Professional Women. Hers was a small, high room, looking out into a deep well, surrounded by black red brick walls. The light always had a struggle there. To-day the struggle was too much for it, and it died. She turned on the electric light in the ceiling. Darkness and black walls were nothing to the electric light. It leapt forth at once, and exposed the ugliness of the room. Nothing was old, and all was soiled and shabby save Miss Perrin's shelf of favourite books, her Wordsworth, Browning, Ruskin and Carlyle.

She went downstairs to hostel breakfast. On her way they told her she was wanted on the telephone.

"Is that you, Perks?" came a jolly voice. "It's too bad to bother you so early. Happy Christmas, and many of them, at least not many like this. What a day! I'm so dreadfully sorry, but George and Billy have gone and got mumps, bless their hearts, so all our Christmas do's are off. Isn't it too bad? Yes, I'll let you know how we go on, and you must come the minute we're out of quarantine."

She was very, very much disappointed. She was a teacher by profession, and felt herself still capable of work, though head mistresses knew she was too old. She had lately come to live forlornly in London. She had been invited to spend Christmas with a favourite former pupil, the joyous mother of five boys. She had counted the days to sharing Christmas with children, to looking on at merriment.

"Might I speak to you, Miss Dart?" said she to the secretary with the Eton crop.

"Oh, happy Christmas, Miss Perrin," said Miss Dart officially.

"I only wanted to tell you," she said apologetically, "that I shall be in to dinner and supper."

"Oh, really, I wish you could have let me know beforehand. Didn't you see the notice? It makes it so much easier for the staff; of course they all want to get off for Christmas. I'm afraid it's absolutely nothing but cold to-night."

"I'm very sorry," said Miss Perrin. "They've just started mumps, so they've had to put me off at a moment's notice."

"Dear, yes, how unfortunate. Did you want me, Miss Hardy?"

Miss Dart liked active residents under forty, doing work that showed in the world; social, political, journalistic. "One wants to eliminate the decayed governess type," said she.

It was now ten o'clock, and the day decided it would turn into night. There was no fog, but the sky was dark brown, and black rain was dripping down the gutter. She must give up morning church too. She sat in her bedroom by the grate, and tried to think the central heating was a fire. She read the Christmas service. "His name shall be called Wonderful, Counsellor, the mighty God, the Everlasting Father, the Prince of Peace." She felt a tear roll down her cheek. Was she really so foolish as to cry because she was missing the Christmas tree?

"In the Beginning was the Word, and the Word was with God, and the Word was God." Her thoughts turned to Christmas long ago. They were all so excited with the stockings, they could not walk to church, they must skip. She was holding her father's hand, and made him run too. On their way they almost quarrelled over their favourite hymns, "While Shepherds watched," "Christians awake." Gilbert was there; he did not mean much to her now, he was a prosperous business man in Liverpool. And Edith, she did not get on very well with Edith, she disliked her husband. And Lancy—he was dead.

"And there went forth a decree from Cæsar Augustus that all the world should be taxed." Once she could not hear those words without tears, because they began what seemed then the most touching story ever written. Now she shed tears, because they moved her no more. She put her Bible and Prayer Book away and took out Wordsworth. She read *Tintern Abbey.* But she could no longer respond to the poet's serenity; her mind was numb, she felt with a pang that this was growing old.

There was a knock, and a smart, much made-up girl, whom the hostel called Pam, walked into the room. Her low-necked, sleeveless, orange frock came well above her knees.

"Hullo," cried she, "I see you've cut saying prayers in church. You'll go to Hell, won't you, and *how* lucky you'll be—the one thing to-day is to frizzle. The furnace being out of order, as ever, I've got the shudders."

"Of course you're shivering, if you wear a dress like that in mid winter," replied Miss Perrin.

"I thought you must rise at that. I hoped Hell would do it, but you don't rise as you did. Now I've told you many times that the *more* you wear the colder you are. It's been scientifically proved. I say," breaking off erratically, "what freaks you read—Bible, Prayer Book, Wordsworth. How deadly, and I want cheering. Picture it: I'm going to a family party where we shall prance round a Christmas tree with small kids, and sing 'Once in royal David's City.' Why, because someone chose to be born in a manger should we have to go on singing about it nineteen hundred years afterwards?"

"Does Christmas mean nothing at all to you then?"

"Oh, much worse than nothing," she replied gaily. "I have a religious complex. Carols depress me to the depths, and wherever you go you hear carols. Apparently they depress you, for you don't seem very gay either, my fair one." She said this kindly.

"You'll think me very absurd," said Miss Perrin, "but I'm disappointed because I'm *not* going to prance round a Christmas tree with small kids."

"Yes, you see you've got to second childhood, and I daresay

that is really the best time of life. Now I've got something to buck you up." She unwrapped a very décolleté doll, dressed as a ballet girl. "She was the most depraved doll I could find. It's so good for you to be shocked." She tickled Miss Perrin under the chin. "No, but I have got something *really* bucking. Here's your mail. Eight, you lucky beggar; I've only got four."

As a conscientious schoolmistress and good churchwoman, Miss Perrin shivered at such talk, but misery makes strange bedfellows. Pam was her crumb of comfort in the hostel. Though much sought after, she alone found time to come and be pleasant to one so mossy.

Miss Perrin opened her envelopes. They contained remembrances from steady old friends, who had been sending the same robins and kittens for thirty years. But there was one letter in a large, decided hand, which made her heart leap; she kept it to the last.

> 29 Felix Street, S.W.
> "My dear old Ethel,
>
> "You know, I hope, that Wednesday is Innocent's Day. Do you remember more than fifty years ago my father used to say, 'It's Innocents' Day, let's ask the little Perrins and Fanny Fleet to come to tea'? I'm afraid Edith is too far to get at, but I'm asking dear Fanny, she's living in London now, and as you've been so delightful as to settle fairly near us, you must come too. Four o'clock sharp. If you can get 'bus 22, and make it stop at the dullest road you see, that will be Felix Street, which is ours, and we're half-way down.

"I know I'm a pig to write so seldom, but I really scarcely get a moment, and I don't change, but am as always your faithful and affectionate

"NELL."

Ethel and Edith Perrin, the doctor's daughters, Fanny Fleet, the vicar's daughter, Rosa and Eleanor Danvers, the squire's daughters, had all been children together at Lawton. Ethel had been fond of Fanny and Rosa, but Eleanor she had adored and, though life had parted them for years, she adored her still. As she walked down Felix Street next Wednesday, she overtook a stout heavy woman, trudging along with difficulty.

"Fanny," she cried.

"Is that you, Ethel?" said Fanny, now the widow, Mrs. Bentley, "Nell told me she was asking you. I hobble along very slowly, I'm so rheumatic, also stout. I wonder you recognized me. You're lucky to have gone thin. Well, it's very nice to be meeting you again after all these years."

"I've often wondered about you. It was no good writing, for you never answered my letters."

"You don't get much time in the Bush. Now the children are all dispersed, I've come back to lay my bones in England. Have you seen Rosa and Nell?"

"Not for seventeen years, I think. I was in a remote school in Ireland, and I never came back to England all that time."

"Then I'd better warn you. Rosa's speech is affected, she had a queer sort of attack, and her mind too a little. I suppose you knew Colonel Danvers speculated, and he had to sell Lawton, and lost almost all their money as well as his own, so they're just in lodgings. You remember Eric, the youngest brother? He lived close to us in New South Wales."

They were shown into a dull lodging-house parlour. The picture above the mantelpiece, one of the few relics from Lawton, shone out from its meanness. It was a portrait of the two Danvers at seventeen and twenty in the 'eighties. The sisters stood arm-in-arm smiling sweetly at life. Their smile was so disarming it seemed as if life must be kind to them. But it was pitiless, and struck them hard.

They had large fringes coming down over their large blue eyes, soft hats with feathers, worn at the back of the head, blue velvet frocks to match their eyes, with ruffles and gold lockets, little bustles and tapered waists. Miss Perrin well remembered the pretty frocks and the delight at the new gold lockets. As she took her thoughts back, one of the sitters came into the room.

"You two darling people," cried Nell kissing them. "How wonderful it is to get you both together again."

Her dark hair had turned grey, her blue eyes were faded, her cheek had paled; she looked as if a lifetime of rest would not sweep away her wanness. Miss Perrin could have wept to see such a ruin of her loveliness, but for her Nell still had the fascination which had brought her to subjection fifty years ago.

"Fancy our not being on the doorstep to bring you up," said Nell. "But Rosa slept so badly; she was excited at the thought of the party. Will you come to her now? She is longing to see you. She's rather difficult to understand, but she loves to talk."

The fire flickered brightly in the bedroom, and candles threw interesting shadows on the walls. By this light the visitors saw the poor invalid on the bed, her face a little twisted, and every attraction gone.

"Here they are, dear one," said Nell, "and this is nurse, or

Nanna as we call her; Mrs. Bentley, Miss Perrin. Now, Rosa, you and Nanna must entertain the guests, while Mrs. Bone and I get tea."

Nanna and the landlady were under the same spell as Miss Perrin. Nell had exactly the right shade of manner for each; just as she used to have for the retinue at Lawton. The tea was charming; there were crackers, and an iced cake. It had "A Happy Christmas to Fanny, Ethel, Rosa, Nell and Nanna" in pink letters with silver stars and fairies.

"I made that," said Miss Danvers, "so please like it." She interpreted Rosa's uncouth murmurings, and when they were incomprehensible, she laughed cheerfully, and made the invalid laugh too.

When tea was over and cleared away, they blew out the lights, and sat in the red firelight. Miss Danvers went out and came back with a miniature Christmas tree, hung with little candles and the bright balls and tinsel they had all loved in childhood. On the tree there were five tiny dolls.

"There's a settler with a kangaroo for Fanny," said Nell, "and a don in a cap and gown with books for Ethel, and a lady dressed for a drawing-room for Rosa, because we always have to read her the Court Intelligence first thing, Mrs. Gamp for Nanna, for obvious reasons, and that's me in a riding habit, because I always was mad on hunting, and I'm quite as mad still, when I get the chance."

The dolls were made with exquisite finish.

"I suppose they're all the work of your ten fingers, Nell," said Fanny Bentley. "You always were such a needlewoman."

"Yes, I was a clever creature, and it comes in handy here. Now let's have a carol to end up with, or it won't be really Christmas."

The thin elderly voices, singing harshly, huskily and sweetly, touched young, happy Nanna. "It was perfectly pathetic to hear the old dears," she wrote to the man she was marrying next year.

When the carol was finished, the singers did not speak for some moments. Each was thinking: Ethel of the child she once was, long, long lost and gone; Nell of the children she had so much desired and never had; Fanny of the children who had been her all, now well content without her.

"After all this excitement you must rest, Rosa," said Nell, "I'll take these two into the parlour."

They sat round the fire; she leant back wearily in her chair, as if it was a relief to rest from the burden of gaiety.

Sometimes in the jog-trot of life comes a week, a day, an afternoon, lit up with some special sweetness, which sets it apart, and makes it treasured in the memory. The humble Christmas tree would be such a remembrance to Miss Perrin.

"You don't know what a treat you've given me," she said to Miss Danvers. "I wept because I thought I wasn't going to have a tree."

"I'm so glad you liked it. Nanna and I are babies, and love Christmas trees, and I wanted Rosa particularly to have one this year, for it may be the last she can enjoy. She'll gradually get worse, and lately it seems to me the progress has been quicker. Poor Rosa," she whispered to herself.

"What dreadful changes you've had," said Fanny, "and it was all so prosperous when I went to Australia. I thought you were going to be a marchioness."

"I used to think of marriage, but I aimed too high. I don't mean I was waiting for a prince of the blood, but I thought you mustn't marry unless you were carried off your feet by an overwhelming passion, and I never was. I daresay it wasn't in me, and I believe I might have married very happily just on good, respectable love."

"Mine was the other way," said Fanny. "I thought something short of love would do, I wanted badly to get away from home just then, but it didn't work."

"But you had the children," said Nell.

"Yes, and they were wonderful years, but they're very short, they don't last."

"But don't you think the children come back?" said Nell taking Fanny's hand. "I believe they will, and you've had them. What would some of us have given to have had them?"

"Thank you, I must just go on and hope," said Mrs. Bentley. "Now tell me about Rosa. I thought she was going to marry Major Finch."

"Yes, but things went wrong; he didn't behave well. But sometimes I wonder, if she was to be ill like this, whether it was better she didn't marry. A husband would have loved her as much, but he would have found this illness very frazzling; men do. Now little Ethel," turning to Miss Perrin, as if she were still the little girl of seven, while Nell and Fanny were nine and ten. "We've been telling the secrets of our lives, and you sit by silent and think the more."

"I always liked listening to you and Fanny," said Miss Perrin.

"But what happened to you? You were going to be Head of Newnham."

"Yes, everything seemed possible at eighteen. I don't think anything happened to me. But I know I've regretted I spent so much time on study. Perhaps I've been unlucky, but being intellectual cuts you off; people don't want it. I used to think books could take the place of home and love, but they can't; you can suck books very dry."

"Still I'm grateful to books," said Nell. "*The Woman in White* has brought me through sometimes, when things seemed getting rather much."

"Oh, the dear old *Woman in White,*" said Fanny. "Do you remember your mother reading it to us on Saturday afternoons?"

They laughed over the recollection. Then Miss Danvers said almost solemnly:

"Life's been very different for all of us from what we expected."

"It's been very hard for all of us," said Mrs. Bentley, sighing heavily, "particularly for Rosa."

"And as one gets older, it seems to get harder still," said Miss Perrin. " 'The best is yet to be' is quite untrue."

"But dear Fanny and Ethel," said Nell. "This is Christmas time, I won't let you be so sad." She spoke playfully, but with earnestness.

"But does Christmas really mean anything to you still?" said Miss Perrin. "When one was a child of course——"

Miss Danvers had always talked without reserve. The country doctor's daughter, living in a less outspoken circle, sometimes wondered at her. But of one thing the squire's daughter never spoke, her own religious beliefs.

At first she did not answer, and when she did speak, she turned her head away, and the words came out with difficulty.

"When you're a child, you love it all, but it's quite unreal, because you know nothing. Now I'm old, it means much, much more, because I've been through more, and feel more."

"How do you mean exactly?"

"I can't explain. But isn't there a poem 'Love came down at Christmas'? only I like to think it's 'comes' not 'came.' "

"Say some more, Nell, you don't know how hungry I am."

"My dear child, I would in an instant if I could, but I *can't.* I have endless thoughts, but I have no words, you know I never have. Besides there aren't any, except the carol we used to sing at Lawton." She sang with a strong Gloucestershire accent:

" 'The King of all Kings to this world being brought,
Small store of fine linen to wrap Him was sought.
But when she had swaddled her young Son so sweet,
Within an ox manger she laid Him to sleep' "

"That was my favourite verse. Can't you hear Ben Mathers? He was always so *concerned* at the small store of fine linen." She would say no more. Ethel felt herself gently silenced. She was reminded of their childhood, when she had sometimes been put in her place by the quelling dignity of the little beauty.

The door opened, and Nanna looked in. "Miss Danvers, could you come, please?"

"All right, Nanna. I'm so sorry, dears, she sometimes gets a little difficult, and then it's better for Nanna to have someone. It's done me so much good, being all four together again. Do come often and cheer us up. Will you let yourselves out? Mind that nasty turn on the stairs." She gave a hand to each and kissed them.

The two friends walked along the shining road. It had stopped raining, and the long streams of light reflected from the small shop windows made the dull little street bright and homely.

"What pluck Nell has," said Fanny. "It makes one ashamed of one's grousing."

"Yes," said Ethel, "and didn't you love what she said about Christmas? I had come to think it was only fun for children. But I see just to be jolly children again is only a small part of it."

"Yes, but the children's fun is very sweet," said Fanny uncomprehending.

"I know, but I wonder if sometimes people aren't so loaded with presents and fun, and warm with love, that there is no room for Him in the fun. What Nell said makes me feel He comes especially to those who are in trouble, and perhaps to people like me too, who are not in trouble, but just stupid and lonely. So that at Christmas He setteth the solitary in families."

"I always liked to hear you holding forth," said Mrs. Bentley, "though you were slow in getting under way," and then with motherly encouragement: "I think what you say is very nice. But," breaking off, "there's your 22 over there: you must run, child, if you want to catch it."

Merry Christmas

by Stephen Leacock

"My dear young friend," said Father Time, as he laid his hand gently upon my shoulder, "you are entirely wrong."

Then I looked up over my shoulder from the table at which I was sitting and I saw him.

But I had known, or felt, for at least the last half hour that he was standing somewhere near me.

You have had, I do not doubt, good reader, more than once that strange uncanny feeling that there is some one unseen standing beside you—in a darkened room, let us say, with a dying fire, when the night has grown late, and the October wind sounds low outside, and when, through the thin curtain that we call Reality, the Unseen World starts for a moment clear upon our dreaming sense.

You *have* had it? Yes, I know you have. Never mind telling me about it. Stop. I don't want to hear about that strange presentiment you had the night your Aunt Eliza broke her leg. Don't let's bother with *your* experience. I want to tell mine.

"You are quite mistaken, my dear young friend," repeated Father Time, "quite wrong."

"*Young* friend?" I said, my mind, as one's mind is apt to in such a case, running to an unimportant detail. "Why do you call me young?"

"Your pardon," he answered gently—he had a gentle way with him, had Father Time, "the fault is in my failing eyes. I took you at first sight for something under a hundred."

"Under a hundred?" I expostulated. "Well, I should think so!"

"Your pardon again," said Time, "the fault is in my failing memory. I forgot. You seldom pass that now-a-days, do you? Your life is very short of late."

I heard him breathe a wistful hollow sigh. Very ancient and dim he seemed as he stood beside me. But I did not turn to look upon him. I had no need to. I knew his form, in the inner and clearer sight of things, as well as every human being knows by innate instinct the Unseen face and form of Father Time.

I could hear him murmuring beside me—"Short—short, your life is short"—till the sound of it seemed to mingle with the measured ticking of a clock somewhere in the silent house.

Then I remembered what he had said.

"How do you know that I am wrong?" I asked. "And how can you tell what I was thinking?"

"You said it out loud," answered Father Time; "but it wouldn't have mattered, anyway. You said that Christmas was all played out and done with."

"Yes," I admitted, "that's what I said."

"And what makes you think that?" he questioned, stooping, so it seemed to me, still further over my shoulder.

"Why," I answered, "the trouble is this. I've been sitting here for hours, sitting till goodness only knows how far into the night, trying to think out something to write for a Christmas story. And it won't go. It can't be done—not in these awful days."

"A Christmas Story?"

"Yes. You see, Father Time," I explained, glad with a foolish little vanity of my trade to be able to tell him something that I thought enlightening, "all the Christmas stuff—stories and jokes and pictures—is all done, you know, in October."

I thought it would have surprised him, but I was mistaken.

"Dear me!" he said, "not till October! What a rush! How well I remember in Ancient Egypt—as I think you call it—seeing them getting out their Christmas things, all cut in hieroglyphics, always two or three years ahead."

"Two or three years!" I exclaimed.

"Pooh," said Time, "that was nothing. Why in Babylon they used to get their Christmas jokes ready—all baked in clay—a whole Solar eclipse ahead of Christmas. They said, I think, that the public preferred them so."

"Egypt?" I said, "Babylon! But surely, Father Time, there was no Christmas in those days. I thought——"

"My dear boy," he interrupted gravely, "don't you know that there has always been Christmas?"

I was silent. Father Time had moved across the room and stood beside the fireplace, leaning on the mantel. The little wreaths of smoke from the fading fire seemed to mingle with his shadowy outline.

"Well," he said presently, "what is it that is wrong with Christmas?"

"Why," I answered, "all the romance, the joy, the beauty of it has gone, crushed and killed by the greed of commerce and the horrors of war. I am not, as you thought I was, a hundred years old, but I can conjure up, as anybody can, a picture of Christmas in the good old days of a hundred years ago—the quaint old-fashioned houses, standing deep among the evergreens, with the light twinkling from the windows on the snow—the warmth and comfort within—the great fire roaring on the hearth—the merry guests grouped about its blaze and the little children with their eyes dancing in the Christmas firelight, waiting for Father Christmas in his fine mummery of red and white and cotton wool to hand the presents from the Yule-tide tree. I can see it," I added, "as if it were yesterday."

"It was but yesterday," said Father Time, and his voice seemed to soften with the memory of by-gone years. "I remember it well."

"Ah," I continued, "that was Christmas indeed. Give me back such days as those, with the old good cheer, the old stage coaches and the gabled inns and the warm red wine, the snapdragon and the Christmas tree, and I'll believe again in Christmas, yes, in Father Christmas himself."

"Believe in him?" said Time, quietly, "you may well do that. He happens to be standing outside in the street at this moment."

"Outside?" I exclaimed. "Why won't he come in?"

"He's afraid to," said Father Time. "He's frightened and he daren't come in unless you ask him. May I call him in?"

I signified assent, and Father Time went to the window for a moment and beckoned into the darkened street. Then I heard footsteps, clumsy and hesitant they seemed, upon the stairway. And in a moment a figure stood framed in the doorway—the figure of Father Christmas. He stood shuffling his feet, a timid, apologetic look upon his face.

How changed he was!

I had known in my mind's eye, from childhood up, the face and form of Father Christmas as well as that of Old Time himself. Everybody knows, or once knew him,—a jolly little rounded man, with a great muffler wound about him, a packet of toys upon his back and with such merry, twinkling eyes and rosy cheeks as are only given by the touch of the driving snow and the rude fun of the North Wind. Why, there was once a time, not yet so long ago, when the very sound of his sleigh-bells sent the blood running warm to the heart.

But now how changed.

All draggled with the mud and rain he stood, as if no house had sheltered him these three years past. His old red jersey was tattered in a dozen places, his muffler frayed and ravelled.

The bundle of toys that he dragged with him in a net seemed wet and worn till the card-board boxes gaped asunder. There were boxes among them, I vow, that he must have been carrying these three years past.

But most of all I noted the change that had come over the face of Father Christmas. The old brave look of cheery confidence was gone. The smile that had beamed responsive to the laughing eyes of countless children around unnumbered Christmas trees was there no more. And in the place of it there showed a look of timid apology, of apprehensiveness, as of one who has asked in vain the warmth and shelter of a human home—such a look as the harsh cruelty of this world has stamped upon the races of its outcasts.

So stood Father Christmas shuffling upon the threshold, fumbling his poor tattered hat in his hand.

"Shall I come in?" he said, his eyes appealingly on Father Time.

"Come," said Time; and added, as he turned to speak to me, "Your room is dark. Turn up the lights. He's used to light, bright light and plenty of it. The dark has frightened him these three years past."

I turned up the lights and the bright glare revealed all the more cruelly the tattered figure before us.

Father Christmas advanced a timid step across the floor. Then he paused, as if in sudden fear.

"Is this floor mined?" he said.

"No, no," said Time soothingly. And to me he added in a murmured whisper—"He's afraid. He was blown up in a mine in No Man's Land between the trenches at Christmas time in 1914. It broke his nerve."

"May I put my toys on that machine gun?" asked Father Christmas timidly, "it will help to keep them dry."

"It is not a machine gun," said Time gently; see, it is only a pile of books upon the sofa." And to me he whispered: "They turned a machine gun on him in the streets of Warsaw. He thinks he sees them everywhere since then."

"It's all right, Father Christmas," I said, speaking as cheerily as I could, while I rose and stirred the fire into a blaze, "there are no machine guns here and there are no mines. This is but the house of a poor writer."

"Ah," said Father Christmas, lowering his tattered hat still further and attempting something of a humble bow, "a writer? Are you Hans Andersen, perhaps?"

"Not quite," I answered.

"But a great writer, I do not doubt," said the old man, with a humble courtesy that he had learned, it well may be, centuries ago in the Yule Tide season of his northern home. "The world owes much to its great books. I carry some of the greatest with me always. I have them here."

He began fumbling among the limp and tattered packages that he carried—"Look! *The House that Jack Built*—a marvellous, deep thing, sir—and this, *The Babes in the Wood*. Will you take it, sir? A poor present, but a present still—not so long ago I gave them in thousands every Christmas time. None seem to want them now."

He looked appealingly towards Father Time, as the weak may look towards the strong, for help and guidance.

"None want them now," he repeated, and I could see the tears start in his eyes. "Why is it so? Has the world forgotten its sympathy with the lost children wandering in the wood?"

"All the world," I heard Time murmur with a sigh, "is wandering in the wood."—But out loud he spoke to Father Christmas in cheery admonition—"Tut, tut, good Christmas," he said, "you must cheer up. Here, sit in this chair—the biggest one—so—beside the fire—let us stir it to a blaze—more wood—that's better—and listen, good old Friend, to the wind outside—almost a Christmas wind, is it not? Merry and boisterous enough, for all the evil times it stirs among."

Old Christmas seated himself beside the fire, his hands outstretched towards the flames. Something of his old-time cheeriness seemed to flicker across his features as he warmed himself at the blaze.

"That's better," he murmured. "I was cold, sir, cold, chilled to the bone: of old I never felt it so; no matter what the wind, the world seemed warm about me. Why is it not so now?"

"You see," said Time, speaking low in a whisper for my ear alone, "see how sunk and broken he is? Will you not help?"

"Gladly," I answered, "if I can."

"All can," said Father Time, "every one of us can."

Meantime Christmas had turned towards me a questioning eye, in which, however, there seemed to revive some little gleam of merriment.

"Have you, perhaps," he asked half timidly, "schnapps?"

"Schnapps?" I repeated.

"Aye, schnapps. A glass of it to drink your health might warm my heart again, I think."

"Ah!" I said, "something to drink?"

"His one failing," whispered Time, "if it is one. Forgive it him. He was used to it for centuries. Give it him if you have it."

"I keep a little in the house," I said, reluctantly perhaps, "in case of illness."

"Tut, tut," said Father Time, as something as near as could be to a smile passed over his shadowy face. "In case of illness! They used to say that in ancient Babylon. Here, let me pour it for him. Drink, Father Christmas, drink!"

Marvellous it was to see the old man smack his lips as he drank his glass of liquor neat after the fashion of old Norway.

Marvellous, too, to see the way in which, with the warmth of the fire and the generous glow of the spirits, his face changed and brightened till the old-time cheerfulness beamed again upon it.

He looked about him, as it were, with a new and growing interest.

"A pleasant room," he said, "and what better, sir, than the wind without and a brave fire within!"

Then his eye fell upon the mantel piece, where lay among the litter of books and pipes a little toy horse.

"One," I answered, "the sweetest boy in all the world."

"I'll be bound he is!" said Father Christmas, and he broke

now into a merry laugh that did one's heart good to hear. "They all are! Lord bless me! The number that I have seen, and each and every one—and quite right, too—the sweetest child in all the world. And how old, do you say? Two and a half all but two months except a week? The very sweetest age of all, I'll bet you say, eh, what? They all do!"

And the old man broke again into such a jolly chuckling of laughter that his snow-white locks shook upon his head.

"But stop a bit," he added. "This horse is broken—tut, tut,—a hind leg nearly off. This won't do!"

He had the toy in his lap in a moment, mending it. It was wonderful to see, for all his age, how deft his fingers were.

"Time," he said, and it was amusing to note that his voice had assumed almost an authoritative tone, "reach me that piece of string. That's right. Here, hold your finger across the knot. There! Now, then, a bit of bee's wax. What? No bee's wax? Tut, tut, how ill-supplied your houses are to-day. How can you mend toys, sir, without bee's wax? Still, it will stand up now."

I tried to murmur my best thanks.

But Father Christmas waved my gratitude aside.

"Nonsense," he said. "That's nothing. That's my life. Perhaps the little boy would like a book too. I have them here in the packet. Here, sir, *Jack and the Bean Stalk,* a most profound thing. I read it to myself often still. How damp it is! Pray, sir, will you let me dry my books before your fire?"

"Only too willingly," I said. "How wet and torn they are!"

Father Christmas had risen from his chair and was fumbling among his tattered packages, taking from them his children's books, all limp and draggled from the rain and wind.

"All wet and torn!" he murmured, and his voice sank again

into sadness. "I have carried them these three years past. Look! These were for little children in Belgium and in Serbia. Can I get them to them, think you?"

Time gently shook his head.

"But presently, perhaps!" said Father Christmas, "if I dry and mend them. Look, some of them were inscribed already! This one, see you, was written *'With father's love.'* Why has it never come to him? Is it rain or tears upon the page?"

He stood bowed over his little books, his hands trembling as he turned the pages. Then he looked up, the old fear upon his face again.

"That sound!" he said. "Listen! guns—I hear them!"

"No, no," I said, "it is nothing. Only a car passing in the street below."

"Listen," he said. "Hear that again—voices crying!"

"No, no," I answered, "not voices, only the night wind among the trees."

"My children's voices!" he exclaimed. "I hear them everywhere—they come to me in every wind—and I see them as I wander in the night and storm—my children—torn and dying in the trenches—beaten into the ground—I hear them crying from the hospitals—each one to me, still as I knew him once, a little child. Time, Time," he cried, reaching out his arms in appeal, "give me back my children!"

"They do not die in vain," Time murmured gently.

But Christmas only moaned in answer, "Give me back my children!"

Then he sank down upon his pile of books and toys, his head buried in his arms.

"You see," said Time, "his heart is breaking, and will you not help him if you can?"

"Only too gladly," I replied. "But what is there to do?"

"This," said Father Time, "listen."

He stood before me grave and solemn, a shadowy figure but half seen though he was close beside me. The fire-light had died down, and through the curtained windows there came already the first dim brightening of dawn.

"The world that once you knew," said Father Time, "seems broken and destroyed about you. You must not let them know—the children. The cruelty and the horror and the hate that racks the world to-day—keep it from them. Some day he will know—" here Time pointed to the prostrate form of Father Christmas—"that his children, that once were, have not died in vain: that from their sacrifice shall come a nobler, better world for all to live in, a world where countless happy children shall hold bright their memory forever. But for the children of To-day, save and spare them all you can from the evil hate and horror of the war. Later they will know and understand. Not yet. Give them back their Merry Christmas and its kind thoughts, and its Christmas charity, till later on there shall be with it again Peace upon Earth, Good Will towards Men."

His voice ceased. It seemed to vanish, as it were, in the sighing of the wind.

I looked up. Father Time and Christmas had vanished from the room. The fire was low and the day was breaking visibly outside.

"Let us begin," I murmured. "I will mend this broken horse."

A Christmas White Elephant

by W. A. Wilson

FRED WAS IN A SAD quandary. There were certain things in the house which managed themselves, that is, were attended to by Agnes, his wife. There were others which required careful and judicious treatment, he said. These were left to him, of course. He found them, usually, more or less disagreeable. This case, however, was particularly difficult to deal with; the more so as it was plain to him that not only his own feelings, but those of Cecie, his little five-year-old daughter, had become involved. Now, he was much attached to his only child, and, whatever might happen to his own feelings, he objected to hers being wounded in any way. The situation, therefore, became more and more perplexing. As a natural consequence, he put off, from day to day, deciding what was to be done.

Agnes had expressed herself with her customary decision. "We simply cannot keep it in the house," she said, one evening when Fred went into the matter once for all.

"That is true," admitted her husband.

"Very well, then; we may as well get rid of it at once," she concluded.

"Yes, but how?" asked Fred, with an air of clinching the matter with a question she would find it difficult to answer.

"How? That is simple enough, surely."

"Don't see it."

"Why, open the door and put it out."

"Wh-a-at!" cried Fred, "and let it *die* in the yard?"

"Why, yes. You don't need to be so silly about it."

"Silly about it! Silly about it!! It's all very well to say 'silly' about it, but I couldn't do it. I couldn't sleep at nights. It's a good thing Cecie is not here to hear her mother."

"Really, Fred, it seems to me that you are driving matters a little too far," remarked Agnes, in a tone of great severity.

"Driving! That's not bad. I am not driving; I am being driven," said Fred, pleased, however, that he seemed to have the better of the argument.

"Well, I don't know," she said. "You agree that it cannot stay, and yet you object to letting it go."

"I do nothing of the kind," said Fred, helplessly. "I only said it wasn't feasible. It simply cannot be put out to die. It doesn't cost much to feed it, you must admit."

"That is true," said Agnes; "but that has nothing to do with it. Surely there is no use going over all the reasons again."

"Then," said Fred, in desperation, "let us get a man to take it out into the country somewhere and leave it to its fate. Perhaps some one would take a fancy to it," he added, rising.

"That would cost more than it is worth. Besides, it is a good thing Cecie is not here to hear her father," laughed Agnes, and the subject was allowed to drop once more.

Fred felt that the matter was becoming serious. If Agnes were so unreasonable, what would Cecie say to a proposal to turn her newly found friend out of doors? If it had only not been so very large!

Cecie had become quite a personage of importance in the household. Her father was reminded so often of himself by things she said and did that he strove in every way to protect her from being, as he called it, badly used—that is, from being misconstrued and misunderstood. A strong feeling had, consequently, grown up between them. This case, this Green White Elephant of a Christmas-tree, was a characteristic instance. Only Cecie could have caused such a fuss about such a trifle. The more he thought about it the more ridiculous it seemed. Yet, as he said, it was easier to laugh than to say what was to be done.

Toward the end of the previous month, Robin, a friend, having sent a present consisting of a large Christmas-tree growing in an earthen pot, Fred went into town—unknown, of course, to Cecie—to purchase decorations for it. The same evening that young lady, having danced about the house all day and feeling tired, begged her father to read to her, as she expressed it, a nice fairy-tale. Fred was an artist, and had been occupied for some months illustrating a new edition of Hans Christian Andersen. He took up an old volume of his fairy-stories and opened it at random. It chanced that he stumbled upon the story of "The Fir-tree." This, as it happened, had not yet been read to his daughter, and as her father prepared to read he noticed that she settled herself on her stool at her mother's feet, and elaborately smoothed her pinafore out before her, as she was wont to do on great occasions; for no occasion was so great to Cecie as the first reading of a new fairy-tale.

He did not stop to think. It did not occur to him precisely what the result of reading that particular story at that particular time would most likely be. Otherwise, he would probably have kept it for another day. But he did not; he read innocently on, and Cecie listened. When he had finished she surprised him by saying nothing. She sat quite still, and seemed to have become very thoughtful. After a time she rose and went quietly into the room where the Christmas-tree was standing.

Presently a small voice called out: "Papa!"

Fred, suspecting what had happened, rose and went in. Agnes remained. She had an important piece of sewing to do.

"Papa," asked Cecie, whose blonde curls scarcely reached the lowest branches of the tree, "it never moves, does it?"

"No, dear."

"And it *is* alive just like us?"

"Yes. That is—well, yes; not exactly, you know, but it is quite alive."

"What does it feed on all the time, then?"

"The juices of the earth," said Fred, with the air of an experienced gardener. "That is why we must give it water. It requires air, too, for it sucks moisture in with these as well." And he pinched the branch nearest him, and few needles came off between his fingers.

"Doesn't that hurt the tree?" cried Cecie.

"Oh, no; it won't mind that."

"Wouldn't it like some juices just now, papa?"

"I think not. The earth is moist enough."

"Oh, let me! I'll go and get some water," said Cecie, starting toward the door.

"No, no; it has sufficient."

"But perhaps it would like a long drink. I do sometimes," pleaded the little girl, in tones which usually had the desired effect.

"No!" said the head of the family, to satisfy himself that he could be firm occasionally.

There was a pause. Cecie stood still, looking up at the handsome stranger as if she had never seen a tree before. "Do you think it hears us talking about it, papa?" she said after a moment.

"Perhaps."

"Perhaps it is asleep," she suggested, moving closer to her father and putting her little hand in his.

"Perhaps it is," said Fred, feeling that, after all, the tree might as well have had some water.

"But how does it sleep when it has no eyes?"

"Oh, it just sleeps in its own way."

"Standing up like that always?"

"Yes, just as, just as—let me see—as horses do, for example."

"Oh, but horses don't always," retorted Cecie; because the baker had told her, the other day, that his horse lay down on the straw and went to sleep whenever it got home at night.

"They sometimes do," observed Fred, in the interests of parental authority, meaning at the first opportunity to get reliable information on the subject of the private life of horses.

"Then will it like to live with us?"

Fred thought it would, if they were kind to it.

"And we will be kind to it, won't we?"

"Of course we will," Fred promised, in the innocence of his heart; for he was a child of nature himself, fond of flowers and trees and everything that lived a free and healthy life.

Then Cecie said good night to her tree, "and pleasant dreams"; and when she had closed the door for the night and left her new friend alone, she went contentedly away with her nurse; and Fred sat down, blissfully unconscious that he had committed himself in any way.

The following forenoon, after struggling for an hour to get into his work, Fred had just got fairly settled when he was startled by a fall, a crash of crockery, and a loud wail in the room adjoining his studio. Laying down his drawing-board and pen, with a sigh, he went to the folding doors and opened them.

Cecie had already been picked up. She was standing like a little model for a statuette, holding out her limp and dripping hands. Her pinafore and dress were soaked with water, and there was a pond on the bright waxed floor, dotted with islands of broken stoneware jug. The cat, in the center of the farther room, was excitedly licking its back. Cecie's lips were puckered up in great distress, and her eyes were lost in a spasm of tears, for she had startled no one more than she had herself.

Fred could not help smiling. He bent down and comforted her, and, after the tears had ceased, said that to prevent confusion in future, either he or mama, or at all events nurse, would see that the tree got sufficient water. Cecie was to give herself no concern whatever. There was no need to trouble herself about it. Would she be good and not do so any more?

"Y-y-yes," promised Cecie, feeling, however, that she was promising away her entire interest in life.

"Oh, I will tell you," said Fred. "Every evening at tea-time remind me that the tree is thirsty. Nurse can fetch us water, and we can give it some."

Cecie was led away for a change of clothes, with an expression on her face like sunshine breaking through the clouds on an April day. Fred, with a reflection of it glistening in his eyes, went back to his room and took up his board.

That evening he was busy decorating the tree for some time after Cecie had gone to sleep.

The next evening was Christmas eve; but when the happy moment arrived, and the doors were flung open, disclosing the tree in a blaze of light, Cecie did not seem to rise to the occasion quite so enthusiastically as her parents had expected; and yet this was not only the largest but the finest tree she had ever had. Cecie, however, was not one who could be gay to order; and with her the unexpected usually happened. This time it was not that she did not think her protégé beautiful. She was divided between admiration and another feeling. She was wondering if it would care to be lighted up with candles within an inch of its life like that, and covered with glittering ornaments till it could scarcely breathe; whether it liked to have molten wax run all over its fresh green branches; and whether it were being treated with proper respect in being made to hold up such a load of things.

Fred laughed heartily when she confided her anxieties to him, and said, "Oh, that won't matter. Don't mind that, little woman."

"But don't you remember that the story said when the trees had bark-ache it was as bad as headache is to us?"

"Oh, but it is strong," said her father. "It doesn't feel such little things."

"Well, I would have barkache—headache, I mean," said Cecie, laughing at her slip, "if I had to carry all those burning candles."

Later, when the little party had broken up and Fred was left alone, he sat down in an easy-chair. A question had occurred to him while Cecie was speaking. This tree of hers—what was to be done with it when its time came?

He and mama had no means of disposing of it, living in the city as they did, and it could not be kept in the house. Moreover, Cecie would require to know what had been done with it. Previous Christmas-trees had had their death-blows dealt them in the forest. With this one it was different. It was not only still living, but, thanks to Cecie, was becoming from day to day more and more a personality in the house.

Parents, he reflected, really ought to remember to tell their children, when talking of the duty of kindness to all dumb creatures, that there are exceptions to every rule—that is to say, if they wish to avoid drifting into ridiculous situations. To think of the father of a family hesitating about such a paltry thing as this! He looked up at the moment, and his eyes fell upon the tree. How beautiful it certainly was, in spite of all the finery and tinsel!

Cecie was an odd child! However, when Christmas was over, other things would distract her attention, he hoped, and then it would be time enough to—well, that could be determined when the time came. Perhaps something would turn up before then.

The next day, being Christmas, was a holiday. Fred sat reading in his easy-chair before the studio fire. Cecie, not far away, lay upon the floor, propping her head up with her arms, deeply engrossed in an illustrated spelling-book. For a few moments there was no sound but the grave beat of the old timepiece hanging on the wall and the nervous ticking of two modern clocks in the adjoining room. A thin fall of snow had slid down the studio windows and collected at the bottom of the panes.

Presently Fred laid down his book, and said, over his shoulder: "Where is Dolly to-day?"

"She's asleep just now," she said, rising and going to her father's side. "She's been making plum-pudding." Taking the watch from her father's pocket, and holding it sideways, she continued: "What time is it?"

"A quarter past three."

"But you said it was twelve when the hands were together."

"Yes; but when they are together at the *top*."

Cecie gave it up. Replacing the watch, she said, in an altered tone of voice: "Papa!"

"Well, dear?"

"Trees don't care for anything but growing, do they?"

"Well, I don't know that they care much even for that. They have to grow just as you, just as I, must do."

"Must you grow, papa?"

"I? Well, I suppose I am done growing now," said Fred.

"Will you never grow, never any more?" asked Cecie, so seriously that her father turned around and looked at her, and smiled.

"Well, dear," he said, stroking her hair, "it wouldn't do, you know, if we never stopped. Think how big we should get to be!"

Cecie burst into a gay laugh. "We couldn't get in by the door, unless we bent down and crept in on our hands and knees, could we?"

"Of course we couldn't," laughed Fred.

"But it is funny, too, that we have to stop growing. Tell me, papa," she continued, looking earnestly at him, "are you *very* old?"

"Who? I?" said Fred, aghast. "No—of course not. I am quite young."

"How old is old, then?"

"Old? Let me see. Fifty is old, or sixty—thereabouts," said Fred.

After a silence Cecie began again:

"Will *I* ever be old, papa?"

"Why, certainly, my dear," said Fred, cheerfully; "that is," he added, as if feeling guilty of some vague ungallantry, "I hope so."

"And never grow any more, like you?"

"Y-yes."

"But wouldn't you like to keep growing always?"

"I don't know. I feel pretty comfortable as I am. If I were a little girl like you it might be different."

"Do people only want to grow when they are young?"

Fred shifted in his chair, and then, drawing her closer to him, said: "Why do you ask about the tree caring to grow?"

"Because you read in the story that the tree said to itself: 'Let me grow, only let me grow; there is nothing so beautiful in all the world.' "

"I don't remember."

"Wait, and I will get the book," said Cecie.

She returned with the volume, which she had opened at the proper place, and declared that it was at the very beginning.

"How did you know that that is the place?"

"Because the picture of the tree is there," replied the child, simply.

Fred patted her on the cheek, and ran his eye rapidly down the page. At length he said:

"Oh, yes; you are right. Here it is:

> " 'Be happy,' said the Sunshine, 'that you are young. Rejoice in your growth, and in the young life that is within you.' And the Wind kissed the tree by day, and the Dew wept over it by night: but the Fir-tree did not understand."

"What didn't it understand?" asked Cecie.

"Oh, I don't know," said her father, carelessly.

"I know."

"What, then?"

"That some day it would stop growing, like you, and might want to grow some more, and couldn't," cried Cecie, breaking into a dance of joy; for she had a great belief that her father knew nearly everything, and it was a great treat to her to be able to tell him something he did not know.

Finally, as if by way of further relieving her feelings, she caught up one foot, and hopped round the studio and out at the open door.

As she did so, Fred's book slipped from his knee and fell. He picked it up again, but laid it on the table. Resuming his chair, he sat for some time with his head resting on his hand, looking absently at the fire.

Cecie sometimes had fits of not knowing what to do with her limbs; or it might, perhaps, be more correct to say that her limbs had fits of not knowing what to do with themselves and her. At one moment she would be seen lounging about like a marionette, hanging on her father or mother or whoever happened to be near. The next minute she had gone. She was likely, however, to reappear at any moment, like a kitten, the innocent victim of some strange galvanic power.

These moods had the additional peculiarity of usually occurring when every one else was disposed to be quiet. This occasion being no exception, Fred was soon startled from his reverie by warm lips sending a sudden "Boo-o-o!" near his ear.

"What's the matter?" he cried out, twitching as if from an electric shock.

Cecie applied her lips to his ear again.

"I don't know," he said, laughing, and rubbing that organ energetically.

"Guess!"

"Can't. There isn't anything forgotten."

"Oh, yes, there is," said Cecie, and whispering a second time.

"Oh, not just now, I think," said Fred, smiling, as she retreated a pace, to watch the effect of the joyful communication.

"But you said you would."

"It won't require any water to-day."

"Oh, yes. You know it has all the candles and things to hold."

Fred rose resignedly, and went into the room, and the tree was ceremoniously and most delicately watered, to the complete satisfaction of its patroness.

It was large enough, certainly (its top just touched the ceiling of the room in which it stood), but it was very kind of Robin, Fred reflected, to have sent such a handsome tree. If, therefore, this newly born enthusiasm of Cecie's for growing were to be encouraged, it might soon be necessary to take her friend into the studio. But that was entirely out of the question. He could not afford the space. Sooner or later he must come to a decision. There seemed to be no resource but to break it up for fire-wood. Cecie could be sent for a walk while that was being done. Who was to do it, however? It was not work for his wife, and he—well, he did not care to do it. He was not accustomed to use an ax, for one thing; besides, work of that sort was bad for an artist's hands.

Nurse would do it. Why not? She was a great, strong woman.

It was not until the first week of the new year, when the mistletoe and holly and other relics of Christmas were being cleared away, that the subject of their silent visitor came up again.

"If Cecie would only tire of it," he would say to himself at times, "or if it would only die!" Of the latter, unfortunately, there seemed to be very little prospect, unless, indeed, it died by drowning. Thanks to Cecie's watchfulness, there seemed a distant possibility of that.

Once he pulled himself together, and, without daring to address himself directly to his daughter, spoke about the matter, in a seemingly casual manner, in her presence.

"What shall we do when the tree is away?" he said to mama.

"It isn't going away, is it, papa?" asked Cecie, looking up in great surprise. "You said it was to be allowed to stay."

"C-certainly, my dear. I mean, what would we have done if it had been going away?"

Cecie's calmness had quite disarmed him.

"Where could it have gone, poor thing?" asked Cecie, tenderly.

"I—don't—know," said Fred, hopelessly.

Again he and Agnes were talking obscurely about it, so that the child might not understand.

Presently Cecie said in a low whisper:

"S-sh, mama, s-sh! Don't talk like that. The tree might hear you, and think you were talking about *it*."

"But, my dear," said her mother, seizing the opportunity, "we *are* talking about it." Suddenly lowering her voice, in response to an expression in Cecie's face, she added: "Something must be done, you know. It cannot stay here always."

"Then," said Cecie in a hoarse whisper to her father, who had begun to crumble bread upon the table-cloth, "why did you let it hear you say it could, papa?"

"Me, dear? I didn't."

"Yes, you did; the first night it came," persisted Cecie, her eyes filling suddenly.

"Did I? Well, but we don't need to chop it up, you know," said Fred, soothingly.

"Chop it up!" cried Cecie, horrified. "Who said we would chop it up?"

"Why, why—nobody. Did nurse say so?"

"Nurse? Why, no. She loves it as much as I do now, ever since I told her," said Cecie.

"Oh! I didn't know," said the victim, feeling that the toils were closing around him, and beginning to wonder if Hunding found it inconvenient to have a tree growing through the roof of his abode. It might look picturesque, at least, if the worst came to the worst.

"Poor thing!" said Cecie, turning to their helpless charge; "we promised to be kind to you, and we will, won't we?"

Neither Fred nor Agnes said a word. They felt that their best course was to wait.

Cecie, however, made it difficult for them at the outset by saying good night to her tree that evening with even more kindliness in her voice than usual.

Fred complained to Agnes afterward, as they sat alone together, that it was impossible to work when one was constantly distracted by the small things of life. Agnes said, "Stuff and nonsense!" Moreover, she added, laughing, it was absurd to call Cecie's tree a small thing of life. It was already too large, and, what was worse, seemed to be growing larger.

It was no wonder, therefore, that Fred was in a great quandary.

Whenever he chanced to see the tree, standing on its stool, so submissive or so indifferent,—he could not quite make out which,—but certainly so undeniably fresh and healthy-looking, his conscience gave a twinge. He began to avoid the "prison," as Agnes jestingly called the room in which it stood; for when he met the tree face to face, he always thought of the Good Robber, and how he must have felt when he took the Babes by the hand and led them to the Wood; and when he heard nurse watering it and spraying its branches twice a day, he winced, for he had delegated the work to her in the steadfast hope that she would forget to do it.

Once, with a bitter remembrance of this, he said to Agnes, who had complained of her neglect: "Yes; she does nothing she is told to do, that girl."

"Oh, papa," broke in Cecie, who happened to be in a corner of the room, "you can't say that. Look at the way she keeps the tree. Why, there are buds upon it already!"

At another time, Agnes, who had just decided to take the law into her own hands, and give orders for the execution without saying anything either to Cecie or her husband, was busy arranging her bookcase, when Fred looked up from the letter he was writing and said: "S-sh! Who is that in the next room?"

"It is only Cecie."

"But she is talking to some one."

Agnes laid down the book she was dusting, and, going softly to the door, stood still and listened. As she did so, a curious look, that was half smile and half something else, crossed her face.

"They are having a great time in there," she said in a lowered tone, coming away from the door. "Cecie is telling it a long story about a walk she had in the park with nurse."

Agnes resumed her work among the books, and decided that in the meantime there was no hurry; the tree could remain where it was for a day or two longer.

At last, at the eleventh hour, quite unexpectedly, a solution of the difficulty arrived.

One windy night toward the end of January, Fred was awakened by the slamming of the folding windows in a room down-stairs.

He lay, reluctant to rise, for some moments, but, on the noise being repeated, sprang out of bed and put on his slippers.

Passing the staircase window like a ghost, he reached the hall, and moved toward the parlor door. The shutters were closed, and the room was dark. After feeling about, and upsetting a vase of water filled with flowers, and a few glasses and ornaments on a table, he succeeded in finding the matches, and struck a light.

He opened the door of the room whence the noise was coming; but, as he did so, the window was blown wide open, his lamp was extinguished, and he found himself in an almost forgotten presence.

Majestic and calm, within a few paces of him, stood the

tree, in the great flood of moonlight which streamed in past the fluttering curtains.

Fifteen seconds later, Fred had shuffled up the staircase, and was coiled up in his bed again.

He told Cecie in the morning.

The tree's old friends had missed it, she said, and had come to pay it a visit to see how it was getting on.

"What *friends*?" asked Frederick-of-the-Guilty-Conscience.

"The moonlight and the wind," said Cecie.

"Oh," said Fred.

That this little episode impressed Cecie was evident; but it was not until the following Saturday that she said anything of an idea which it seemed to have suggested to her. It was the first time since New Year's that Fred had found time to run out beyond the city, which he was in the habit of doing as often as he could, to spend a few hours in the pure, fresh air of his favorite woods. Agnes usually accompanied him, and, for the first time, they yielded to Cecie's entreaties and took her also with them.

These snatches of health-giving air, these walks, short though they were, on the country soil, were everything to Fred. Two hours of freedom among the trees, in the silence of the forest, he used to say, were enough to clear a week's cobwebs from the brain. They did more for him that day—they solved the problem of the tree.

To reach their favorite walk it was necessary to go by steamboat to a station down the river, and thence climb a short, steep hill to a wood which stretched for miles beyond. It was apt to be dusty and less attractive in the summer months, but in late autumn and winter and early spring, when deserted by the picnicking crowd, it was a beautiful and peaceful spot. The favorite corner of Fred's was a small pond which lay in the midst of a thicket of young elms and oaks. When Cecie saw this for the first time she remained very quiet for some moments. Two fir-trees growing at a corner of the pond seemed to attract her attention.

"What are you thinking about?" asked her father.

"I am thinking—why not send our tree out here and let it grow beside the others? Look at those two poor trees standing over there, all alone. It would be happier too, I think. It would like to be beside them."

"Do you think it would?" asked Fred, musingly.

"I am sure of it!" cried Cecie, excitedly. "It would get the dew, and the wind, and the rain, and the sun, and could grow and grow all the time. I am afraid it won't grow much with us."

An hour afterward they stood on the pier watching their steamboat coming up the river.

"Now," said Fred, who seemed to be in unusually good spirits, "we have only to ask Robin if he is willing."

"Willing—what to do?"

"To let us send his present into the woods to live, instead of keeping it ourselves," said Fred, quite gravely.

"Oh, he will," said Cecie, confidently. "I will go and ask him. Nurse can take me—to-morrow morning—before break-fast-time."

"I think I wouldn't go quite so soon," said her father, with an amused look. "Robin doesn't—I mean Robin is very busy in the early mornings."

The snow and ice had disappeared from the streets and avenues, and in the mild skies of the early days of February there was a glad respite from the cold, and a welcome promise of the coming spring.

The sun no longer hid behind banks of fog, but rose from day to day with clear and lustrous face. The mists had gathered up their trains and fled, and the skies were filled with armies of fleecy clouds. The grass in the parks seemed already to feel the breath of April, the crocuses peeped out from their beds of earth and hurried on their yellow garments, while the trees donned a livery of tiny buds and stood in sleepy readiness for the festival. The busy steamers plying up and down the river became suddenly gay with color for the passengers no longer huddled together in heated cabins, but crowded out upon the deck that they might breathe the fresh air.

Beyond the city, nature seemed less eager to listen to fair promises, for her landscapes lay still as they had been left by the marauding winds of winter. The country roads were bleak and bare, the shrubs and hedges stripped of their leaves and left stifled with snow and mud, and the deserted foot-paths wandered listlessly through the maze of trunks and branches and lawless thorns. Yet when the sun shone into the thickets and down upon the inert ground, everything seemed to quicken: the ice retreated into the shady corners of the ponds, the drowsy trees lazily stretched themselves, and here and there in the recesses a bird took courage and began piping feeble snatches of almost forgotten song.

On the afternoon of one of these early February days the deserted woods seemed quieter even than they had been in the dead of winter. There was not a breath of wind to ruffle the surface of the pond, beside which a young fir-tree had recently been planted. Far in the distance a dog's bark or a cock-crow might be heard; still farther, perhaps, a long, faint whistle from a train winding along the river's bank; or, nearer at hand, the rustle of a falling leaf: but these only served to make the silence more profound. Close beside two other firs, standing in friendly reserve somewhat aloof from the attendant herd of young oaks and elms, the new member of the mute community depended its lustrous green reflection into the somber mirror at its feet. Behind it rose the slender stems of two silver birches. In a corner near at hand a marsh-willow had burst into a mist of downy buds; and, still nearer, an old oak, as if to show an example to the younger members of its family, who still clung to their tattered covering of leaves, stretched its bare and rugged limbs far up above its neighbors, and stood, stern and weather-beaten, on its carpet of grass and fallen acorns.

The mossy foot-path which skirted the pond led to a clearing in the wood where it joined a broader way. This crossed a more open tract of ground covered with bushes and clogged with heather and dark-leaved brambles, until at one corner the country road appeared from behind a clump of trees. Between this corner and the point, some distance farther on, where the road descended the wooded hill leading to the river, a gardener's cottage was situated.

At the gate of this cottage, toward sunset on a February afternoon, three figures were standing. The one in colored shirt-sleeves and ample corduroys wore a gardener's blue apron; the others were clad in the more conventional clothing of the city.

One of them wore a dark hat and cloak, and beside him stood a little figure dressed in a quaint gown of blue trimmed with sable. From beneath the felt and feathers of her hat one of her blonde curls escaped and lay gracefully upon her shoulder.

A fourth figure, that of the gardener's wife, a motherly looking woman in a faded cotton dress, presently disappeared into a small greenhouse near the cottage, and closed the door behind her.

"Well," said the owner of the blue apron, in an affable tone, to his visitors, when at length they prepared to leave, "I suppose Missy will be satisfied now."

"I think so," said the figure in the cloak, looking down to "Missy," who smiled a shy assent, "*I* certainly am very well satisfied," he added, with a quizzical look, while buttoning his cloak.

When they set out, a few minutes later, the sun was glittering behind the trees, the earth was deep in color, and the sky was filled with light.

They had reached the point where the road dipped suddenly in the direction of the steamer-pier, when the door of the greenhouse opened, and the woman with the faded gown reappeared, tying up a bouquet as she walked slowly into the garden.

She did not look up at first, but when she did so and found that the strangers had gone, she threw her scissors down upon a table, ran past her husband, who was at the gate, and hastened after them along the road.

They turned on hearing her, and when she reached them she bent down and, with a mixture of hesitancy and tenderness, placed the flowers between two small gloved hands, and retreated.

A minute afterward she was standing in the middle of the empty road, bareheaded, and with cheeks hot and flushed, watching a waving cloak and a little dot of blue gradually disappearing down the avenue.

Jack's Sermon

BY JACOB A. RIIS

JACK SAT ON THE FRONT porch in a very bad humor indeed. That was in itself something unusual enough to portend trouble; for ordinarily Jack was a philosopher well persuaded that, upon the whole, this was a very good world and Deacon Pratt's porch the centre of it on week-days. On Sundays it was transferred to the village church, and on these days Jack received there with the family. If the truth were told, it would probably have been found that Jack conceived the services to be some sort of function specially designed to do him honor at proper intervals, for he always received an extra petting on these occasions. He sat in the pew beside the deacon through the sermon as decorously as befitted a dog come to years of discretion long since, and wagged his tail in a friendly manner when the minister came down and patted him on the head after the benediction. Outside he met the Sunday-school children on their own ground, and on their own terms. Jack, if he didn't have blood, had sense, which for working purposes is quite as good, if not so common. The girls gave him candy and called him Jack Sprat. His joyous bark could be heard long after church as he romped with the boys by the creek on the way home. It was even suspected that on certain Sabbaths they had enjoyed a furtive cross-country run together; but by tacit consent the village overlooked it and put it down to the dog. Jack was privileged and not to blame. There was certainly something, from the children's point of view, also, in favor of Jack's conception of Sunday.

On week-day nights there were the church meetings of one kind and another, for which Deacon Pratt's house was always the place, not counting the sociables which Jack attended with unfailing regularity. They would not, any of them, have been quite regular without Jack. Indeed, many a question of grave church polity had been settled only after it had been submitted to and passed upon in meeting by Jack. "Is not that so, Jack?" was a favorite clincher to arguments which, it was felt, had won over his master. And Jack's groping paw cemented a treaty of good-will and mutual concession that had helped the village church over more than one hard place. For there were hard heads and stubborn wills in it as there are in other churches; and Deacon Pratt, for all he was a just man, was set on having his way.

And now all this was changed. What had come over the town Jack couldn't make out, but that it was something serious nobody was needed to tell him. Folks he used to meet at the gate, going to the trains of mornings, on neighborly terms, hurried past him without as much as a look. Deacon Jones, who gave him ginger-snaps out of the pantry-crock as a special bribe for a hand-shake, had even put out his foot to kick him, actually kick him, when he waylaid him at the corner that morning. The whole week there had not been as much as a visitor at the house, and what with Christmas in town—Jack knew the signs well enough; they meant raisins and goodies that came only when they burned candles on trees in the church—it was enough to make any dog cross. To top it all, his mistress must come down sick, worried into it all, as like as not, he had heard the doctor say. If Jack's thoughts could have been put into words as he sat on the porch looking moodily over the road, they would doubtless have taken something like this shape, that it was a pity that men didn't have the sense of dogs, but would bear grudges and make themselves and their betters unhappy. And in the village there would have been more than one to agree with him secretly.

Jack wouldn't have been any the wiser had he been told that the trouble that had come to town was that of all things most worrisome, a church quarrel. What was it about and how did it come? I doubt if any of the men and women who strove in meeting for principle and conscience with might and main, and said mean things about each other out of meeting, could have explained it. I know they all would have explained it differently, and so added fuel to the fire that was hot enough already. In fact, that was what had happened the night before Jack encountered his special friend, Deacon Jones, and it was in virtue of his master's share in it that he had bestowed the memorable kick upon him. Deacon Pratt was the valiant leader of the opposing faction.

To the general stress of mind the holiday had but added another cause of irritation. Could Jack have understood the ethics of men he would have known that it strangely happens that:

"Forgiveness to the injured does belong,
But they ne'er pardon who have done the wrong,"

and that everybody in a church quarrel having injured everybody else within reach for conscience sake, the season of goodwill and even the illness of that good woman, the wife of Deacon Pratt, admittedly from worry over the trouble, practically put a settlement of it out of the question. But being only a dog he did not understand. He could only sulk; and as this went well enough with things as they were in general, it proved that Jack was, as was well known, a very intelligent dog.

He had yet to give another proof of it, that very day, by preaching to the divided congregation its Christmas sermon, a sermon that is to this day remembered in Brownville; but of that neither they nor he, sitting there on the stoop nursing his grievances, had at that time any warning.

It was Christmas Eve. Since the early Lutherans settled there, away back in the last century, it had been the custom in the village to celebrate the Holy Eve with a special service and a Christmas tree; and preparations had been going forward for it all the afternoon. It was noticeable that the fighting in the congregation in no wise interfered with the observance of the established forms of worship; rather, it seemed to lend a keener edge to them. It was only the spirit that suffered. Jack, surveying the road from the porch, saw baskets and covered trays carried by, and knew their contents. He had watched the big Christmas tree going down on the grocer's sled, and his experience plus his nose supplied the rest. As the lights came out one by one after twilight, he stirred uneasily at the unwonted stillness in his house. Apparently no one was getting ready for church. Could it be that they were not going; that this thing was to be carried to the last ditch? He decided to go and investigate.

His investigations were brief, but entirely conclusive. For the second time that day he was spurned, and by a friend. This time it was the deacon himself who drove him from his wife's room, whither he had betaken him with true instinct to ascertain the household intentions. The deacon seemed to be, if anything, in a worse humor than even Jack himself. The doctor had told him that afternoon that Mrs. Pratt was a very sick woman, and that, if she was to pull through at all, she must be kept from all worriment in an atmosphere which fairly bristled with it. The deacon felt that he had a contract on his hands which might prove too heavy for him. He felt, too, with bitterness, that he was an ill-used man, that all his years of faithful labor in the vineyard went for nothing because of some wretched heresy which the enemy had devised to wreck it; and all his humbled pride and his pent-up wrath gathered itself into the kick with which he sent poor Jack flying back where he had come from. It was clear that the deacon was not going to church.

Lonely and forsaken, Jack took his old seat on the porch and pondered. The wrinkles in his brow multiplied and grew deeper as he looked down the road and saw the Joneses, the Smiths, and the Aliens go by toward the church. When the Merritts had passed, too, under the lamp, he knew that it must be nearly time for the sermon. They always came in after the long prayer. Jack took a turn up and down the porch, whined at the door once, and, receiving no answer, set off down the road by himself.

The church was filled. It had never looked handsomer. The rival factions had vied with each other in decorating it. Spruce and hemlock sprouted everywhere, and garlands of ground-ivy festooned walls and chancel. The delicious odor of balsam and of burning wax-candles was in the air. The people were all there in their Sunday clothes and the old minister in the pulpit; but the Sunday feeling was not there. Something was not right. Deacon Pratt's pew alone of them all was empty, and the congregation cast wistful glances at it, some secretly behind their hymn-books, others openly and sorrowfully. What the doctor had said in the afternoon had got out. He himself had told Mrs. Mills that it was doubtful if the deacon's wife got around, and it sat heavily upon the conscience of the people.

The opening hymns were sung; the Merritts, late as usual, had taken their seats. The minister took up the Book to read the Christmas gospel from the second chapter of Luke. He had been there longer than most of those who were in the church to-night could remember, had grown old with the people, had loved them as the shepherd who is answerable to the Master for his flock. Their griefs and their troubles were his. If he could not ward them off, he could suffer with them. His voice trembled a little as he read of the tidings of great joy. Perhaps it was age; but it grew firmer as he proceeded toward the end:—

"And suddenly there was with the angel a multitude of the heavenly host praising God and saying, 'Glory to God in the highest, and on earth peace, good-will toward men.' "

The old minister closed the Book and looked out over the congregation. He looked long and yearningly, and twice he cleared his throat, only to repeat, "on earth peace, good-will toward men." The people settled back in their seats, uneasily; they strangely avoided the eye of their pastor. It rested in its slow survey of the flock upon Deacon Pratt's empty pew. And at that moment a strange thing occurred.

Why it should seem strange was, perhaps, not the least strange part of it. Jack had come in alone before. He knew the trick of the door-latch, and had often opened it unaided. He was in the habit of attending the church with the folks; there was no reason why they should not expect him, unless they knew of one themselves. But somehow the click of the latch went clear through the congregation as the heavenly message of good-will had not. All eyes were turned upon the deacon's pew; and they waited.

Jack came slowly and gravely up the aisle and stopped at his master's pew. He sniffed of the empty seat disapprovingly once or twice—he had never seen it in that state before—then he climbed up and sat, serious and attentive as he was wont, in his old seat, facing the pulpit, nodding once as who should say, "I'm here; proceed!"

It is recorded that not even a titter was heard form the Sunday-school, which was out in force. In the silence that reigned in the church was heard only a smothered sob. The old minister looked with misty eyes at his friend. He took off his spectacles, wiped them and put them on again, and tried to speak; but the tears ran down his cheeks and choked his voice. The congregation wept with him.

"Brethren," he said, when he could speak, "glory to God in the highest, and on earth peace, good-will toward men! Jack has preached a better sermon than I can to-night. Let us pray together."

It is further recorded that the first and only quarrel in the Brownville church ended on Christmas Eve and was never heard of again, and that it was all the work of Jack's sermon.

*The Feast—by J*s*ph C*nr*d*

by Max Beerbohm

The hut in which slept the white man was on a clearing between the forest and the river. Silence, the silence murmurous and unquiet of a tropical night, brooded over the hut that, baked through by the sun, sweated a vapour beneath the cynical light of the stars. Mahamo lay rigid and watchful at the hut's mouth. In his upturned eyes, and along the polished surface of his lean body black and immobile, the stars were reflected, creating an illusion of themselves who are illusions.

The roofs of the congested trees, writhing in some kind of agony private and eternal, made tenebrous and shifty silhouettes against the sky, like shapes cut out of black paper by a maniac who pushes them with his thumb this way and that, irritably, on a concave surface of blue steel. Resin oozed unseen from the upper branches to the trunks swathed in creepers that clutched and interlocked with tendrils venomous, frantic and faint. Down below, by force of habit, the lush herbage went through the farce of growth—that farce old and screaming, whose trite end is decomposition.

Within the hut the form of the white man, corpulent and pale, was covered with a mosquito-net that was itself illusory like everything else, only more so. Flying squadrons of mosquitoes inside its meshes flickered and darted over him, working hard, but keeping silence so as not to excite him from sleep. Cohorts of yellow ants disputed him against cohorts of purple ants, the two kinds slaying one another in thousands. The battle was undecided when suddenly, with no such warning as it gives in some parts of the world, the sun blazed up over the horizon, turning night into day, and the insects vanished back into their camps.

The white man ground his knuckles into the corners of his eyes, emitting that snore final and querulous of a middle-aged man awakened rudely. With a gesture brusque but flaccid he plucked aside the net and peered around. The bales of cotton cloth, the beads, the brass wire, the bottles of rum, had not been spirited away in the night. So far so good. The faithful servant of his employers was now at liberty to care for his own interests. He regarded himself, passing his hands over his skin.

"Hi! Mahamo!" he shouted. "I've been eaten up."

The islander, with one sinuous motion, sprang from the ground, through the mouth of the hut. Then, after a glance, he threw high his hands in thanks to such good and evil spirits as had charge of his concerns. In a tone half of reproach, half of apology, he murmured—

"You white men sometimes say strange things that deceive the heart."

"Reach me that ammonia bottle, d'you hear?" answered the white man. "This is a pretty place you've brought me to!" He took a draught. "Christmas Day, too! Of all the —— But I suppose it seems all right to you, you funny blackamoor, to be here on Christmas Day?"

"We are here on the day appointed, Mr. Williams. It is a feast-day of your people?"

Mr. Williams had lain back, with closed eyes, on his mat. Nostalgia was doing duty to him for imagination. He was wafted to a bedroom in Marylebone, where in honour of the Day he lay late dozing, with great contentment; outside, a slush of snow in the street, the sound of church-bells; from below a savour of especial cookery. "Yes," he said, "it's a feast-day of my people."

"Of mine also," said the islander humbly.

"Is it though? But they'll do business first?"

"They must first do that."

"And they'll bring their ivory with them?"

"Every man will bring ivory," answered the islander, with a smile gleaming and wide.

"How soon'll they be here?"

"Has not the sun risen? They are on their way."

"Well, I hope they'll hurry. The sooner we're off this cursed island of yours the better. Take all those things out," Mr. Williams added, pointing to the merchandise, "and arrange them—neatly, mind you!"

In certain circumstances it is right that a man be humoured in trifles. Mahamo, having borne out the merchandise, arranged it very neatly.

While Mr. Williams made his toilet, the sun and the forest, careless of the doings of white and black men alike, waged their warfare implacable and daily. The forest from its inmost depths sent forth perpetually its legions of shadows that fell dead in the instant of exposure to the enemy whose rays heroic and absurd its outposts annihilated. There came from those inilluminable depths the equable rumour of myriads of winged things and crawling things newly roused to the task of killing and being killed. Thence detached itself, little by little, an insidious sound of a drum beaten. This sound drew more near.

Mr. Williams, issuing from the hut, heard it, and stood gaping towards it.

"Is that them?" he asked.

"That is they," the islander murmured, moving away towards the edge of the forest.

Sounds of chanting were a now audible accompaniment to the drum.

"What's that they're singing?" asked Mr. Williams.

"They sing of their business," said Mahamo.

"Oh!" Mr. Williams was slightly shocked. "I'd have thought they'd be singing of their feast."

"It is of their feast they sing."

It has been stated that Mr. Williams was not imaginative. But a few years of life in climates alien and intemperate had disordered his nerves. There was that in the rhythms of the hymn which made bristle his flesh.

Suddenly, when they were very near, the voices ceased, leaving a legacy of silence more sinister than themselves. And now the black spaces between the trees were relieved by bits of white that were the eyeballs and teeth of Mahamo's brethren.

"It was of their feast, it was of you, they sang," said Mahamo.

"Look here," cried Mr. Williams in his voice of a man not to be trifled with. "Look here, if you've——"

He was silenced by sight of what seemed to be a young sapling sprung up from the ground within a yard of him—a young sapling tremulous, with a root of steel. Then a thread-like shadow skimmed the air, and another spear came impinging the ground within an inch of his feet.

As he turned in his flight he saw the goods so neatly arranged at his orders, and there flashed through him, even in the thick of the spears, the thought that he would be a grave loss to his employers. This—for Mr. Williams was, not less than the goods, of a kind easily replaced—was an illusion. It was the last of Mr. Williams' illusions.

Christmas by Injunction

by O. Henry

Cherokee was the civic father of Yellowhammer. Yellowhammer was a new mining town constructed mainly of canvas and undressed pine. Cherokee was a prospector. One day while his burro was eating quartz and pine burrs Cherokee turned up with his pick a nugget weighing thirty ounces. He staked his claim and then, being a man of breadth and hospitality, sent out invitations to his friends in three States to drop in and share his luck.

Not one of the invited guests sent regrets. They rolled in from the Gila country, from Salt River, from the Pecos, from Albuquerque and Phoenix and Santa Fe, and from the camps intervening.

When a thousand citizens had arrived and taken up claims they named the town Yellowhammer, appointed a vigilance committee, and presented Cherokee with a watch-chain made of nuggets.

Three hours after the presentation ceremonies Cherokee's claim played out. He had located a pocket instead of a vein. He abandoned it and staked others one by one. Luck had kissed her hand to him. Never afterward did he turn up enough dust in Yellowhammer to pay his bar bill. But his thousand invited guests were mostly prospering, and Cherokee smiled and congratulated them.

Yellowhammer was made up of men who took off their hats to a smiling loser; so they invited Cherokee to say what he wanted.

"Me?" said Cherokee, "oh, grubstakes will be about the thing. I reckon I'll prospect along up in the Mariposas. If I strike it up there I will most certainly let you all know about the facts. I never was any hand to hold out cards on my friends."

In May Cherokee packed his burro and turned its thoughtful, mouse-coloured forehead to the north. Many citizens escorted him to the undefined limits of Yellowhammer and bestowed upon him shouts of commendation and farewells. Five pocket flasks without an air bubble between contents and cork were forced upon him; and he was bidden to consider Yellowhammer in perpetual commission for his bed, bacon and eggs, and hot water for shaving in the event that luck did not see fit to warm her hands by his campfire in the Mariposas.

The name of the father of Yellowhammer was given him by the gold hunters in accordance with their popular system of nomenclature. It was not necessary for a citizen to exhibit his baptismal certificate in order to acquire a cognomen. A man's name was his personal property. For convenience in calling him up to the bar and in designating him among other blue-shirted bipeds, a temporary appellation, title, or epithet was conferred upon him by the public. Personal peculiarities formed the source of the majority of such informal baptisms. Many were easily dubbed geographically from the regions from which they confessed to have hailed. Some announced themselves to be "Thompsons," and "Adamses," and the like, with a brazenness and loudness that cast a cloud upon their titles. A few vaingloriously and shamelessly uncovered their proper and indisputable names. This was held to be unduly arrogant, and did not win popularity. One man who said he was Chesterton L. C. Belmont, and proved it by letters, was given till sundown to leave the town. Such names as "Shorty," "Bow-legs," "Texas," "Lazy Bill," "Thirsty Rogers," "Limping Riley," "The Judge," and "California Ed" were in favour. Cherokee derived his title from the fact that he claimed to have lived for a time with that tribe in the Indian Nation.

On the twentieth day of December Baldy, the mail rider, brought Yellowhammer a piece of news.

"What do I see in Albuquerque," said Baldy, to the patrons of the bar, "but Cherokee all embellished and festooned up like the Czar of Turkey, and lavishin' money in bulk. Him and me seen the elephant and the owl, and we had specimens of this seidlitz powder wine; and Cherokee he audits all the bills, C. O. D. His pockets looked like a pool table's after a fifteen-ball run."

"Cherokee must have struck pay ore," remarked California Ed. "Well, he's white. I'm much obliged to him for his success."

"Seems like Cherokee would ramble down to Yellowhammer and see his friends," said another, slightly aggrieved. "But that's the way. Prosperity is the finest cure there is for lost forgetfulness."

"You wait," said Baldy; "I'm comin' to that. Cherokee

strikes a three-foot vein up in the Mariposas that assays a trip to Europe to the ton, and he closes it out to a syndicate outfit for a hundred thousand hasty dollars in cash. Then he buys himself a baby sealskin overcoat and a red sleigh, and what do you think he takes it in his head to do next?"

"Chuck-a-luck," said Texas, whose ideas of recreation were the gamester's.

"Come and Kiss Me, Ma Honey," sang Shorty, who carried tintypes in his pocket and wore a red necktie while working on his claim.

"Bought a saloon?" suggested Thirsty Rogers.

"Cherokee took me to a room," continued Baldy, "and showed me. He's got that room full of drums and dolls and skates and bags of candy and jumping-jacks and toy lambs and whistles and such infantile truck. And what do you think he's goin' to do with them inefficacious knick-knacks? Don't surmise none—Cherokee told me. He's goin' to load 'em up in his red sleigh and—wait a minute, don't order no drinks yet—he's goin' to drive down here to Yellowhammer and give the kids—the kids of this here town—the biggest Christmas tree and the biggest cryin' doll and Little Giant Boys' Tool Chest blowout that was ever seen west of Cape Hatteras."

Two minutes of absolute silence ticked away in the wake of Baldy's words. It was broken by the House, who, happily conceiving the moment to be ripe for extending hospitality, sent a dozen whisky glasses spinning down the bar, with the slower travelling bottle bringing up the rear.

"Didn't you tell him?" asked the miner called Trinidad.

"Well, no," answered Baldy, pensively; "I never exactly seen my way to.

"You see, Cherokee had this Christmas mess already bought

and paid for; and he was all flattered up with self-esteem over his idea; and we had in a way flew the flume with that fizzy wine I speak of; so I never let on."

"I cannot refrain from a certain amount of surprise," said the Judge, as he hung his ivory-handled cane on the bar, "that our friend Cherokee should possess such an erroneous conception of—ah—his, as it were, own town."

"Oh, it ain't the eighth wonder of the terrestrial world," said Baldy. "Cherokee's been gone from Yellowhammer over seven months. Lots of things could happen in that time. How's he to know that there ain't a single kid in this town, and so far as emigration is concerned, none expected?"

"Come to think of it," remarked California Ed, "it's funny some ain't drifted in. Town ain't settled enough yet for to bring in the rubber-ring brigade, I reckon."

"To top off this Christmas-tree splurge of Cherokee's," went on Baldy, "he's goin' to give an imitation of Santa Claus. He's got a white wig and whiskers that disfigure him up exactly like the pictures of this William Cullen Longfellow in the books, and a red suit of fur-trimmed outside underwear, and eight-ounce gloves, and a stand-up, lay-down croshayed red cap. Ain't it a shame that a outfit like that can't get a chance to connect with a Annie and Willie's prayer layout?"

"When does Cherokee allow to come over with his truck?" inquired Trinidad.

"Mornin' before Christmas," said Baldy. "And he wants you folks to have a room fixed up and a tree hauled and ready. And such ladies to assist as can stop breathin' long enough to let it be a surprise for the kids."

The unblessed condition of Yellowhammer had been truly described. The voice of childhood had never gladdened its flimsy structures; the patter of restless little feet had never consecrated the one rugged highway between the two rows of tents and rough buildings. Later they would come. But now Yellowhammer was but a mountain camp, and nowhere in it were the roguish, expectant eyes, opening wide at dawn of the enchanting day; the eager, small hands to reach for Santa's bewildering hoard; the elated, childish voicings of the season's joy, such as the coming good things of the warm-hearted Cherokee deserved.

Of women there were five in Yellowhammer. The assayer's wife, the proprietress of the Lucky Strike Hotel, and a laundress whose washtub panned out an ounce of dust a day. These were the permanent feminines; the remaining two were the Spangler Sisters, Misses Fanchon and Erma, of the Transcontinental Comedy Company, then playing in repertoire at the (improvised) Empire Theatre. But of children there were none. Sometimes Miss Fanchon enacted with spirit and address the part of robustious childhood; but between her delineation and the visions of adolescence that the fancy offered as eligible recipients of Cherokee's holiday stores there seemed to be fixed a gulf.

Christmas would come on Thursday. On Tuesday morning Trinidad, instead of going to work, sought the Judge at the Lucky Strike Hotel.

"It'll be a disgrace to Yellowhammer," said Trinidad, "if it throws Cherokee down on his Christmas tree blowout. You might say that that man made this town. For one, I'm goin' to see what can be done to give Santa Claus a square deal."

"My co-operation," said the Judge, "would be gladly forthcoming. I am indebted to Cherokee for past favours. But, I do not see—I have heretofore regarded the absence of children rather as a luxury—but in this instance—still, I do not see—"

"Look at me," said Trinidad, "and you'll see old Ways and Means with the fur on. I'm goin' to hitch up a team and rustle a load of kids for Cherokee's Santa Claus act, if I have to rob an orphan asylum."

"Eureka!" cried the Judge, enthusiastically.

"No, you didn't," said Trinidad, decidedly. "I found it myself. I learned about that Latin word at school."

"I will accompany you," declared the Judge, waving his cane. "Perhaps such eloquence and gift of language as I may possess will be of benefit in persuading our young friends to lend themselves to our project."

Within an hour Yellowhammer was acquainted with the scheme of Trinidad and the Judge, and approved it. Citizens who knew of families with offspring within a forty-mile radius of Yellowhammer came forward and contributed their information. Trinidad made careful notes of all such, and then hastened to secure a vehicle and team.

The first stop scheduled was at a double log-house fifteen miles out from Yellowhammer. A man opened the door at Trinidad's hail, and then came down and leaned upon the rickety gate. The doorway was filled with a close mass of youngsters, some ragged, all full of curiosity and health.

"It's this way," explained Trinidad. "We're from Yellowhammer, and we come kidnappin' in a gentle kind of a way. One of our leading citizens is stung with the Santa Claus affliction, and he's due in town to-morrow with half the folderols that's painted red and made in Germany. The youngest kid we got in Yellowhammer packs a forty-five and a safety razor. Consequently we're mighty shy on anybody to say 'Oh' and 'Ah' when we light the candles on the Christmas tree. Now, partner, if you'll loan us a few kids we guarantee to return 'em safe and sound on Christmas Day. And they'll come back loaded down with a good time and Swiss Family Robinsons and cornucopias and red drums and similar testimonials. What do you say?"

"In other words," said the Judge, "we have discovered for the first time in our embryonic but progressive little city the inconveniences of the absence of adolescence. The season of the year having approximately arrived during which it is a custom to bestow frivolous but often appreciated gifts upon the young and tender—"

"I understand," said the parent, packing his pipe with a forefinger. "I guess I needn't detain you gentlemen. Me and the old woman have got seven kids, so to speak; and, runnin' my mind over the bunch, I don't appear to hit upon none that we could spare for you to take over to your doin's. The old woman has got some popcorn candy and rag dolls hid in the clothes chest, and we allow to give Christmas a little whirl of our own in a insignificant sort of style. No, I couldn't, with any degree of avidity, seem to fall in with the idea of lettin' none of 'em go. Thank you kindly, gentlemen."

Down the slope they drove and up another foothill to the ranch-house of Wiley Wilson. Trinidad recited his appeal and the Judge boomed out his ponderous antiphony. Mrs. Wiley gathered her two rosy-cheeked youngsters close to her skirts and did not smile until she had seen Wiley laugh and shake his head. Again a refusal.

Trinidad and the Judge vainly exhausted more than half their list before twilight set in among the hills. They spent the night at a stage road hostelry, and set out again early the next morning. The wagon had not acquired a single passenger.

"It's creepin' upon my faculties," remarked Trinidad, "that

borrowin' kids at Christmas is somethin' like tryin' to steal butter from a man that's got hot pancakes a-comin'."

"It is undoubtedly an indisputable fact," said the Judge, "that the—ah—family ties seem to be more coherent and assertive at that period of the year."

On the day before Christmas they drove thirty miles, making four fruitless halts and appeals. Everywhere they found "kids" at a premium.

The sun was low when the wife of a section boss on a lonely railroad huddled her unavailable progeny behind her and said:

"There's a woman that's just took charge of the railroad eatin' house down at Granite Junction. I hear she's got a little boy. Maybe she might let him go."

Trinidad pulled up his mules at Granite Junction at five o'clock in the afternoon. The train had just departed with its load of fed and appeased passengers.

On the steps of the eating house they found a thin and glowering boy of ten smoking a cigarette. The dining-room had been left in chaos by the peripatetic appetites. A youngish woman reclined, exhausted, in a chair. Her face wore sharp lines of worry. She had once possessed a certain style of beauty that would never wholly leave her and would never wholly return. Trinidad set forth his mission.

"I'd count it a mercy if you'd take Bobby for a while," she said, wearily. "I'm on the go from morning till night, and I don't have time to 'tend to him. He's learning bad habits from the men. It'll be the only chance he'll have to get any Christmas."

The men went outside and conferred with Bobby. Trinidad pictured the glories of the Christmas tree and presents in lively colours.

"And, moreover, my young friend," added the Judge

"Santa Claus himself will personally distribute the offerings that will typify the gifts conveyed by the shepherds of Bethlehem to—"

"Aw, come *off*," said the boy, squinting his small eyes. "I ain't no kid. There ain't any Santa Claus. It's your folks that buys toys and sneaks 'em in when you're asleep. And they make marks in the soot in the chimney with the tongs to look like Santa's sleigh tracks."

"That might be so," argued Trinidad, "but Christmas trees ain't no fairy tale. This one's goin' to look like the ten-cent store in Albuquerque, all strung up in a redwood. There's tops and drums and Noah's arks and—"

"Oh, rats!" said Bobby, wearily. "I cut them out long ago. I'd like to have a rifle—not a target one—a real one, to shoot wildcats with; but I guess you won't have any of them on your old tree."

"Well, I can't say for sure," said Trinidad diplomatically; "it might be. You go along with us and see."

The hope thus held out, though faint, won the boy's hesitating consent to go. With this solitary beneficiary for Cherokee's holiday bounty, the canvassers spun along the homeward road.

In Yellowhammer the empty storeroom had been transformed into what might have passed as the bower of an Arizona fairy. The ladies had done their work well. A tall Christmas tree, covered to the topmost branch with candles, spangles, and toys sufficient for more than a score of children, stood in the centre of the floor. Near sunset anxious eyes had begun to scan the street for the returning team of the child-providers. At noon that day Cherokee had dashed into town with his new sleigh piled high with bundles and boxes and bales of all sizes and shapes. So intent was he upon the arrangements for his altruistic plans that the dearth of childhood did not receive his notice. No one gave away the humiliating state of Yellowhammer, for the efforts of Trinidad and the Judge were expected to supply the deficiency.

When the sun went down Cherokee, with many winks and arch grins on his seasoned face, went into retirement with the bundle containing the Santa Claus raiment and a pack containing special and undisclosed gifts.

"When the kids are rounded up," he instructed the volunteer arrangement committee, "light up the candles on the tree and set 'em to playin' 'Pussy Wants a Corner' and 'King William.' When they get good and at it, why—old Santa'll slide in the door. I reckon there'll be plenty of gifts to go 'round."

The ladies were flitting about the tree, giving it final touches that were never final. The Spangled Sisters were there in costume as Lady Violet de Vere and Marie, the maid, in their new drama, "The Miner's Bride." The theatre did not open until nine, and they were welcome assistants of the Christmas tree committee. Every minute heads would pop out the door to look and listen for the approach of Trinidad's team. And now this became an anxious function, for night had fallen and it would soon be necessary to light the candles on the tree, and Cherokee was apt to make an irruption at any time in his Kriss Kringle garb.

At length the wagon of the child "rustlers" rattled down the street to the door. The ladies, with little screams of excitement, flew to the lighting of the candles. The men of Yellowhammer passed in and out restlessly or stood about the room in embarrassed groups.

Trinidad and the Judge, bearing the marks of protracted travel, entered, conducting between them a single impish boy, who stared with sullen, pessimistic eyes at the gaudy tree.

"Where are the other children?" asked the assayer's wife, the acknowledged leader of all social functions.

"Ma'am," said Trinidad with a sigh, "prospectin' for kids at Christmas time is like huntin' in limestone for silver. This parental business is one that I haven't no chance to comprehend. It seems that fathers and mothers are willin' for their offsprings to be drownded, stole, fed on poison oak, and et by catamounts 364 days in the year; but on Christmas Day they insists on enjoyin' the exclusive mortification of their company. This here young biped, ma'am, is all that washes out of our two days' manœuvres."

"Oh, the sweet little boy!" cooed Miss Erma, trailing her De Vere robes to centre of stage.

"Aw, shut up," said Bobby, with a scowl. "Who's a kid? You ain't, you bet."

"Fresh brat!" breathed Miss Erma, beneath her enamelled smile.

"We done the best we could," said Trinidad. "It's tough on Cherokee, but it can't be helped."

Then the door opened and Cherokee entered in the conventional dress of Saint Nick. A white rippling beard and flowing hair covered his face almost to his dark and shining eyes. Over his shoulder he carried a pack.

No one stirred as he came in. Even the Spangler Sisters ceased their coquettish poses and stared curiously at the tall figure. Bobby stood with his hands in his pockets gazing gloomily at the effeminate and childish tree. Cherokee put down his pack and looked wonderingly about the room.

Perhaps he fancied that a bevy of eager children were being herded somewhere, to be loosed upon his entrance. He went up to Bobby and extended his red-mittened hand.

"Merry Christmas, little boy," said Cherokee. "Anything on the tree you want they'll get it down for you. Won't you shake hands with Santa Claus?"

"There ain't any Santa Claus," whined the boy. "You've got old false billy goat's whiskers on your face. I ain't no kid. What do I want with dolls and tin horses? The driver said you'd have a rifle, and you haven't. I want to go home."

Trinidad stepped into the breach. He shook Cherokee's hand in warm greeting.

"I'm sorry, Cherokee," he explained. "There never was a kid in Yellowhammer. We tried to rustle a bunch of 'em for your swaree, but this sardine was all we could catch. He's a atheist, and he don't believe in Santa Claus. It's a shame for you to be out all this truck. But me and the Judge was sure we could round up a wagonful of candidates for your gimcracks."

"That's all right," said Cherokee gravely. "The expense don't amount to nothin' worth mentionin'. We can dump the stuff down a shaft or throw it away. I don't know what I was thinkin' about; but it never occurred to my cogitations that there wasn't any kids in Yellowhammer."

Meanwhile the company had relaxed into a hollow but praiseworthy imitation of a pleasure gathering.

Bobby had retreated to a distant chair, and was coldly regarding the scene with ennui plastered thick upon him. Cherokee, lingering with his original idea, went over and sat beside him.

"Where do you live, little boy?" he asked respectfully.

"Granite Junction," said Bobby without emphasis. The

room was warm. Cherokee took off his cap, and then removed his beard and wig.

"Say!" exclaimed Bobby, with a show of interest, "I know your mug, all right."

"Did you ever see me before?" asked Cherokee.

"I don't know; but I've seen your picture lots of times."

"Where?"

The boy hesitated. "On the bureau at home," he answered.

"Let's have your name, if you please, buddy."

"Robert Lumsden. The picture belongs to my mother. She puts it under her pillow of nights. And once I saw her kiss it. I wouldn't. But women are that way."

Cherokee rose and beckoned to Trinidad.

"Keep this boy by you till I come back," he said. "I'm goin' to shed these Christmas duds, and hitch up my sleigh. I'm goin' to take this kid home."

"Well, infidel," said Trinidad, taking Cherokee's vacant chair, "and so you are too superannuated and effete to yearn for such mockeries as candy and toys, it seems."

"I don't like you," said Bobby, with acrimony. "You said there would be a rifle. A fellow can't even smoke. I wish I was at home."

Cherokee drove his sleigh to the door, and they lifted Bobby in beside him. The team of fine horses sprang away prancingly over the hard snow. Cherokee had on his $500 overcoat of baby sealskin. The laprobe that he drew about them was as warm as velvet.

Bobby slipped a cigarette from his pocket and was trying to snap a match.

"Throw that cigarette away," said Cherokee, in a quiet but new voice.

Bobby hesitated, and then dropped the cylinder overboard.

"Throw the box, too," commanded the new voice.

More reluctantly the boy obeyed.

"Say," said Bobby, presently, "I like you. I don't know why. Nobody never made me do anything I didn't want to do before."

"Tell me, kid," said Cherokee, not using his new voice, "are you sure your mother kissed that picture that looks like me?"

"Dead sure. I seen her do it."

"Didn't you remark somethin' a while ago about wanting a rifle?"

"You bet I did. Will you get me one?"

"To-morrow—silver-mounted."

Cherokee took out his watch.

"Half-past nine. We'll hit the Junction plumb on time with Christmas Day. Are you cold? Sit closer, son."

A Christmas Mystery

by William J. Locke

Three men who had gained great fame and honour throughout the world met unexpectedly in front of the bookstall at Paddington Station. Like most of the great ones of the earth they were personally acquainted, and they exchanged surprised greetings.

Sir Angus McCurdie, the eminent physicist, scowled at the two others beneath his heavy black eyebrows.

"I'm going to a God-forsaken place in Cornwall called Trehenna," said he.

"That's odd; so am I," croaked Professor Biggleswade. He was a little, untidy man with round spectacles, a fringe of greyish beard and a weak, rasping voice, and he knew more of Assyriology than any man, living or dead. A flippant pupil once remarked that the Professor's face was furnished with a Babylonic cuneiform in lieu of features.

"People called Deverill, at Foullis Castle?" asked Sir Angus.

"Yes," replied Professor Biggleswade.

"How curious! I am going to the Deverills, too," said the third man.

This man was the Right Honourable Viscount Doyne, the renowned Empire Builder and Administrator, around whose solitary and remote life popular imagination had woven many legends. He looked at the world through tired grey eyes, and the heavy, drooping, blonde moustache seemed tired, too, and had dragged down the tired face into deep furrows. He was smoking a long black cigar.

"I suppose we may as well travel down together," said Sir Angus, not very cordially.

Lord Doyne said courteously: "I have a reserved carriage. The railway company is always good enough to place one at my disposal. It would give me great pleasure if you would share it."

The invitation was accepted, and the three men crossed the busy, crowded platform to take their seats in the great express train. A porter, laden with an incredible load of paraphernalia, trying to make his way through the press, happened to jostle Sir Angus McCurdie. He rubbed his shoulder fretfully.

"Why the whole land should be turned into a bear garden on account of this exploded superstition of Christmas is one of the anomalies of modern civilization. Look at this insensate welter of fools travelling in wild herds to disgusting places merely because it's Christmas!"

"You seem to be travelling yourself, McCurdie," said Lord Doyne.

"Yes—and why the devil I'm doing it, I've not the faintest notion," replied Sir Angus.

"It's going to be a beast of a journey," he remarked some moments later, as the train carried them slowly out of the station. "The whole country is under snow—and as far as I can understand we have to change twice and wind up with a twenty-mile motor drive."

He was an iron-faced, beetle-browed, stern man, and this morning he did not seem to be in the best of tempers. Finding his companions inclined to be sympathetic, he continued his lamentation.

"And merely because it's Christmas I've had to shut up my laboratory and give my young fools a holiday—just when I was in the midst of a most important series of experiments."

Professor Biggleswade, who had heard vaguely of and rather looked down upon such new-fangled toys as radium and thorium and helium and argon—for the latest astonishing developments in the theory of radio-activity had brought Sir Angus McCurdie his world-wide fame—said somewhat ironically:

"If the experiments were so important, why didn't you lock yourself up with your test tubes and electric batteries and finish them alone?"

"Man!" said McCurdie, bending across the carriage, and speaking with a curious intensity of voice, "d'ye know I'd give a hundred pounds to be able to answer that question?"

"What do you mean?" asked the Professor, startled.

"I should like to know why I'm sitting in this damned train and going to visit a couple of addle-headed society people whom I'm scarcely acquainted with, when I might be at home in my own good company furthering the progress of science."

"I myself," said the Professor, "am not acquainted with them at all."

It was Sir Angus McCurdie's turn to look surprised.

"Then why are you spending Christmas with them?"

"I reviewed a ridiculous blank-verse tragedy written by Deverill on the Death of Sennacherib. Historically it was puerile. I said so in no measured terms. He wrote a letter claiming to be a poet and not an archaeologist. I replied that the day had passed when poets could with impunity commit the abominable crime of distorting history. He retorted with some futile argument, and we went on exchanging letters, until his invitation and my acceptance concluded the correspondence."

McCurdie, still bending his black brows on him, asked him why he had not declined. The Professor screwed up his face till it looked more like a cuneiform than ever. He, too, found the question difficult to answer, but he showed a bold front.

"I felt it my duty," said he, "to teach that preposterous ignoramus something worth knowing about Sennacherib. Besides I am a bachelor and would sooner spend Christmas, as to whose irritating and meaningless annoyance I cordially agree with you, among strangers than among my married sisters' numerous and nerve-racking families."

Sir Angus McCurdie, the hard, metallic apostle of radio-activity, glanced for a moment out of the window at the grey, frost-bitten fields. Then he said:

"I'm a widower. My wife died many years ago and, thank God, we had no children. I generally spend Christmas alone."

He looked out of the window again. Professor Biggleswade suddenly remembered the popular story of the great scientist's antecedents, and reflected that as McCurdie had once run, a bare-foot urchin, through the Glasgow mud, he was likely to have little kith or kin. He himself envied McCurdie. He was always praying to be delivered from his sisters and nephews and nieces, whose embarrassing demands no calculated coldness could repress.

"Children are the root of all evil," said he. "Happy the man who has his quiver empty."

Sir Angus McCurdie did not reply at once; when he spoke again it was with reference to their prospective host.

"I met Deverill," said he, "at the Royal Society's Soirée this year. One of my assistants was demonstrating a peculiar property of thorium and Deverill seemed interested. I asked him to come to my laboratory the next day, and found he didn't know a damned thing about anything. That's all the acquaintance I have with him."

Lord Doyne, the great administrator, who had been wearily turning over the pages of an illustrated weekly chiefly filled with flamboyant photographs of obscure actresses, took his gold glasses from his nose and the black cigar from his lips, and addressed his companions.

"I've been considerably interested in your conversation," said he, "and as you've been frank, I'll be frank too. I knew Mrs. Deverill's mother, Lady Carstairs, very well years ago, and of course Mrs. Deverill when she was a child. Deverill I came across once in Egypt—he had been sent on a diplomatic mission to Teheran. As for our being invited on such slight acquaintance, little Mrs. Deverill has the reputation of being the only really successful celebrity hunter in England. She inherited the faculty from her mother, who entertained the whole world. We're sure to find archbishops, and eminent actors, and illustrious divorcées asked to meet us. That's one thing. But why I, who loathe country house parties and children and Christmas as much as Biggleswade, am going down there to-day, I can no more explain than you can. It's a devilish odd coincidence."

The three men looked at one another. Suddenly McCurdie shivered and drew his fur coat around him.

"I'll thank you," said he, "to shut that window."

"It is shut," said Doyne.

"It's just uncanny," said McCurdie, looking from one to the other.

"What?" asked Doyne.

"Nothing, if you didn't feel it."

"There did seem to be a sudden draught," said Professor Biggleswade. "But as both window and door are shut, it could only be imaginary."

"It wasn't imaginary," muttered McCurdie.

Then he laughed harshly. "My father and mother came from Cromarty," he said with apparent irrelevance.

"That's the Highlands," said the Professor.

"Ay," said McCurdie.

Lord Doyne said nothing, but tugged at his moustache and looked out of the window as the frozen meadows and bits of river and willows raced past. A dead silence fell on them. McCurdie broke it with another laugh and took a whiskey flask from his hand-bag.

"Have a nip?"

"Thanks, no," said the Professor. "I have to keep to a strict dietary, and I only drink hot milk and water—and of that sparingly. I have some in a thermos bottle."

Lord Doyne also declining the whiskey, McCurdie swallowed a dram and declared himself to be better. The Professor took from his bag a foreign review in which a German sciolist had dared to question his interpretation of a Hittite inscription. Over the man's ineptitude he fell asleep and snored loudly.

To escape from his immediate neighbourhood McCurdie went to the other end of the seat and faced Lord Doyne, who had resumed his gold glasses and his listless contemplation of obscure actresses. McCurdie lit a pipe, Doyne another black cigar. The tram thundered on.

Presently they all lunched together in the restaurant car. The windows steamed, but here and there through a wiped patch of pane a white world was revealed. The snow was falling. As they passed through Westbury, McCurdie looked mechanically for the famous white horse carved into the chalk of the down; but it was not visible beneath the thick covering of snow.

"It'll be just like this all the way to Gehenna—Trehenna, I mean," said McCurdie.

Doyne nodded. He had done his life's work amid all extreme fiercenesses of heat and cold, in burning droughts, in simoons and in icy wildernesses, and a ray or two more of the pale sun or a flake or two more of the gentle snow of England mattered to him but little. But Biggleswade rubbed the pane with his table-napkin and gazed apprehensively at the prospect.

"If only this wretched train would stop," said he, "I would go back again."

And he thought how comfortable it would be to sneak home again to his books and thus elude not only the Deverills, but the Christmas jollities of his sisters' families, who would think him miles away. But the train was timed not to stop till Plymouth, two hundred and thirty-five miles from London, and thither was he being relentlessly carried. Then he quarrelled with his food, which brought a certain consolation.

The train did stop, however, before Plymouth—indeed, before Exeter. An accident on the line had dislocated the traffic. The express was held up for an hour, and when it was permitted to proceed, instead of thundering on, it went cautiously, subject to continual stoppings. It arrived at Plymouth two hours late. The travellers learned that they had missed the connection on which they had counted and that they could not reach Trehenna till nearly ten o'clock. After weary waiting at Plymouth they took their seats in the little, cold local train that was to carry them another stage on their journey. Hot-water cans put in at Plymouth mitigated to some extent the iciness of the compartment. But that only lasted a comparatively short time, for soon they were set down at a desolate, shelterless wayside junction, dumped in the midst of a hilly snow-covered waste, where they went through another weary wait for another dismal local train that was to carry them to Trehenna. And in this train there were no hot-water cans, so that the compartment was as cold as death. McCurdie fretted and shook his fist in the direction of Trehenna.

"And when we get there we have still a twenty miles' motor drive to Foullis Castle. It's a fool name and we're fools to be going there."

"I shall die of bronchitis," wailed Professor Biggleswade.

"A man dies when it is appointed for him to die," said Lord Doyne, in his tired way; and he went on smoking long black cigars.

"It's not the dying that worries me," said McCurdie. "That's a mere mechanical process which every organic being from a king to a cauliflower has to pass through. It's the being forced against my will and my reason to come on this accursed journey, which something tells me will become more and more accursed as we go on, that is driving me to distraction."

"What will be, will be," said Doyne.

"I can't see where the comfort of that reflection comes in," said Biggleswade.

"And yet you've travelled in the East," said Doyne. "I suppose you know the Valley of the Tigris as well as any man living."

"Yes," said the Professor. "I can say I dug my way from Tekrit to Bagdad and left not a stone unexamined."

"Perhaps, after all," Doyne remarked, "that's not quite the way to know the East."

"I never wanted to know the modern East," returned the Professor. "What is there in it of interest compared with the mighty civilizations that have gone before?"

McCurdie took a pull from his flask.

"I'm glad I thought of having a refill at Plymouth," said he.

At last, after many stops at little lonely stations they arrived at Trehenna. The guard opened the door and they stepped out on to the snow-covered platform. An oil lamp hung from the tiny pent-house roof that, structurally, was Trehenna Station. They looked around at the silent gloom of white undulating moorland, and it seemed a place where no man lived and only ghosts could have a bleak and unsheltered being. A porter came up and helped the guard with the luggage. Then they realized that the station was built on a small embankment, for, looking over the railing, they saw below the two great lamps of a motor car. A fur-clad chauffeur met them at the bottom of the stairs. He clapped his hands together and informed them cheerily that he had been waiting for four hours. It was the bitterest winter in these parts within the memory of man, said he, and he himself had not seen snow there for five years. Then he settled the three travellers in the great roomy touring car covered with a Cape-cart hood, wrapped them up in many rugs and started.

After a few moments, the huddling together of their bodies—for, the Professor being a spare man, there was room for them all on the back seat—the pile of rugs, the serviceable and all but air-tight hood, induced a pleasant warmth and a pleasant drowsiness. Where they were being driven they knew not. The perfectly upholstered seat eased their limbs, the easy swinging motion of the car soothed their spirits. They felt that already they had reached the luxuriously appointed home which, after all, they knew awaited them. McCurdie no longer railed, Professor Biggleswade forgot the dangers of bronchitis, and Lord Doyne twisted the stump of a black cigar between his lips without any desire to relight it. A tiny electric lamp inside the hood made the darkness of the world to right and left and in front of the talc windows still darker. McCurdie and Biggleswade fell into a doze. Lord Doyne chewed the end of his cigar. The car sped on through an unseen wilderness.

Suddenly there was a horrid jolt and a lurch and a leap and a rebound, and then the car stood still, quivering like a ship that has been struck by a heavy sea. The three men were pitched and tossed and thrown sprawling over one another onto the bottom of the car. Biggleswade screamed. McCurdie cursed. Doyne scrambled from the confusion of rugs and limbs and, tearing open the side of the Cape-cart hood, jumped out. The chauffeur had also just leaped from his seat. It was pitch dark save for the great shaft of light down the snowy road cast by the acetylene lamps. The snow had ceased falling.

"What's gone wrong?"

"It sounds like the axle," said the chauffeur ruefully.

He unshipped a lamp and examined the car, which had wedged itself against a great drift of snow on the off side. Meanwhile McCurdie and Biggleswade had alighted.

"Yes, it's the axle," said the chauffeur.

"Then we're done," remarked Doyne.

"I'm afraid so, my lord."

"What's the matter? Can't we get on?" asked Biggleswade in his querulous voice.

McCurdie laughed. "How can we get on with a broken axle? The thing's as useless as a man with a broken back. Gad, I was right. I said it was going to be an infernal journey."

The little Professor wrung his hands. "But what's to be done?" he cried.

"Tramp it," said Lord Doyne, lighting a fresh cigar.

"It's ten miles," said the chauffeur.

"It would be the death of me," the Professor wailed.

"I utterly refuse to walk ten miles through a Polar waste with a gouty foot," McCurdie declared wrathfully.

The chauffeur offered a solution of the difficulty. He would set out alone for Foullis Castle—five miles farther on was an inn where he could obtain a horse and trap—and would return for the three gentlemen with another car. In the meanwhile they could take shelter in a little house which they had just passed, some half mile up the road. This was agreed to. The chauffeur went on cheerily enough with a lamp, and the three travellers with another lamp started off in the opposite direction. As far as they could see they were in a long, desolate valley, a sort of No Man's Land, deathly silent. The eastern sky had cleared somewhat, and they faced a loose rack through which one pale star was dimly visible.

"I'm a man of science," said McCurdie as they trudged through the snow, "and I dismiss the supernatural as contrary to reason; but I have Highland blood in my veins that plays me exasperating tricks. My reason tells me that this place is only a commonplace moor, yet it seems like a Valley of Bones haunted by malignant spirits who have lured us here to our destruction. There's something guiding us now. It's just uncanny."

"Why on earth did we ever come?" croaked Biggleswade.

Lord Doyne answered: "The Koran says, 'Nothing can befall us but what God hath destined for us.' So why worry?"

"Because I'm not a Mohammedan," retorted Biggleswade.

"You might be worse," said Doyne.

Presently the dun outline of the little house grew perceptible. A faint light shone from the window. It stood unfenced by any kind of hedge or railing a few feet away from the road in a little hollow beneath some rising ground. As far as they could discern in the darkness when they drew near, the house was a mean, dilapidated hovel. A guttering candle stood on the inner sill of the small window and afforded a vague view into a mean interior. Doyne held up the lamp so that its rays fell full on the door. As he did so, an exclamation broke from his lips and he hurried forward, followed by the others. A man's body lay huddled together on the snow by the threshold. He was dressed like a peasant, in old corduroy trousers and rough coat, and a handkerchief was knotted round his neck. In his hand he grasped the neck of a broken bottle. Doyne set the lamp on the ground and the three bent down together over the man. Close by the neck lay the rest of the broken bottle, whose contents had evidently run out into the snow.

"Drunk?" asked Biggleswade.

Doyne felt the man and laid his hand on his heart.

"No," said he, "dead."

McCurdie leaped to his full height. "I told you the place was uncanny!" he cried. "It's fey." Then he hammered wildly at the door.

There was no response. He hammered again till it rattled. This time a faint prolonged sound like the wailing of a strange sea-creature was heard from within the house. McCurdie turned round, his teeth chattering.

"Did ye hear that, Doyne?"

"Perhaps it's a dog," said the Professor.

Lord Doyne, the man of action, pushed them aside and tried the doorhandle. It yielded, the door stood open, and the gust of cold wind entering the house extinguished the candle within. They entered and found themselves in a miserable stone-paved kitchen, furnished with poverty-stricken meagreness—a wooden chair or two, a dirty table, some broken crockery, old cooking utensils, a fly-blown missionary society almanac, and a fireless grate. Doyne set the lamp on the table.

"We must bring him in," said he.

They returned to the threshold, and as they were bending over to grip the dead man the same sound filled the air, but this time louder, more intense, a cry of great agony. The sweat dripped from McCurdie's forehead. They lifted the dead man and brought him into the room, and after laying him on a dirty strip of carpet they did their best to straighten the stiff limbs. Biggleswade put on the table a bundle which he had picked up outside. It contained some poor provisions—a loaf, a piece of fat bacon, and a paper of tea. As far as they could guess (and as they learned later they guessed rightly) the man was the master of the house, who, coming home blind drunk from some distant inn, had fallen at his own threshold and got frozen to death. As they could not unclasp his fingers from the broken bottleneck they had to let him clutch it as a dead warrior clutches the hilt of his broken sword.

Then suddenly the whole place was rent with another and yet another long, soul-piercing moan of anguish.

"There's a second room," said Doyne, pointing to a door. "The sound comes from there."

He opened the door, peeped in, and then, returning for the lamp, disappeared, leaving McCurdie and Biggleswade in the pitch darkness, with the dead man on the floor.

"For heaven's sake, give me a drop of whiskey," said the Professor, "or I shall faint."

Presently the door opened and Lord Doyne appeared in the shaft of light. He beckoned to his companions.

"It is a woman in childbirth," he said in his even, tired voice. "We must aid her. She appears unconscious. Does either of you know anything about such things?"

They shook their heads, and the three looked at each other in dismay. Masters of knowledge that had won them world-wide fame and honour, they stood helpless, abashed before this, the commonest phenomenon of nature.

"My wife had no child," said McCurdie.

"I've avoided women all my life," said Biggleswade.

"And I've been too busy to think of them. God forgive me," said Doyne.

The history of the next two hours was one that none of the three men ever cared to touch upon. They did things blindly, instinctively, as men do when they come face to face with the elemental. A fire was made, they knew not how, water drawn they knew not whence, and a kettle boiled. Doyne accustomed to command, directed. The others obeyed. At his suggestion they hastened to the wreck of the car and came staggering back beneath rugs and travelling bags which could supply clean linen and needful things, for amid the poverty of the house they could find nothing fit for human touch or use. Early they saw that the woman's strength was failing, and that she could not live. And there, in that nameless hovel, with death on the hearthstone and death and life hovering over the pitiful bed, the three great men went through the pain and the horror and squalor of birth, and they knew that they had never yet stood before so great a mystery.

With the first wail of the newly born infant a last convulsive shudder passed through the frame of the unconscious mother. Then three or four short gasps for breath, and the spirit passed away. She was dead. Professor Biggleswade threw a corner of the sheet over her face, for he could not bear to see it.

They washed and dried the child as any crone of a midwife would have done, and dipped a small sponge which had always remained unused in a cut-glass bottle in Doyne's dressing-bag in the hot milk and water of Biggleswade's thermos bottle, and put it to his lips; and then they wrapped him up warm in some of their own woollen undergarments, and took him into the kitchen and placed him on a bed made of their fur coats in front of the fire. As the last piece of fuel was exhausted they took one of the wooden chairs and broke it up and cast it into the blaze. And then they raised the dead man from the strip of carpet and carried him into the bedroom and laid him reverently by the side of his dead wife, after which they left the dead in darkness and returned to the living. And the three grave men stood over the wisp of flesh that had been born a male into the world. Then, their task being accomplished, reaction came, and even Doyne, who had seen death in many lands, turned faint. But the others, losing control of their nerves, shook like men stricken with palsy.

Suddenly McCurdie cried in a high pitched voice, "My God! Don't you feel it?" and clutched Doyne by the arm. An expression of terror appeared on his iron features. "There! It's here with us."

Little Professor Biggleswade sat on a corner of the table and wiped his forehead.

"I heard it. I felt it. It was like the beating of wings."

"It's the fourth time," said McCurdie. "The first time was just before I accepted the Deverills' invitation. The second in the railway carriage this afternoon. The third on the way here. This is the fourth."

Biggleswade plucked nervously at the fringe of whisker under his jaws and said faintly, "It's the fourth time up to now. I thought it was fancy."

"I have felt it, too," said Doyne. "It is the Angel of Death." And he pointed to the room where the dead man and woman lay.

"For God's sake let us get away from this," cried Biggleswade.

"And leave the child to die, like the others?" said Doyne.

"We must see it through," said McCurdie.

A silence fell upon them as they sat round in the blaze with the new-born babe wrapped in its odd swaddling clothes asleep on the pile of fur coats, and it lasted until Sir Angus McCurdie looked at his watch.

"Good Lord," said he, "it's twelve o'clock."

"Christmas morning," said Biggleswade.

"A strange Christmas," mused Doyne.

McCurdie put up his hand. "There it is again! The beating of wings." And they listened like men spellbound. McCurdie kept his hand uplifted, and gazed over their heads at the wall, and his gaze was that of a man in a trance, and he spoke:

"Unto us a child is born, unto us a son is given—"

Doyne sprang from his chair, which fell behind him with a crash.

"Man—what the devil are you saying?"

Then McCurdie rose and met Biggleswade's eyes staring at him through the great round spectacles, and Biggleswade turned and met the eyes of Doyne. A pulsation like the beating of wings stirred the air.

The three wise men shivered with a queer exaltation. Something strange, mystical, dynamic had happened. It was as if scales had fallen from their eyes and they saw with a new vision. They stood together humbly, divested of all their greatness, touching one another in the instinctive fashion of children, as if seeking mutual protection, and they looked, with one accord, irresistibly compelled, at the child.

At last McCurdie unbent his black brows and said hoarsely:

"It was not the Angel of Death, Doyne, but another Messenger that drew us here."

The tiredness seemed to pass away from the great administrator's face, and he nodded his head with the calm of a man who has come to the quiet heart of a perplexing mystery.

"It's true," he murmured. "Unto us a child is born, unto us a son is given. Unto the three of us."

Biggleswade took off his great round spectacles and wiped them.

"Gaspar, Melchior, Balthazar. But where are the gold, frankincense and myrrh?"

"In our hearts, man," said McCurdie.

The babe cried and stretched its tiny limbs.

Instinctively they all knelt down together to discover, if possible, and administer ignorantly to, its wants. The scene had the appearance of an adoration.

Then these three wise, lonely, childless men who, in furtherance of their own greatness, had cut themselves adrift from the sweet and simple things of life and from the kindly ways of their brethren, and had grown old in unhappy and profitless wisdom, knew that an inscrutable Providence had led them, as it had led three Wise Men of old, on a Christmas morning long ago, to a nativity which should give them a new wisdom, a new link with humanity, a new spiritual outlook, a new hope.

And, when their watch was ended, they wrapped up the babe with precious care, and carried him with them, an inalienable joy and possession, into the great world.

About the Authors

Willis Boyd Allen (1855–1938). Maine born and Harvard educated, Allen was a member of a prominent Boston law firm until 1888 when he left the bar to turn his energies to writing. He wrote for the *Atlantic Monthly, Scribner's,* the *Century* and other celebrated magazines of that era, editing two popular but now lesser-known weeklies himself—*The Cottage Hearth Magazine* and *Our Sunday Afternoon.* Among his many books are: *Silver Rags* (1886), *Cloud and Cliff, or Summer Days at the White Mountains* (1889), *John Brownlow's Folks* (1891), *Around the Yule Log* (1898) and *Sword and Plowshare* (1904).

Louisa May Alcott (1832–1888). One of the best-loved of all American writers, Alcott grew up in New England, the daughter of Bronson Alcott, a visionary educator and utopian thinker. At the age of seventeen she began contributing to the support of her family. She served as a nurse during the Civil War and wrote the memoir *Hospital Sketches* (1863) about her experiences. In 1868, when her novel *Little Women*—it featured a loving household of four girls based on her own—came out, it was an instant success. She followed it with such other favorites as *An Old-Fashioned Girl* (1870), *Little Men* (1871), *Eight Cousins* (1874) and *Rose in Bloom* (1876) Her final book, *Jo's Boys,* was published in 1886.

Mary E. Wilkins Freeman (1852–1930). Like Alcott, Freeman came from a financially precarious New England background and was forced by necessity to seek work when still in her teens. She began contributing to various children's magazines of the day in the early 1880s, but by the end of the decade had published the first of the two adult short story collections which would secure her reputation. *A Humble Romance and Other Stories* (1888) was followed three years later by *A New England Nun and Other Stories* (1891); each book contained telling portraits of ordinary women facing everyday conflicts. Both were published as by Mary E. Wilkins; she married Dr. Charles Freeman late in life, at which point she began using his name.

M. E. Braddon (1835–1915). Mary Elizabeth Braddon quickly experienced the rewards of Victorian blockbuster status with the publication of her second novel, the highly lurid *Lady Audley's Secret* (1862). Dubbed the "queen of the circulating libraries" and admired by such contemporaries as Tennyson, Dickens, Thackeray and Henry James, she produced more than eighty other titillating melodramas, including *Charlotte's Inheritance* (1868), *To the Bitter End* (1872), *Willard's Weird* (1885) and *Her Convict* (1908). Born in London two years before Queen Victoria took the throne, Braddon lived long enough to see a screening of the silent film of her second book, *Aurora Floyd* (1863).

Armando Palacio Valdés (1853–1938). A native of the province of Asturias, Palacio Valdés first studied law at the University of Madrid. His reputation as a novelist rests upon such works as *El señorito Octavio* (1881), *Marta y Maria* (1883), *José* (1885), *La hermana San Sulpicio* (1889) and *La aldea perdida* (1911). His other writing includes the critical study, *Los Novelistas españoles* (1878) and part of an unfinished autobiography, *El idilio de un enfermo.* Called "Spain's most beloved writer" and "patriarch of contemporary Spanish letters," he was once considered to be his country's leading contender for the Nobel Prize in literature. There are few recent translations of his work, an exception being *Alone, and Other Stories* (1993).

Zona Gale (1874–1938). Portage, the small Wisconsin town, where she grew up an only child, provided the background for much of Gale's work. A journalist before turning fiction writer, she worked for newspapers in Milwaukee and New York, then moved back to

Portage in 1912, making it her home for the rest of her life. Her best-known creation is *Miss Lulu Bett* (1920), which she wrote first as a novel and went on to adapt for the stage; it was awarded the 1921 Pulitzer Prize for drama. (She was the first woman to win in that category.) Gale's other novels include *Faint Perfume* (1923), *Papa La Fleur* (1933) and *Light Woman* (1937).

Myra Kelly (1875–1910). The daughter of an Irish physician who emigrated to New York City where he established a thriving practice, Kelly taught public school after graduating from Columbia University's Teachers College. Her first book, *Little Citizens: The Humours of School Life* (1904), drew upon her experiences with the children of Jewish tenement families, and, after its success, others soon followed, including *Wards of Liberty* (1907) and *Little Aliens* (1910). Among her admirers were President Theodore Roosevelt, who sent her a fan letter from the White House.

Ida M. H. Starr (1859–1938). Brought up in Cincinnati, Ohio, Ida May Hill attended Vassar College for two years before returning home to the University of Cincinnati where she studied music. Leaving there, she traveled to Germany where she was accepted as a pupil of the legendary Clara Schumann. In 1886 she married William J. Starr, who would become a distinguished Wisconsin judge, and at this point began to shift her artistic attention to writing. Among Starr's novels are *Gardens of the Caribees* (1903), *Beyond the Sunset* (1921) and *Amazing Finale* (1927).

John Kendrick Bangs (1862–1922). Born in Yonkers, New York, Bangs briefly studied law at Columbia—where he'd earned his undergraduate degree—but quit to take a magazine job, progressing through the offices of *Harper's Weekly* and *Munsey's*, among others, before winding up, briefly, the editor of *Puck* in 1904. His whimsical fictions include *A House-Boat on the Styx* (1898), *The Enchanted Type-Writer* (1899) and *Mrs Raffles* (1905), and his use of aspects of the afterlife for comic effect led to writings in this style being dubbed "Bangsian fantasy." In 1894 he ran for mayor of Yonkers, losing narrowly but getting a book out of the experience, *Three Weeks in Politics* (1894).

Anthony Trollope (1815–1882). Soon after his birth, Trollope's parents moved from London to the then-rural village of Harrow, where he began his education at that ancient public school. Later, after failing to secure a university scholarship, he entered into a clerkship at the General Post Office, the branch of the English civil service in which he would make his career for more than thirty years. Many people would call Trollope's most beloved novels the ones comprising the slyly comic Barset series, a half-dozen titles beginning with *The Warden* (in book form, 1855) and ending with *The Last Chronicle of Barset* (1867). His other great achievement is the Palliser cycle, the six books of which—beginning with *Phineas Finn, the Irish Member* (1869)—are more worldly, more complex and more concerned with the larger social and political issues of the day. *Rachel Ray* (1863), *The Belton Estate* (1865), *The Claverings* (1867), *Ralph the Heir* (1871) and *The American Senator* (1877) are among the thirty-five remaining novels by this most splendid of Victorian storytellers.

Paul Laurence Dunbar (1872–1906). A native Ohioan and the son of former slaves, Dunbar was the only African-American student in his high school class yet became editor of the school paper and president of the literary society, With his mother's encouragement he'd begun writing and reciting poetry as a small boy; on his twentieth birthday, he gave the first public reading of his own work. Supported by such early prominent mentors as the Wright brothers (Orville had been a classmate), James Whitcomb Riley, Frederick Douglass and William Dean Howells, Dunbar had a New York publisher—Dodd, Mead, for *Lyrics of a Lowly Life*—by the time he was tweny-four. During the course of his brief career, he published a dozen books of poetry, four short story collections, five novels and a play, and also wrote widely for magazines.

William Dean Howells (1837–1920). Another Ohioan, Howells made his career in his native state until he was twenty-three, at which point he set out for Boston and then Europe, where for four years he held the post of American consul in Venice. Back in the United States, he worked for the *Atlantic Monthly* from 1866 to 1881—the last ten years as its editor—where he published Mark Twain and Henry James, both of whom became personal friends. Later, as a columnist for *Harper's New Monthly Magazine,* he was an influential champion of such new writers as Emily Dickinson, Paul Laurence Dunbar, Mary E. Wilkins Freeman, Hamlin Garland and Stephen Crane. Howells wrote over a hundred books in various genres, but among the most acclaimed are the novels A *Modern Instance* (1881), *The Rise of Silas Lapham* (1885) and *A Hazard of New Fortunes* (1890). He was the first president of the American Academy of Arts and Letters.

Mark Lemon (1809–1870). Another Londoner, Lemon, the son of a hop merchant, became in 1841, along with proto-London journalist Henry Mayhew, the co-founder and co-editor of *Punch,* one of the most celebrated comic magazines of any era.He was also an actor and playwright, and since *Punch* did not initially find its audience, he kept it afloat until it did with the profits from his popular plays such as *Mr. Nightingale's Diary* (which he co-wrote with Charles Dickens in 1851). Lemon also produced more than a hundred songs, several triple-decker novels, numerous short stories and compiled the *Jest Book: The Choicest Anecdotes and Sayings* (1865).

J. Edgar Park (1879–1956). Born in Ireland the son of a Protestant clergyman, John Edgar Park himself was ordained after attending Princeton Theological Seminary. Later he became president of Wheaton College in Norton, Massachusetts, while continuing to preach at Harvard, Yale, Cornell and other universities.His many books include *The Keen Joy of Living* (1907), *Bad Results of Good Habits and Other Lapses* (1920), *The Merrie Adventures of Robin Hood and Santa Claus* (1922) and *The Miracle of Preaching* (1939). From 1937 to 1956 he served as head of the American Congregational Association.

F. M. Mayor (1872–1932). Flora Macdonald Mayor's father was a clergyman, as well, who taught classics and moral philosophy at

King's College, London. She herself read history at Cambridge University's Newnham College before going on the stage, a highly unconventional choice for a young woman of her upbringing. Mayor's best known book is *The Rector's Daughter* (1924), but she also wrote *The Third Miss Symons* (1913) and *The Squire's Daughter* (1929). Her early fans included such contemporaries as Virginia Woolf, E. M. Forster, John Masefield and Lytton Strachey, while aficionados of the ghost story have long admired her posthumously published collection of short stories, *The Room Opposite* (1935).

Stephen Leacock (1869–1944). Considered one of the leading early spirits of Canadian literature, Leacock was born in rural England and emigrated with his family to a 100-acre farm in Ontario when he was seven. As one of eleven children he had to struggle to gain an education but, perservering, went on to take a graduate degree at the University of Chicago. Although his field was political economy —he was the longtime chair of the department of Economics and Political Science at McGill University in Montreal, and wrote a standard textbook, *Elements of Political Science* (1906)—Leacock's greatest fame derived from his gently satirical comic stories and parodies. Among the earliest collections of these were *Literary Lapses* (1910) and *Nonsense Novels* (1911). Since 1947, the Stephen Leacock Medal for Humour has been awarded annually to the best humorous book by a Canadian author.

W. A. Wilson. I could find no information whatsoever (not even with the expert help of Thomas Mann, author of *The Oxford Guide to Library Research*) on the delightful story, "A Christmas White Elephant"—perhaps my favorite of all my discoveries. All I know is that Wilson's creation appeared in *The St. Nicholas Christmas Book* (1899) and gives us as heroine five-year-old Cecie, a thoughtfully stubborn child who shows herself to be "green" far ahead of her time. Its sense of modernity—her parents remind me of a great many I know today—caught my attention, and each time I read it I fall under its oddly timeless spell again. Naturally, I welcome any help from readers on the subejct of its author.

Jacob A. Riis (1849–1914). Jacob August Riis, born in Denmark, arrived in America when he was twenty-one. Starting his journalistic career as a police reporter, he made his name as a reform-minded investigator, exposing to newspaper readers the wretched conditions of the urban poor, those immigrants crowded into the tenements and sweatshops of New York. His most famous work, *How the Other Half Lives* (1890), combined text and pictures in an innovative style that would inspire such later works as James Agee and Walker Evans' *Let Us Now Praise Famous Men*. Other works by Riis include: *Children of the Poor* (1892), *Out of Mulberry Street* (1898), *Making of an American* (1901) and *Hero Tales of the Far North* (1910).

Max Beerbohm (1972–1956). Born in London and educated at Oxford, Beerbohm was a professional dandy and humorist celebrated for his satirical writing and witty caricature portraits. However, he also was a drama critic (following George Bernard Shaw in that job on the *Saturday Review*) and, much later, a radio broadcaster delivering occasional highly amusing talks on the BBC. His first book of drawings, *Caricatures of Twenty-five Gentleman*, and his first literary collection, *The Works of Max Beerbohm*, both appeared in 1896, when he was just twenty-four. Perhaps his most famous work is the book of literary parodies, *A Christmas Garland* (1912), from which "The Feast—by J*s*ph C*nr*d" is taken. It contains irreverent pastiches of Hardy, Kipling, Shaw and Chesterton, among others, and was admired by Henry James, despite being himself parodied in it. Beerbohm wrote only a single novel, *Zuleika Dobson* (1911), and his last volume of essays, *A Variety of Things*, was published in 1928.

O. Henry (1862–1910). Born in North Carolina, William Sydney Porter—whose pen name would become synonymous with the American short story—was a convict, imprisoned for embezzlement, when he began to publish as "O. Henry." He had no formal education and was licensed as a pharmacist before taking the job as a bank teller that led to the accusation of misappropriation of funds, a charge which caused him to flee the country alone, without his family. When he returned—owing to his wife's ill health—he was sentenced to five years in an Ohio penitentiary. "The Gift of the Magi" (1906) and "The Last Leaf" (1907) are undoubtedly his two most famous tales and date from the last decade of his life when he produced nearly 300 stories. His first collection, *Cabbages and Kings,* appeared in 1904 and his second, *The Four Million,* two years later. Since 1919, the O. Henry Prize has been given to American and Canadian short stories of exceptional merit which then are collected in an annual volume.

William J. Locke (1863–1930). Born in Barbados, William John Locke was a popular novelist and short-story writer who, though forgotten today, had a string of annual top-ten bestsellers in the early years of the twentieth century. These included *Simon the Jester* (1910), *Fortunate Youth* (1914), *Jaffery* (1915) and *The Red Planet* (1917). In his heyday his work frequently made the transition from page to screen, and, recently, it did again: *Ladies in Lavender* (2004), starring Judi Dench and Maggie Smith, was adapted from his 1916 short story of the same name. Among his other novels are *At the Gate of Samaria* (1894), *Viviette* (1910) and *The Great Pandolfo* (1925)